Praise for Linda Lenhoff and her debut novel
Life à la Mode

"A surprise ending tops off Lenhoff's delightful novel and leaves readers satisfied and hopeful."
—*County Times (San Mateo, California)*

"In her zesty literary debut, Linda Lenhoff serves up a warm slice of twentysomething life laced with a satisfying blend of sugar and spice, saucy dialogue and a sprinkling of sharply drawn secondary characters. Readers are sure to relish *Life à la Mode* and will likely be left craving seconds."
—Wendy Markham, author of *Slightly Settled*

"A lighthearted romp . . . a very funny look at singles life in Manhattan . . . readers will laugh loudly."
—*The Midwest Book Review*

"The satisfaction of a great slice of pie without any of the calories. *Life à la Mode* is sweet, rich, and tasty. Read and enjoy!"
—Lynne Hinton, bestselling author of *Friendship Cake*

Books by Linda Lenhoff

LIFE À LA MODE

LATTE LESSONS

Published by Kensington Publishing Corporation

Latte Lessons

Linda Lenhoff

KENSINGTON BOOKS
www.kensingtonbooks.com

STRAPLESS BOOKS are published by

Kensington Publishing Corp.
850 Third Avenue
New York, NY 10022

To my dad,

and to Casey and Michael

(with a marshmallow on top)

I Owe at Least a Latte to:

Everyone who was so supportive of my first book, *Life à la Mode*, especially Doug McLaurine, Rick Mumma, and Angioline Loredo, for being so persuasive in getting others to read the book. Or so I've heard.

My e-pen pal Beverly Ball, whose thanks in the first book really should have been in boldface type, anyhow, and who has shown the most creativity in marketing techniques for that book. Also my other e-pals Rich Klin and Jill Yesko, for commiserating about writing and life interchangeably. And Christina Pitcher for all things word related and friendship related.

My editor, John Scognamiglio, for unwavering confidence in me and leniency with deadlines, and Sally Hill McMillan, my agent, for the same plus so much Southern charm, as well as inspiration for one of my characters. Both John and Sally deserve extra tall lattes with chocolate sprinkled on top, at the very least.

The wonderful workers at the Lafayette Library, and you just know who you are, for often being the highlight of the week for my daughter and me, and not just because of the air-conditioning on hot days. Not that we mind that at all.

And Michael and Casey Everitt, as always, for all things related to hugs and kisses, and for suggesting title after title. I still like *Popcorn in My Cowgirl Boots*, but maybe next time. Sorry Casey, no latte for you yet, but you can have some whipped cream. I'll owe you the rest.

Chapter 1

What Love Connection?

My friend Jackie recently acquired a list of all the single men in our town who are between the ages of 24 and 45, which she somehow feels is the correct age range for two just-turned-thirty-year-olds—that would be us. I'm not too sure how she came across this convenient information, but I'm not complaining, either. Jackie works with political campaigns doing demographics—creating inventories of potential voters and their ages, incomes, and other data that they'd probably prefer to keep secret. So I've seen lots of lists around her house, besides the ones that say milk, cheese, cookies. This list, though, is the first one we've ever read together, with a bottle of wine ready to mark the right spots.

We're going over the pages tonight, spreading them out on Jackie's blue hypoallergenic carpet. She says it's hypoallergenic, and although I've never seen a tag or anything to prove this, I also don't recall ever sneezing at her condo. So I believe her. We leave a trail of stone-ground crackers from eligible bachelor to eligible bachelor, Jackie especially noting the more British-sounding names, me trying to avoid any more Daves or Andys. We know what we want.

This isn't to say that I would in any way try to meet one

of these 24- to 45-year-olds with an income above sixty-five thousand dollars. Jackie's a different story. My oldest friend, Jackie Steinem (no relation to Gloria) was known in college to wear her hair straight and parted in the middle, and even went so far as to purchase some aviator frames, through which she would stare defiantly at our male college professors. Those who lacked the courage to ask about her relation to Gloria (really, there wasn't any) suffered her most painful glares. She got all As.

Now it's several pairs of contact lenses later, but here we are ten years older, singles bars and personal ads behind us, reading lists of strong-sounding names that live in zip codes our mothers would approve of. It has come to this. This list has something to do with *The New Yorker* magazine's subscribers, and Jackie insists they are all local. Some names may also appear on a list Jackie has of *Playboy* subscribers, but naturally, we will scratch them off as possibilities. We have standards.

"*Blind Date* was calling around at our office today, looking for eligibles," I tell her.

Jackie's cracker falls out of her mouth into her wine glass. She leaves it there. "I think you should go on it," she tells me, crossing off George McDermott from the list with a black marker. She knows him.

"I am not going on that show," I say, looking through the Ds. Matt Damon is on the list, although I'm pretty sure he's not the same one. Still, he's a possibility, and his street name sounds nice. It's a house, not an apartment. You learn to notice these things.

"I don't see the point of going to work every day," Jackie says, "if you're not going to take advantage of extracurricular activities."

"Yeah, yeah." I nod and rip a perforated page.

"Didn't your mother ever tell you the office was a valuable place to meet men?" Jackie asks wide-eyed.

"Eleanor? Are you kidding? When I told her I was going to work in a small advertising firm on Main Street, she said, 'That's nice, dear, just make sure you eat lunch at a restaurant where there are lots of single lawyers.' "

Jackie shrugs. "Yes, but what she really meant was, 'Can't you work in Century City where all the high-paid lawyers are?' "

"She'd settle for an accountant," I say reasonably. "Her demands are fair."

"Good to hear," Jackie says, circling a man. I notice her putting an asterisk by his name. When I try to get closer, she grabs it away. "Mine," she says.

"You controlling female," I say, well into the Fs by now. I haven't circled any possibilities yet. I do have several question marks, though.

"And what would Eleanor say about this scheme?" I wonder, preferring the way Jackie thinks of my mother to my actually having to think about her myself.

"Eleanor would be pleased that we were using our over-educated little minds on such a task. Then she'd take us to the beauty salon to get our nails done."

"So we could keep our priorities straight," I say.

"Hmm," Jackie says, looking at a nail, then biting at it.

I will not go on *Blind Date*, despite my officemate Dennis's requests that we go on together.

"Come on, Claire. That way we could go out to a really great dinner," Dennis says. A great free dinner, he means.

"You're thinking of the old *Love Connection*," I tell him. "You don't get dinner on *Blind Date*."

"You're thinking of *Elimidate*," he says. "You get a lot more than dinner on *Elimidate*. It takes years to get rid of it, I hear."

He's right, I was thinking of *Elimidate* and now can't figure out what *Blind Date* is. Dennis tells me it's like *Elimidate*, only the people dress up more.

"They wear more clothes, anyway," he says. "Well, the women do."

Let me just say that Dennis Cooper is not gay, that we have never had sex and never even kissed, but we did get very drunk one night and go dancing at one of those ballroom dancing places where everyone else was over sixty. Maybe seventy. We danced to something an elderly gentleman swore to us was the rumba, and it did involve body parts touching on occasion, and if I hadn't had so much wine that night, I might even be able to remember which parts.

Dennis is one year younger than I am, and at his 29 to my 30, he sometimes seems to me to be part of an entirely different species, the not-quite-thirty-year-old male, someone without the wisdom you magically seem to get when you cross the big 3-0 threshold. Or at least the wisdom you like to think you get, because you might as well get something for turning a year older and leaving behind the last decade most people I know attribute to youth. Dennis just isn't there yet, and it's a good thing to tease him about, not that I need extra things to tease him about.

Dennis and I are copywriters at a small advertising and promotion company in Venice, California, although our job descriptions don't involve half of what we do in our small firm. Technically, we've never really seen any job descriptions. We arrived on the same day at the same time for the copywriting job interview, and the owner, whose name is Persephone, although we're allowed to call her Perri, hired us both. This job fulfills us, we joke, unlike the jobs we had in grad school (we both went to the same school, UCLA, and were in the same English department even, although we didn't know each other well). My grad school part-time job was in publishing, where I was responsible for the letters to the editor section of a bimonthly magazine for young girls in love with horses and not particularly interested in commas. Dennis was a plumber while writing his almost useless thesis on French themes in English literature and the symbolism of water, believe it or not. I think he found his plumbing work somewhat fulfilling, actually. He joined an otherwise all-woman group that formed their own plumbing service. They took courses for about six months at the tech college, then plumbered by day and read classics by night, among other things, in a huge old house many of them lived in. Dennis has a lot of sordid stories he tries to keep to himself, but on a really slow day he'll slip one in. Our small advertising office here has found him invaluable, one because everyone loves him (he has a furry brown beard, which I think is what makes the occasional intern we have around here so quick to get him coffee), and two because he has fixed the bathroom sink five times. I find him invaluable too, if we're admitting things here.

Dennis has agreed to come over tomorrow night to watch *Blind Date* with Jackie and me. He knows exactly when it is on, and on what channel. This, I think, is something I didn't want to know about him.

Dennis scratches his bearded left cheek. "We can watch *Blind Date*, but just for you, I'll dress like I'm *The Bachelor*," he says, as I notice his mismatched socks, not quite hidden by his frayed old jeans.

I invite Jackie over because she has met Dennis but never wanted to dance with him, as she finds beards too harsh on the skin. We wouldn't want anyone here to feel like they have to impress anyone else, as it really detracts from the TV-watching, we've found. Jackie has commented on Dennis's appearance: "When he's done with the interns, he'll lose the beard," she's said to me. Actually, Dennis isn't interested in interns, I know, and pretty much seems to have given up dating after his last and very serious, not to mention serious-minded, girlfriend, Annie.

I'm fiddling with my remote, going through my thirty or is it sixty channels of cable you pretty much need out here in Venice just to get even the blurriest reception. My mother insists on paying for my overpriced cable in hopes that we'll watch the same melodramatic shows and have something to talk about. It will bring us together, I guess she thinks, and in a way I suppose it does. I simply do not watch enough television for my mother's taste, it seems. She would agree, though, that I watch far too much of it alone.

"Did you know that *Golden Girls* is on like nine times a day now?" Jackie asks me, daintily eating the non-buttered pieces of popcorn from the bowl. I have a really large bowl for such occasions.

"Why do we know these things?" I ask her. I knew about *Golden Girls*.

"We're single, we live alone. TV is our friend."

Dennis is late, and I'm no longer at my best, which I'm convinced is somewhere between 11:15 and 11:30 in the morning, and now it's about twelve hours later. "We could be watching David Letterman," I tell her.

"I hear he already has a girlfriend."

Realizing I'll get no help here, I put the TV on *Bonanza* for a minute and look at the pudgy men. Jackie and I exchange a look, then make fun of their clothes.

Dennis arrives with a thud at my front door. I open it.

"A simple knock will do," I say.

Dennis has dropped his backpack and books have spilled out all over my doorstep. They have French titles. I don't even ask why he's got books with him to watch TV, or why he didn't major in French instead of English. Some things you just get used to about a person.

"Hi," he says, dropping a book for the second time.

Maybe he's just doing that helpless male routine. I can't tell, and Jackie's glued to Little Joe, so she's no help.

I pick up a few books as Dennis comes in. I hand them to him.

"You just want me to feel sorry for you, right? It's a male manipulative thing," I tell him. "I've had a lot of experience with this type of behavior."

"Passive-aggressive," Jackie says, mouth full.

"Give me the popcorn," Dennis says loudly.

"So much for that theory," I say.

Dennis looks at the *Bonanza* boys.

"If you don't change this, I'll sing the theme song."

"Be nice," I say, "or we'll make you watch *Golden Girls.*"

We have counted only three references to dating in the half hour of *Blind Date* and even fewer references to vision. I'm really disappointed that it wasn't more lurid.

"Isn't *The Bachelor* better than this?" I ask.

"Depends what you mean by better," Jackie says. "It's more demeaning toward women, but the men are cleaner."

"*Bachelor* repeats come on next," Dennis says. Both Jackie and I respond with "Oh, good," which makes Dennis look at us funny. Really, it's very late.

"It's like looking at *Vogue*," she tries to explain to him. "It's something you can make fun of without really losing any karma points for."

"Harmless critical behavior," I add. "While yelling at an inanimate electronic household item." Really, sometimes it doesn't get much better than that.

Jackie is right in her assessment of *The Bachelor*. The guy is better groomed as well as far more capable of stringing together the responses that have been written for him. Dennis says the girls are more "Penthouse" than the ones that used to be on the old *Love Connection*. We don't answer him, but we know what he means. We spend a good portion of the rest of our time together talking about the carefully rounded holes in the guy's jeans, and whether women find this attractive. Dennis really wants to understand the appeal. Most of his jeans are ripped, I've noticed, but not really in the same places as the bachelor's. I wonder if he has even noticed.

At work all week I'm trapped in a writing frenzy where I'm trying to devise several new radio and newspaper ads for a local store that sells cowboy boots. I have lost all track of time and friends, and Jackie appears late one night at my apartment with a bottle of Chablis and a quart of chocolate chip. She is my true friend.

"It's time you had a home-cooked meal," she tells me.

I agree and immediately wash two spoons and two wine glasses. I know how to entertain.

Jackie, who's an even better entertainer, has come with what she calls a "bedtime" story. It seems not only did she find a nice-sounding man on a nice-sounding street from her list, but she went right out and met him. I am so impressed that I go back to the kitchen to wash a bowl for her. I think she appreciates the gesture.

"Details," I begin.

"I headed for his house with a bunch of old handouts, you know, fliers from the last election, a guy running for city council. I also had some fliers for a woman running for school board, but I thought they might be distracting, so I left them behind."

"The woman in the black turtleneck?" I ask.

"Yeah, the blonde."

"Good move," I say, toasting her.

"Wait, wait, listen," she says, beginning to shape the air with her hands. "He answers the door in a blue denim shirt—"

"Clean?"

"Yeah, freshly washed, and he listened. Really listened. He said something about meaning to get more involved in local politics himself someday."

"Hmm," I say, trying to picture him. "Levi's or khakis?"

"Levi's."

"Good."

"With white socks, no shoes," Jackie adds.

"Really good," I say, feeling my heart race a little from too much chocolate and the thought of a man out there alone in soft denim.

"Oh, and no TV in the background," Jackie says. "He did ask if it wasn't some time before the next election."

"Sharp," I say.

"Right. I told him it was several months away, but that we needed to keep the public informed. He said he admired me."

"I admire you."

"Yes, but you never pay for dinner. Anyway, he offered me a glass of ice water—"

"He had a clean glass handy?"

"Some people are like that," Jackie says, looking at my wine glass from a fund-raiser about ten years ago. It's aged some. "And since the glass was clean and it didn't have a decal from a bar on it, I decided to flirt with him."

"My mother would be very proud of you. Did you ask if he wanted children?"

"I'm saving that for the second date. The first one's Saturday."

I'm envious of Jackie, naturally. But then, I have a root canal scheduled for Saturday, so I'd be jealous if she were just going to do her laundry. Jackie pushes her red hair behind an ear—a gesture she's told me drives her own mother crazy—and rubs at a freckled spot to the left of her nose, as if trying to rub the freckles off.

"You aren't nervous, are you?" I ask her.

"I tend to get a little anxious without fliers in my hand," she says. I nod, knowing the value of a good prop. A stack of papers can keep you from making swooping movements that scare people away. A wine glass in your hand, however, can be a dangerous thing, especially on a first date, especially if someone keeps filling it.

"You could hold on to a pair of gloves," I suggest.

"Gloves look pretentious, unless it's snowing. Do you think it will snow?"

Since it's about 70 degrees, I doubt it, and tell her we need a Plan B. We finally agree that she'll bring a small leather accessory she has that doubles as a wallet/date book. It looks professional but also classy, like she's a woman who's going places, but isn't in a big hurry, in case she's having a good time. Since Jackie never has a problem properly dressing herself, she doesn't ask my advice there. I might lose all respect for her if she did.

"I've had him checked out, of course," Jackie says, closing the subject. "We ran a TRW at the office, and a friend checked through FBI files."

Honestly, I don't know why I worry about her.

In the morning Dennis comes into the office and puts a cup overflowing with frothy liquid down on a small side table we share. His morning latte, not to be confused with his afternoon and/or evening latte, or any of the other lattes I don't even want to know about. His desk is such a clutter that he often puts really important things, like food, on the side table. I'm not sure if it's an offer to share, but I usually take some.

I stare at the froth with a look of general displeasure.

"I know, I know, I shouldn't be drinking it."

Dennis looks down at his stomach and I follow his look. Really, he's not fat, but I can tell it worries him.

"It's not that," I say, removing the cup to find a brownish ring on my papers. "It's that."

"Sorry," Dennis says, "I'll make it up to you. I'll come over and feed you Jell-O after your root canal."

"I prefer to think of it as mild dental work, thanks."

"You're only kidding yourself," Dennis says.

"Yes, but it doesn't cost anything," I say.

Dennis begins searching his desk for something. He does this every morning for about ten minutes, then stops abruptly and begins making notes. He scribbles frantically for about five minutes, then puts the notes away and never seems to be able to find them again. He's a creature of habit, I guess. It's funny, but I find I can't really start the day until I watch him all the way through his routine.

"I don't like Jell-O," I say.

Dennis thinks a minute. I hear our office clock tick. Finally, he raises an eyebrow and slowly says, "Chocolate pudding."

It's a date, sort of.

Chapter 2

On a Night Like This

It's probably perfectly normal chocolate pudding, even though it's the plain-wrap kind and not a brand name you might recognize. Not that I expected Dennis to slave over a hot bowl of Junket, like my mother used to make—once every five years or so. She'd stand there with her handheld electric beater, and I could scoop up the wet chocolaty stuff with my finger before it hardened. Sometimes my dad would make it for me, and we'd take turns with the beater, then scrub the walls to get off the bits we'd sent flying around the room. Dennis's pudding, though, tastes strangely metallic, as if it has been trapped in an aluminum can for a few years. This is especially odd since it came in one of those plastic cups. Of course, it could be my dayful of root canal work, which has left me not only with disturbed taste buds but also feeling shaky and unloved, as spending hours with a strange man's hands in your mouth will do. But I want name-brand chocolate pudding, something expensive. I guess I want mousse.

I've been waiting for Dennis to arrive so I could start moaning for real. Somehow, moaning by yourself just doesn't satisfy all that much. As soon as I got home from my root canal, I put on my ugliest curly yellow sweater, which is soft as can be but has been known to make others sneeze around me, or at the least shoot me very nasty looks, as the color takes some getting used to. Yellow is a kind word for it; it's really sort of a dirty golden-grayish color. But it's very comforting, and I'm in pain and I want my sweater. I'm wearing yellow leggings that my mother gave me—how else in the world would anyone come by yellow leggings? So I kind of look like a dying canary with a puffy face, a bloated chicken, maybe, and not the free-range healthy kind. But I don't much care. I've taken Vicodan, by prescriptive order, of course, not that I tend to take much in the way of medicine. Vicodan and chocolate pudding cups. Really, I should be much happier than this.

"Great sweater," Dennis says. He seems not at all sarcastic, I think, for which I'm grateful, even though I'm a bit druggy. Along with his pudding, he's brought mashed potatoes and applesauce. I somehow have the feeling they'd all taste about the same. I tell Dennis this.

"We could blindfold you," he suggests, "then I could trade off giving you tastes and you could try to tell which is which." He begins looking around, I guess for something to blindfold me with.

"Maybe later," I say. It's a slow night for television, so we may have to resort to this.

Dennis fixes himself a bowl of mashed potatoes and applesauce and begins to eat, scooping them both up together, which starts to make me feel a little woozy. The phone rings, and as usual, I make no move toward it whatsoever. Before my advertising career, I once worked as a phone operator at school. I've been pretty lax about answering my own phone ever since. Knowing my character flaws, Dennis rises and reaches for the phone. Suddenly, it hits me, that fear, that realization.

"Hello," Dennis answers, mouth full of softened apples and potatoes.

I try to get his attention by throwing still-unopened cups of pudding at him. "Not Eleanor," I whisper as loudly as I can while still making it a whisper. I realize this could well be my mother on the phone—I always know when it's her. I get a feeling inside, sort of like you get a day or two before you come down with the flu. It's indescribable, but it happens every time. And I like my mother.

Dennis manages to ignore his shower of pudding cups.

"How are you, Eleanor," he says, sitting back down, cradling the phone on his shoulder and reaching for his mush.

I don't want to talk to my mother right now, though, first because I didn't tell her about the root canal—not wanting to hear another lecture about what happened to Aunt Louise's teeth—and second because it's Saturday night, and if I were any kind of daughter at all, I'd be out on a date in a beaded cocktail dress. Better yet, I'd have given her grandchildren and still be able to fit nicely into a beaded cocktail dress.

"She's sleeping," Dennis says, taking my cue after dodging three pudding cups and an assortment of plaid throw pillows. The fourth pudding cup swipes his left earlobe, which seems to irritate him a bit. "She had a root canal," he says, as I bury my face in the couch and moan. My nubby pink-and-white flowery couch smells a little like lavender, which reminds me of Aunt Louise again. But then, I could be hallucinating.

"I know, it's terrible the stuff she eats," Dennis says. I peek at him as he opens one of the pudding cups and digs in.

Dennis and Eleanor hit it off when they met, which they did despite my efforts against this sort of thing. I firmly believe it's not a great idea to have your mother know your friends, let alone their phone numbers. These things can get ugly. Eleanor came by work that day to give me some blue shoes she bought that were too small for her. When this happens, I have learned to stop asking why she buys things that are too small for her. I have learned to be grateful, because every time she's done this, she's said, "You should be grateful." And besides, she's right. I have never much needed blue shoes, though.

When they met, Eleanor began instantly treating Dennis like an old friend, or a small child.

"I recognize that your relationship is strictly platonic," she said to me once after meeting Dennis, "and as a modern woman myself, I know to respect this, even though he is single and there's nothing wrong with him that can't be fixed at Macy's." This may have had something to do with Dennis's outfit that day, which consisted of a faded gray—I think it used to be blue—flannel shirt missing the front pocket, and pants that may have once been blue also. This was someone a bit too disheveled at the moment to be boyfriend material, Eleanor's voice implied, but plenty good enough to bring her daughter pudding on a night like this. One thing I know Eleanor and Jackie have in common is a general distrust of beards.

"I think beards show a lack of a certain quality in men," Eleanor once said to Jackie and me over tea and finger sandwiches at Nordstrom's Tea Room. "A certain," she started forming circles of air in front of her, circles that got larger and larger until she just puffed up her cheeks, let all the air out, and said, "don't you think?" Jackie nodded. I let it go.

Now I lift my head off of my pillow—the only one I didn't throw from the couch at Dennis—as he seems to be finishing his conversation with my mother. He hangs up and says, "She said to try some room-temperature cottage cheese, which she says will be easy for you to eat. She also didn't forget to mention that a little low-cal food wouldn't hurt you any."

I feel the pain in my teeth everywhere all at once, and look down at my body, wondering what pouches of fat my mother has imagined on me.

"She's nuts," Dennis says.

* * *

I dream that my therapist is trying to kill me. She has followed me around my office building, which is an old converted warehouse, with a hidden revolver and one of those large pink cartons of Knudsen's low-fat cottage cheese. Every few steps, she takes out the carton and waves it at me, and I approach, wanting it. Then she pulls out the revolver and I run again. This goes on for what seems like hours, until we get to where Dennis's and my office is. I slip through the doors, and when I look back I see a band of small, gray-flannel canaries blocking my therapist's way to the entrance. They shake their little heads at her, then pull out pudding cups and throw them. Then I wake up.

Once awake, I consider telling my therapist that in my dreams she tried to kill me, but I'm suddenly afraid she'll tell me that she has had this dream, also. The paranoia reminds me that I must still have drugs in my bloodstream, so I go back to sleep.

The next time I wake up, I think I'm feeling much better. I'm surprised, though, to find that it's still Saturday night. Okay, maybe it's early Sunday morning, but I feel like I've been asleep for days, not hours. Clearly, I'm falling to pieces: First I lose my taste buds, now my sense of time. And I can't feel anything in my left hand, which I must have been sleeping on. I hit it against the couch, which doesn't help much, but at least now I feel something like massive acupuncture below my wrist.

Over on the other side of my aging soft couch, Dennis sleeps under the weight of two French texts, which cover him from just under his chin across both shoulders. I'm suddenly quite sure that Dennis has been poisoned by the applesauce, that he's not breathing. I can't hear any noise, no snoring, not even a wheeze, so I crawl up next to him and push a finger against his arm. This does nothing. Finally, I

punch him in the arm, and he rolls his head to the other side
and says, "Pooh Bear." Somehow, this is all I needed to hear.

I find my way to the bedroom and get into bed, canary
sweater and all.

In the morning I'm awakened by a vision of a female figure
through my blurry eyes. Wisps of long hair dangle from her
head down around me as she says "Sleeping Beauty, Sleeping
Beauty" and touches me with her magic wand. I sense this is
my fairy godmother come to save me after all these years and
send me to the ball, but then I realize I may have my fairy tales
mixed up. As my vision clears I see it's just Jackie with a pancake flipper summoning me to breakfast. I cannot begin to
describe my disappointment.

Hearing my groans, Jackie replies, "Real maple syrup!"
It does have an effect.

It is time, after I take a long, hot shower then drench my
taste buds with some maple-syrupy pancakes (Dennis has filled
them with bananas, my favorite) to hear about Jackie's evening.
We sit around my chipped kitchen table, Dennis and I staring at Jackie in anticipation. This is how we live.

I push away my plate after running one last finger through
the syrup. "Spill it," I say.

Dennis looks at Jackie, too, twisting a syrupy fork in his
mouth.

"We met at that bar/saloon place with the brown awning
on Main, you know, and he was punctual."

"Name," Dennis says.

"Kit Jackson."

"Frontier-ish," I say, impressed.

"Age," Dennis says.

"Thirty-four and seven months, medium tall, good build.
Nice teeth, too," she says, smirking at me.

"Yeah, yeah," I say.

"Conversation?" Dennis asks.

"He told me he started his own computer software company two years ago and now has two full-time and three part-time associates."

"Was this before or after dinner?" Dennis asks.

"Before."

"Eew," he replies, fork in his mouth again. Sounded like eew, anyway.

"Yeah, I don't like guys who talk about their income before the main course even arrives," I say.

"Better than guys who talk about their divorce before the main course arrives," Jackie says. She's right.

"I don't like guys with incomes," Dennis says.

"Well, what else are you supposed to talk about before dinner?" Jackie asks.

"Not sports," I say.

"Not politics," Dennis says.

"Not religion, not world crises, not diets," Jackie says. "This leaves work."

"Personal hygiene?" Dennis suggests.

"I think that's second-date material," Jackie says, "depending on how well the first date went."

"What did he order?" I ask.

"Fish."

"Specifics," Dennis says.

"Salmon, blackened, carrots and broccoli, small Caesar salad."

"Blackened is bad for you," I say, running another finger through syrup.

"So is dating," Jackie says. Really, she looks a bit tired.

"Did he spill any food?" Dennis asks.

"No," Jackie says.

Dennis stops playing with his fork. "Come on."

"Okay, there was this one carrot I lost track of."

"It's one carrot," I say, in Jackie and her date's defense. Dennis shrugs okay.

"Second-date possibilities?" I ask.

Jackie looks down at her bits of pancake left on the plate. She never finishes anything, preferring to leave large holes in her food. She tugs at the left side of her hair a little.

"He didn't really have that look, when he looked at me, you know? He just looked at me." Jackie keeps her eyes on her plate, then watches her hand twirl her hair round and round.

"Oh," Dennis and I say, nearly in unison. Dennis gets up to clear the dishes, and I just sit there trying to think of something consoling to say that I haven't already said at least fifty to one hundred times to Jackie, or she hasn't already said to me. I think we're out of consolations for this sort of thing.

After a minute or two of quiet, Dennis walks back over to the table and places a pudding cup on top of Jackie's head. She removes it, then hits him, but lightly.

Chapter 3

Not Your Mother's Dating Service

I really think it's one thing for Jackie and me to sit around looking at lists of men's names, searching for that certain something—maybe it's a first name like Gabriel or Raphael, something foreign and romantic—that little something that makes your heart think, *Well, maybe . . . ?* despite your mind saying, *Too much wine, too much wine.*

It's another thing entirely, I have to think, to learn your mother has been computer dating.

"Eleanor having e-sex?" Jackie asks me one night, as we try to make sushi ourselves—one of those dinners that's not really worth the effort, and that you know will only make you reach for the Tater Tots and frozen French toast for dessert.

"I don't know about sex, but she seems into the *e* part," I say. "It could be worse," I say. "It could be your mom."

Jackie's parents have been married steadily since the late 1960s when they (honestly) met roller-skating. They still go out together for milkshakes (honestly), which they get now at smoothie shops, as both are fitness-crazed fifty-five-year-olds. They fast-walk together each late afternoon, then stop for a quick malted/smoothie—although usually a soy one.

Jackie just shakes her head at this. "They think lattes are for cowards," Jackie has told me. We really just don't understand them at all.

But back to Eleanor, my recently widowed mother.

"I thought Eleanor dreaded the computer," Jackie says.

"At first she thought it was wrecking her manicure," I say. "But she says she's figured out a way to type using what she calls her 'finger pads.' " We both look at our fingers. "I didn't even know there was such a thing as a finger pad," I say.

"It's the part that's not worth biting," Jackie says, then takes a piece of sushi and douses it with soy sauce. I watch her.

"It's lite soy sauce," she adds.

"Not your mother's soy sauce," I say after tasting some. We go and cook the Tater Tots.

"Electronic dating," Dennis ponders when I tell him about my mom. "Still, it's good to see Eleanor trying new things. Maybe getting out a little."

We are back in our small shared office, which has adobe-style archways that someone swore to me were made out of straw. It does explain some of the sneezing around here.

"Eleanor getting out." I think about this. "My mom, on the computer, well, that's strange enough," I say. "But out there," I point westward, although there's mostly ocean in that direction, as we're that close to the beach. "Out there among the world of, well, dating?" I think about my mom meeting a man at a trendy café in Santa Monica. I picture her a little surprised at what she meets. I picture her disappointed. It's almost too sad to think about. Or maybe I'm just projecting.

"Maybe it's you who's not ready for her to move on," Dennis says.

I think about my dad. I think about him often, and it doesn't always bring tears to my eyes after a year and a half. I know my therapist would say this is a good thing, but still, I wonder if Dennis is right. Dennis who is not a good one at moving on himself, I happen to know. Which doesn't mean he doesn't have a good point.

"Let's just have a look," Dennis says, turning to his computer. "Where do you start, when you're a woman over fifty—"

"But not necessarily willing to admit it," I add.

"Oh, Eleanor's okay," Dennis says. "A guy could do worse."

I have to admire Dennis for saying this. It's true, his own mom, whom I met when she was visiting from her home in Vermont, is a bit preachy and goody-goody, the kind who has just seen the latest Broadway show and isn't ashamed to say so, and who only went to see it after visiting each new art exhibit at the major museums, of which she's probably a member. To be honest, I find her intimidating, and not even in a way that makes me envious.

"Here's a Web site," he says. And it's not like we don't have work to do, but I can tell this is important to Dennis, for some reason, so I humor him. Not that I'm not dying for a peek.

"Is it I-Village?" I ask. "I hear a lot of women like that one for shopping, but I don't know if you can find men in your size there."

"No," Dennis says. We look at the site. It's called Romance Redux, as in www.romance-redux.com.

"You know," I say, "that it's got a dot-com address says something seedy to me. If it were a dot-org, I might have more respect for it. A nonprofit organization aiming to fix your widowed mom up for second-time love might be a worthy thing."

"A dot-org is a terrible thing to waste," Dennis says. "Then again, maybe that it's a dot-com and still in business means it's actually having some success."

We consider this.

"Here's a chat room called Ladies Longing for Candle-light," Dennis says.

"As opposed to ladies longing for direct overhead light, I suppose. Should we go in?"

"No," Dennis says, "it seems like voyeurism, unless you're low on candles yourself, so to speak?" Dennis asks, hinting.

"I'm not the candlelight type," I say. "I like to see the person in daylight. It's hard to get a good look into some-one's eyes by candle. And the burning wicks make my eyes sting."

"You need a chat room for the allergic," Dennis says. I hadn't thought of this, but he might be right.

"Hypoallergenic dating," I say. "You may be on to some-thing."

"Hypoallergenic dating," Dennis repeats. "Sounds like an oxymoron to me," former English major that he is.

We do, as I say, on occasion, work here at our small adver-tising and promotion agency. It's called Persephonia!, named after our leader, Persephone, and if you saw her you might know why. She is a commanding presence of a woman, and I do mean it as a compliment, most of the time at least. Today, her hair—which is semi-long and always curly in that way that makes you wonder how much she paid for her perma-nent and why yours never looks that good—is red specked with gold, like a fairy godmother should look. Perri, as we all call her, changes her hair color frequently and with gusto. She often passes out ballots and allows us to vote on our fa-vorite color for the year. She's unashamed and fearless. She calls herself "fortysomething-plus," I know, as I've heard her say it more than once.

Perri has created this company herself, thus the name, and although most of our clients are pretty small scale—

along with doing promotions for the cowboy boot store, we represent several performers, including an if-Elvis-were-a-woman impersonator. And she's a she, not really trying to look like a he, although I find it a bit confusing. Her name is Elvissa, although her real name is Suzy, and she does a mean "Jailhouse Rock." We also have a fifties crooner type as well as a few up-and-coming singers who mostly do commercials and open for larger acts. Still, it keeps us busy, us being me and Dennis, Perri, our art director, David, an assistant named Josie, interns who come and go to answer our phones and copy and file, and Malcolm, Perri's twentysomething son, who does anything and everything around here that Perri tells him to do. Malcolm's sort of Perri's opposite—not very brave, not very outlandish, nobody's dream fairy godmother. Dennis teases him a lot, which, for some reason, Malcolm actually seems to appreciate.

My mom calls me at ten-thirty that morning.

"Hello, Claire, it's Mom," my mother always announces.

"Hi, Mom," I say. "I'm kind of busy—"

"Not that you're not glad to hear from me," Mom says.

"Of course," I say.

"I know that I shouldn't take time from your workday, as you know I fully support young women settling themselves into a good career," she says.

"I appreciate that, Mom."

"Before taking off those few years to marry and beget, of course, so that their lives—and mine—will be complete," Mom says.

"Of course," I say again.

"It's the way of the world, no stopping it," Mom says, but not unkindly. In fact, a little tiredly.

I put aside an ad I'm working on for Elvissa, who has a gig in Reno. I settle in. "Aren't you at work, Mom?"

"Yes, dear. I'm here at Billie's, straightening things up."

My mother has long been a bookkeeper, and a respected one, for a lengthy list of very feminine places of business. Billie's is a hair salon owned by, naturally, Billie, a fiftysomething, very elegant woman whose own hair is a very respectable salt-and-pepper. But it doesn't mean she doesn't recommend any color of the rainbow to her clients. She's often tried to get me to entertain a little color in my own long, brown, slightly curly hair when I've visited there (at my mother's request). One thing I do like about Billie's is that despite the ruffly curtains and four shades of pink on the walls, the only magazines Billie keeps for her clients to read are financial ones—mostly about women and business. Billie started her shop thirty years ago in a small spot on La Cienega, and it has grown to a large, well-placed spot on trendy Beverly. My mother's other clients are similarly feminine and successful, like a nail salon called Fly Away Nails that has a sign with fingernails painted to look like butterflies, a dress store called Très Elegant, and a few other places, including, I've recently learned, a shop that specializes in bikini waxing. Mom says it's very refined there, but I'm not sure how she means it.

Eleanor suggests we meet for tea on Saturday to catch up, after her weekly appointment at Billie's.

"You can tell me what's new in your life," Mom says, "face to face, rather than by impersonal electronic communication."

"Okay," I say.

"Really," Mom says, "I think all this new technology, computers, faxes, cell phones, is really keeping mothers and daughters farther apart. What ever happened to family dinners and Sunday brunches?"

"I thought you were getting into the computer these days, Mom."

"Actually, I have been," Mom says, then giggles. "See you Saturday."

*   *   *

My mother and I have arranged to meet, with Jackie as interpreter/intermediary, not that we need one all that much, at a place called the Tea Cozy in my Venice neighborhood. Naturally, you can find all kinds of tea there, not to mention very fancy scones that they insist are low-fat, but I think they mean low-fat in a relative way, as opposed to eating a container of Crisco, say. Not that we care, because scones are worth a little something extra in the calorie department. And it can be a plus to have something to put in your mouth when your mom is around. As long as you don't make crumbs.

Eleanor actually likes this place, even though my neighborhood at large doesn't thrill her, and she flat out refuses to visit the sandwich shop next door to the Tea Cozy, which proudly displays its name in large letters above the door: Bite Me.

"You have to admit it isn't that appetizing a name," even Jackie has said to me.

"I really think it's the guys with the tattoos on their noses that keep Eleanor away," I've replied to Jackie, and to be honest, it's not a look I feel all that comfortable with either. Still, it's the kind of place you'd feel free to visit barefoot and in your pajamas even if they had holes in them, and no one would say anything.

But for now it's the Tea Cozy for us girls, as Mom likes to call us. Mom dresses in a very presentable light blue knit T-shirt and matching pants, the kind of thing you find in catalogs where the women look of a certain age, and maybe retired, but still trendy enough. They usually wear Keds in the ads as well, or what used to be called boat shoes. There are, in fact, often boats featured behind the women. I find the catalogs relaxing, frankly. And while I'm admitting things, I should say that my mother looks fabulous in light blue, and

I tell her so, knowing how much she loves both light blue and the word fabulous. It goes well with her frosted Candice Bergen-color hair, which Billie does just right every time, I also know. Jackie and I are dressed in jeans and faded T-shirts— our Saturday gear—and it's doubtful that either of us has much combed her hair, at least more than a swipe-swipe with a comb. My jeans aren't even that clean, but they're tucked under the table at least. Jackie's knees are starting to appear through rips, which I can sometimes hear her tugging at under the table. She likes to keep her hands busy. I just know that in minutes she'll be dissecting her scone. It's one reason why we often don't get to share our food. Hers is a pile of crumbs in no time.

"So tell me the most fascinating thing in your lives right now," Mom starts. "Don't hold back."

"Even the shocking stuff?" Jackie asks. Jackie has a good kidding relationship with my mom.

"Oh," Mom says, "I wouldn't drive out to the beach for anything less."

My mother and I lean in happily for Jackie's news. It would take me a while to think of something fascinating myself, let alone shocking, so I'm glad for the break. Plus, my low-fat wild cherry scone came with low-fat chocolate dipping sauce, and I'm pretty much enjoying the dipping part.

"Okay," Jackie says. "My company has taken on a campaign for a man who's running for the congressional seat in our district."

"In this area?" Mom asks, a little horrified as Jackie nods. "He doesn't look like one of those boys in the shop next door, I hope. Not that there's anything wrong with you young people expressing yourselves. Just why you have to do it with permanent ink is beyond me," Mom says.

"No, no," Jackie says. "He's very presentable. Um, very."

"This sounds like the fascinating part to me," I say. I'm a little jealous, but I'm pretty happy to live vicariously through Jackie's life, especially until the chocolate sauce runs out.

"What are his views on gentrification, on education, on enhancing the arts?" Mom asks.

"He's very progressive and yet protective of individual rights of expression," Jackie says, practiced. She is a demographer, after all, and she's worked on hundreds of campaigns for local politicians, many of them progressive yet protective of individual rights of expression. Even Mom's heard this part before.

Mom waves the comment away. She wants the good stuff.

"Let's get down to it," I say. "Are we talking datable material?" It's not beyond Jackie to have considered this before agreeing to work with the guy.

"That is," my mother says, daintily cutting her scone into little triangles, which I can never manage to do without breaking the things into crumbs, "are we talking marriage-able?"

"Not that marriage is the goal for every single woman in the metropolitan area here," I add, although not convincingly, I have to admit.

"Of course not," Mom says. "But let's just say theoretically, as in just in case you were to like one another and walk by a bridal store and find a dress you must have and need an occasion to wear it to. Just say," Mom says.

I notice we haven't even asked his name yet. First things first.

"Well," Jackie says, starting to rub a freckle, which I know is a bad sign. "Theo is technically married."

"The technical marriages are always such a problem," Mom says.

"Is it technically," I say, "as opposed to theoretically? Or as opposed to philosophically?"

"Well," Jackie starts again. "It's important that Theo maintains his marital status. But he's admitted the marriage isn't going well."

"Was this before or after the first date?" my mother asks. I'm a little shocked at her being so calm about these things. Mom catches my mouth open. "I'm a woman of the world, dear. One hears all sorts of things at Billie's salon, after all these years."

"I haven't dated him," Jackie says proudly. "I have standards, you know."

"That's wonderful, dear," my mother says, a little doubtfully.

"And it's news!" I say, poking at Jackie jokingly, even though I do know she has standards. We all do. They just get challenged sometimes.

"He has the loveliest soft graying hair, though," Jackie says a little dreamily.

"Prematurely gray?" I ask. I can see Mom wants to know, too.

"He's thirty-nine, exactly nine years and nine months my senior," Jackie, mistress of statistics, says.

"Thirty-nine," my mother says dreamily.

"Something intriguing you want to tell us, Mom, about thirty-nine?" I say.

"It's a fine age for a man," she says, still mysteriously. She takes a sip of tea. "Not to mention the last age many women I know will admit to being."

We all consider this. Jackie and I trade scones, as she's noticed me staring at her vanilla bean almond one, and she hasn't started to dissect it yet. I've picked most of the cherries out of mine, but Jackie doesn't seem to mind. She's that good a friend. We order more dipping sauce.

"What about the e-dating, Eleanor?" Jackie asks. I feel my stomach slip a bit, not that I don't want to know. But maybe I don't want to know too much.

"Ah," Eleanor starts. "It's certainly an interesting avenue. I've had a few chats, I think you girls call them. But men with poor grammar," she sighs, "I just have to draw the line."

"Yes, men who don't use spell checkers," Jackie nods.

"It just makes you wonder what else they don't bother with," Eleanor says.

Jackie nods. "I hear you."

"Anyway," Mom says, "I believe in shopping around, waiting for just the right bargain to appear. Plus, I'm joining a group at the city college, a book group for the over-fifty crowd. No romance novels, just good clean fiction, to attract male and female readers."

"Wow," I say. "Literature as lure."

"And what about you, dear," Mom says. "Tell us something fascinating about your week."

I dwell for a moment. Perri came in wearing a red cape this week, but no one dared say anything. Dennis spilled an entire light chocolate latte decaf on his pants, but it really didn't show after a couple of minutes.

"My cable went out again on Wednesday," I say.

"I'll call the company and complain. They'll prorate, you know," Mom says. Jackie nods. "But we were hoping for something a bit more personal," Mom adds.

"Juicy," Jackie says, "If not seamy and downright sluttish, no offense, Eleanor."

"Please," my mother says, "speak freely. Pretend I'm not even here."

"Well, Perri is in search of new clients. She mentioned she's found a boy singing group. They're called the Heartthrobs, if you can believe that." Most of our clients are what might nicely be called B acts on a bill, and not high in demand, but most of them can sing pretty well.

"A boy band," Jackie says. "Hmm."

"Do I sense potential?" Eleanor asks. "And just what is it

you girls mean by 'boy' anyway, agewise? Not that age is everything."

"Although legal age does have some importance," Jackie says.

"Even here in this neighborhood?" Eleanor says. "I wouldn't have guessed."

A pair of twin girls, maybe thirteen, come crashing down the sidewalk on their skateboards. One twin has purple hair. The other has chartreuse, although it could have just been a hair-dye mistake. The neighborhood discourages skateboarders down the sidewalk, but this doesn't stop them much. I think the girls were headed for Bite Me, anyhow.

"The singers are boys in the generic sense, I'm told," I say.

"That's the important sense, of course," Jackie says.

"But they're all over eighteen now, although they've been singing together since they were little kids."

"Over eighteen," my mother muses again. We're a little alarmed.

"Shocking, Eleanor," Jackie kids her.

"You girls are such fuddy-duddies."

"How much over eighteen?" Jackie asks. Remember, numbers are important to her.

"I think the lead singer is twenty-three, the rest somewhere around there," I say.

"How many boys are we talking about here?" Eleanor asks.

"Five," I say. "Not that I've met them." I think about this. I'm not that good with groups of boys. Only-child syndrome and all. It's not really a meeting I'm looking forward to.

"Five heartthrobs," my mother says, raising an eyebrow. "Enough to pass around to your friends." Jackie just shakes her head no. Mom looks disappointed.

"Five boy singers who we hope will soon be surrounded by swarms of underage girls, screaming and throwing their clothes at them."

"Oh," Eleanor says, as if a bubble has just burst.

"Do girls still do that?" Jackie asks. "Throw clothing?"

"Beats me," I say. "Maybe they throw nose rings. Although that sounds a bit dangerous if you're on the receiving end."

"Maybe they throw thongs now," Jackie says. "Leopard print, Victoria's Secret."

"Not at those prices," my well-dressed mother says somewhat primly. We just stare at her for a moment, wondering, unable to bring ourselves to ask the unmentionable about unmentionables. Even Jackie hesitates.

"You girls forget I'm on-line," Eleanor says innocently, picking up a sliver of scone. "Secure shopping."

It may be more than I need to know.

Chapter 4

Who's That Boy?

I arrive at work Monday after a night where I could not sleep, probably because I watched a special on TV where old TV stars were forced to eat slimy creatures while watching their old TV shows. It might be a good question to ask why I even watched this, but part of it is that I used to love those old TV shows. I'm afraid the memories of sitting with my dad and a big bowl of popcorn watching really unsophisticated shows—and it really didn't get much better than that for me at about age eleven—those memories are now ruined by slimy creatures you wouldn't even want to eat in an end-of-the-world scenario. I'm not sure I understand TV anymore at all.

To make it worse, of course, I was completely out of anything at all with caffeine in it this morning, unless you count a bag of emergency chocolate chips, the kind you're supposed to put in cookies, which I keep way in the back of my cupboard, just behind the marjoram. I don't know what you're supposed to do with marjoram, but it hides the chips from my sight, relatively well, at least. For breakfast I ate a rice cake (I'm even out of jam to put on top). There's really nothing at all cakelike about a rice cake that I can figure. I can't say that it made me happy.

I'm afraid I don't arrive at work in my best mood but feeling needy and unloved by congealed rice. In my office, I notice that there's a young guy sitting in my chair, listening attentively to Dennis, whose shirt pocket is hanging half off his shirt again, but in an almost fashionable way, although I doubt he planned it that way. The other guy nearly falls off his chair when he sees me, or, I should say, falls off my chair.

"Hello," I say. "You're in my chair, and I'm territorial." We rarely have guests.

"I'm so sorry," he says. I've flustered him, which I like to do to Dennis's friends when I can, not that he has that many friends, actually. This one can't be much over twenty.

"Claire Duncan, this is Brendan Baker," Dennis says formally. "You have to be nice to him because he's a client."

"Oh," I say, really a little ashamed of myself, but Brendan is looking embarrassed anyhow, I guess so that I won't feel I have to.

"No, it's okay," Brendan says.

"I'm not usually rude to clients," I say, apologetically.

"Claire's never rude to anyone but me, usually." Dennis turns to me. "You must have been out of coffee this morning," Dennis says. He knows me that well.

"Please, it's okay," Brendan says. "I'm in your chair, and you must have work to do."

Dennis actually laughs.

"I have some work to do," I say defensively. "Are you really a client?"

Dennis has brought an uncomfortable-looking metal stool into the office, as our usual blue guest chair is out for repairs. Brendan jumps over to sit on the stool.

"No, no, you're the guest," Dennis says shaking his head. "Here, you should have a padded chair."

"It's true," I tell him, as I can see he's kind of timid for such an attractive (I just noticed) young person. "Plus, you're a paying guest."

"This stool is fine, really. I love it. I have a lot of these in my apartment," he says. I have to wonder how much of a paying client he can be. It's a pretty old stool.

"Brendan is the lead guitarist for the Heartthrobs," Dennis says.

"Oh, you're a Heartthrob," I say, kind of excited. It's not like I throw any clothes or anything, but I can see how it might happen, someday, at least somebody else's throwing. It's just a first impression, but it works for me.

"I don't like the name," Brendan says. Dennis nods and points to his desk, where he's been making notes.

"You mean Brendan Baker or the Heartthrobs?" I say. I need clarity on so little real food.

Dennis gives me a look. "The Heartthrobs, of course."

"I'm sorry, I only had a rice cake this morning," I admit.

"Oh," they both say, completely understanding. I do feel comforted. I can see we'll be able to work together. Brendan is one of us, clearly lacking appreciation for crunchy tasteless food.

"Not that Brendan Baker is all that great," Brendan Baker says.

"No, it's good," I say. "Alliteration is important for name recognition."

"Really?" he says.

"We were English majors," Dennis says. Brendan looks relieved. I, for some reason, am starting to feel much better about myself.

"The Heartthrobs," I say, sitting back in my chair.

"It's bad," Brendan says.

"It's sixties," Dennis says.

"But not in the way you wish it were," I say. They nod. "What have you come up with so far? Oh, and is this okay with the rest of the band?"

"No one likes the name. It's what our moms used to call us."

"Say no more," I say. "Time to rebel." I point at their list.

Dennis reads the list: "If we stick with the theme, we have Heartbreak, Heartbeat, Heartache—"

"Do we want to stick with the theme?" I ask.

"I don't think we want to stick with the theme," Dennis says, "although apparently they have a lot stationery with hearts on it."

"From my mom," Brendan says, truly embarrassed.

"We believe firmly, here at Persephonia!, in recycling," I suggest.

"Whenever possible," Dennis says. "Okay, moving down the list: Stillwater, Black Lake, Everclear."

"What's with the water imagery?" I ask.

"We thought it was peaceful," Brendan says.

I have to wonder how long they've been working on these. It's not like I was late this morning, so I guess it wasn't long.

"Is your music especially peaceful?" I ask.

"Not exactly," Brendan says.

"Is it that you want your audience to feel—rested, relaxed, or, let's face it, sleepy?"

Brendan almost smiles. "We're really kind of loud, but we have a firm belief in the melodic standards of rockabilly music, too."

"So napping amongst the audience wouldn't be a goal of yours," I say.

"I guess that if someone fell asleep at our concert—" Brendan starts to seriously consider it, but Dennis and I just look at each other, recognizing that Brendan is not capable of serious kidding. We make a mental note. Brendan goes on: "I would hope that someone else in the audience would try to wake that person and make sure that he or she didn't need to be taken to the hospital. There's really no other good reason for a sleeping audience member. Not that I can think of."

"You don't use drugs, do you," Dennis says, half-disparaging, half-disappointed. I guess Dennis has fallen asleep at a few concerts, one way or another, in his day.

"No," Brendan says, alarmed. It actually goes through my mind: *Kids these days.*

"Good," Dennis says, not that convincingly. "Okay, any positive, useful ideas, Claire?"

"Okay, rockabilly-like, kind of loud. Positive, happy music."

"Sometimes covers," Brendan says. "When appropriate."

"Appropriate covers for special times, special feelings." He nods. Oh boy. I need to think of a name for a boy singing group, and I don't think this was in my job description. I can see it wasn't in Dennis's, as he looks stumped.

"I like the area kind of names," I say. "You know, Alabama, Chicago."

"Santana," Dennis says. I look at him. "Not that it's a place," he admits, "but it feels like it could be."

"Montana," I say. "Like Santana but with the real place imagery."

"Montana," Dennis says. "I can't think of any cracks to make about it. Give me a minute."

"Montana," Brendan says, rolling the word around his lyricist mouth, which, by the way, is quite nice. Thousands of girls will want to kiss it. I can just tell this kind of thing, as I was under thirty once myself. Dennis sees me looking at Brendan's mouth and raises his eyebrows. I just shake my head no, no, of course not, no.

"Montana," Brendan says again, snapping our attention back to him.

"What do you guys usually wear on stage?" I say.

"Jeans," Brendan says, "shirts." He points to Dennis's torn shirt, as if that might be the very one he'd wear.

"We'll get to work," I say. "We'll get coffee, though, first."

"Maybe a muffin?" Brendan suggests. I like him a lot, I realize, and even Dennis looks like Brendan has just risen in his estimation. Brendan notices the new looks of approval on our faces.

"Or maybe pancakes?" he suggests quietly but bravely.

After work I reward myself with a trip to my therapist's office, or, what my mother calls Seeing That Woman. I try to think of therapy as a reward, something I've earned, rather than something I have to do, like buying floss, which is something else I have to do tonight. But the fact is, I've been in therapy for a year or so now, although I've tried it before once or twice (it's twice). If it helps, I stick with it, if not, I make fun of it with Jackie, who I know has a preference for male therapists. I tend to figure I have enough problems without needing the extra one of lusting after my therapist.

"It gives me something to think about, between complaints," Jackie says, as she's currently lusting after her Asian-American therapist, aged thirty-five, very handsome and confident. We once saw him at one of our Saturday morning coffee shops where you have to wait if you arrive after 8:30, which is what we were doing, in a line pressed flat against the building to avoid the morning beachy drizzle. He had clearly arrived right on time to get a seat, as well as one for his wife and approximately nine-month-old child dressed in a gender-free green one-piece.

"He has an attractive family," I mentioned to Jackie. "I find that comforting in a therapist."

"It wouldn't be my first choice," Jackie said. Her therapist waved when he saw us, his wife smiled, and the green-suited infant dropped a bottle of something about the same green color as its clothing.

But I'm fairly happy to stick with my own therapist, whose name—and my mother thinks I'm just hiding it from her—is really Claire, just like mine. My therapist and I share the same name. We also have similar hairstyles—mine is long and somewhat curly, hers a little straighter and, I'm sure my mother would say, better tended. It has that cut so it can curve around her face. What we used to call a shag, only longer. Claire also dresses a little like I do, liking long skirts like mine topped with Ts, although I often (but not always) tie an old blue denim work shirt around my waist, a habit left over from gym class, where I used a sweatshirt to hide my always-white thighs from view under those ugly blue gym shorts. I think there may be two kinds of women in the world, the kind who tie on an extra shirt (thin sweaters work, too) and the kind who don't feel the need. I've never gotten past the tie-around-your-waist phase of life, although my mother says that it's completely unnecessary for what she always refers to as my "barely size eight body," which she'll also claim is really a size six if I'd only shop in the better women's department.

"Really, you have such a nice little figure, why not show it off," my mother has said. Jackie's view of my extra layer is less imposing: "If it makes you feel better and is in no way carcinogenic, I think it's fine," Jackie has said. I like this theory and use it in much of my daily life. It also works for nail-biting and lying around the house watching old Disney movies from my childhood, just to name two activities.

But Claire the Therapist, as Jackie and I call her between ourselves, is unafraid to show off her figure, I guess, as she just wears her skirts and tops as is. I'm not sure, actually, that I would continue to see a therapist who perhaps compulsively covered her bottom with a spare shirt, although I still say it isn't hurting anyone if a plain old copywriter does it. Sometimes it's even right in style.

"Look, *Vogue* has Julianne Moore with a Gap sweatshirt tied around her waist," Jackie once showed my mother and me at brunch. Jackie's always trying to support my fashion statements, as well as my compulsions and phobias, as that's what best friends are for.

"Well, I guess they forgot to invite her mother to the photo shoot," my own mom said. "Plus, she needs a barrette." The poor star's hair was blowing uncontrollably at a beach, although she seemed like she was trying to keep it together.

"I think they wanted that windswept look," I said, although it looked like she was about to eat her hair. My mom just shook her head.

"Maybe a headband," I said, giving in. My mother nodded. Jackie turned the page. I thought about picking up a new blue Gap sweatshirt. It would complement my pink and plum skirt, especially from the back.

Claire the Therapist and I always have lots to talk about, although it's really me doing the talking, or it's supposed to be, at least. She's just out of therapy school or whatever you call it and a couple of years younger than I am, which relieves me from ever feeling like perhaps she's mothering me with advice. This is not something I want from a therapist, as my mother does her job perfectly well.

Claire's office is in a busy area of Santa Monica, not that far from my Venice office and borderline Venice/Santa Monica apartment, and despite the cars that find themselves zooming around the blocks here, I always easily find a place to park. She's on the upper floor of an old Spanish-style building, and each time I walk up the stairs, I like to look over into the park next door, where I can just barely see children as they scream insults at one another at the top of their lungs, insults I've really never heard before. So far, I've learned several new ones: duckmouth (yelled at a little girl in yellow, but I didn't see any sort of ducklike feature about her—in fact, she was absolutely beautiful), tweezerface, puttyhead, measlemouth, and my favorite, hairhead, a variation on my own generation's airhead, maybe, albeit more descriptive. I can't always see which child is being called which name, and sometimes it's fun to guess. Writer that I am, I try to remember the insults for use later. Dennis seems intrigued by them, I've learned. And it's only one flight up.

Claire greets me in her office. She has a little outer office where she often hangs dry cleaning, which she insists on airing out thoroughly to get out the chemicals. I don't have this problem as everything I own can be washed. Dry-clean-only tags are just another sign that you shouldn't be buying it or that rules were meant to be broken (so just wash it in cold). I think it's a little funny that Claire the Therapist hangs her blouses in her outer office, but they are nice blouses and, after all, clean. The first time I looked at the blouses she just shrugged and said, "No clothesline." I guess I understand.

Claire doesn't have an assistant in the outer office—one might object to laundry hanging, no doubt—but she does have two answering machines, one black one that blinks red, the other a fluorescent green, modern-looking cube that blinks purple.

"A gift from my mom," she's said, all any girl needs to say to another sometimes. As someone whose own mother has given her two pink cell phones in the last two years (both lost), I understand. The mother-daughter connection requires a world of electronic devices never dreamed of by suffragettes, but I think they'd applaud them all the same. Especially the cell phones that attach to your head with a headband so you can talk and exercise at the same time, if you can do two things at once, that is. My own mother has hinted I have to get one of those, and I do have a birthday coming up, although I don't really exercise very much.

"What shall we talk about today?" Claire the Therapist asks me as we hunker down in a blue denim slip-covered sofa (my seat) and matching chair (her seat), sipping from matching red cups of chamomile tea. Claire swears chamomile tea is the most freeing for her patients, although peppermint works too, she says, and can be cheering in times of need.

She also serves us graham cracker-style biscuits that are actually made of rice flour, as Claire is wheat free. It's a big subject for her, not that we have much time for Claire's subjects.

"I'll serve you the foods I know are better for you," she's always said, "but I won't get into the why. There's nutritional brochures by the door, but I don't feel right charging you for the time it would take to lecture," she has said. I've read the brochures, which cover everything from acne to exhaustion being caused by wheat, dairy, meat, and starch. Really, except for the crackers and tea, I'm not sure what Claire the Therapist finds left to eat. I usually throw in a question before leaving:

"See you next week," I'll say. "By the way, what about smoothies?"

She always knows what I mean. "Watch out for cow's milk, look for goat or soy," she'll say with a nod of approval, although I don't think I've seen goat milk smoothies before.

But back to today. I don't really have a special topic. We've covered the range, a lot of work after my father's death, my main reason for coming back to therapy. Talk about Andy, my former boyfriend and still landlord, a subject even Jackie doesn't like talking about, as she has trouble with the idea of my paying Andy, even though the apartment is wonderful and I'm glad to have it. Then there's my relationship with my mother, ever-changing now that there're just two of us left. There's my work, and there's dating, mostly as in, "Gee, I'm not dating," plus all the fashion magazine stuff you can fill the time in with: food, exercise, how much we need of each, and why we read fashion magazines at all.

I tell her about our new client, Brendan. "Young," I say, "but talented. He sang for us softly at breakfast." It's true, Brendan did sing a song, nearly hiding his head under the table in embarrassment despite a very nice voice and the fact that several young waitresses were very interested in hearing. Dennis made him do it. He told Brendan it was so that I could get a feel for the sound, although it's not like Dennis hadn't just put a demo tape on my desk. He didn't mean it in a mean way, it was just more teasing, he told me after lunch. Dennis has a few older sisters and younger brothers. I tell all this to Claire.

"Boys are different," Claire the Therapist tells me. "Whole different relationships, ways of communicating, means of interaction. Teasing equals tenderness. I have three younger brothers. Running and jumping take on serious levels of importance. But no one's really ever been able to say why."

"That must be kind of fun, a big family," I say. "And helpful, so your parents have more people to pick on at family dinners," I say.

"There are advantages," she says. "But growing up I always just felt that the boys smelled funny."

"My mother just has me now," I say.

"And her work," Claire suggests.

"Yes, she's devoted to the ladies who curl and clip and decorate. The ladies of her boutiques and salons where she's the bookkeeper. She believes in them. Of course, they pay her, so they're successful enough, but I sense she'd believe in them anyway."

"It would have to be a comfort," Claire the Therapist says.

"Yes. More comfort than I am, sometimes, I'm afraid."

"You have to take care of you, first. You can work on helping her, but that's second," Claire says. Claire often likes to number priorities for me although I continually tell her I'm bad at math. Maybe that's why she does it. Maybe that's why she always stays below seven priorities.

"I didn't mean to start talking about my mother," I say.

"But you did," my therapist gets to point out. Really, she does have the easier job here of the two of us, I often have to think.

"How does this happen?" I ask. "I start out talking about this very cute boy singer and end up talking about Eleanor. She doesn't even like rock music."

"He's a rock musician?" Claire says, a little interested.

"Yeah, a good one, and connected to our agency. Imagine." I think about it.

"That's great," Claire says, and I realize it is.

"Yeah, a cute boy singer at our agency," I say, thinking of the last client who left us, who was neither young nor cute, and who dressed like Indiana Jones while playing a harp. Rock music on a harp, sort of. It really didn't work for him. Harpists are usually popular in a certain element of our culture—the wedding circuit especially—but he really didn't fit in to it. Even in Venice. I think of Brendan instead and wonder how he'll fit in.

"A cute boy singer who I get to choose a new name and look for," I say.

"And you say nothing good ever happens," Claire the Therapist says.

"This may be indecent to think about," I say. "I mean, I'm thirty, far too old for a twenty-three-year-old boy—"

"Man," Claire says. "Even at twenty-three you have to call them men. It's in all my therapy manuals."

"No, you don't," I say. "Not when they get the big bucks for being in an all-boy singing group. 'All-men singing group' just doesn't sound right, especially to all girls buying the records."

"Interesting," Claire says, jotting something down on her pad. "Would I have heard of the group?" she asks.

"They were called the Heartthrobs," I say. Claire the Therapist cringes at the Saturday morning cartoonishness of the name, no doubt, then grabs a rice cracker as if to get the bad taste of the Heartthrobs' name out of her mouth.

"I can't say I've heard them," she says.

"You probably haven't touched a *Teen Beat* in years," I say.

"Well," Claire says, "we'll just have to keep my reading habits out of our sessions," she says cryptically. "But I still don't know the group."

I wonder about my therapist, but mostly I'm left thinking about Brendan, the boy singer.

"I'm renaming the group Montana," I try out on Claire. She's proven a very good audience for my writing in the past, especially enjoying my radio ads for a woman named Marie who wears very tight black T-shirts and has billboards placed in Hollywood with her name on them, but otherwise doesn't do much else. Claire's found my ads for her to be "illusive yet still persuasive," which I'll take as a compliment, especially given that we don't know exactly what Marie can do. Jackie has assured me that whatever it is, most radio stations would probably lose their license if they played it. Dennis maintains a more wait-and-see attitude, although I notice he's always stumped about what to write for her promotions, not to mention when she comes into the office. But that's a whole different story.

"I think I might like to hear them," Claire says, taking me back to my new group, Montana.

"I haven't met the other boys yet," I say. "But based on the music, they have actual potential."

"This is a whole new field for you," my therapist says.

"Hmm, clients as potential moneymakers," I say.

"Not to mention boys with potential," Claire says, pouring me more tea and making me wonder just what potential she's referring to, and whether it's okay to wonder.

I wonder all the way home.

Chapter 5

Why We Never Cry Over Spilt Latte

Dennis and I are at work early in our office, engaged in our morning rituals. I guess we all have them, and they do seem to change over the years. I remember there were days and days as a child when I had to have a waffle with a mound of butter in the center, and I had to pour the syrup on without it spilling over the waffle's sides. I in no way found this compulsive, more of a contest with myself, a way to tell how the rest of my fifth-grade-or-so day would go. If I could only keep the syrup on the waffle, I would tell myself, maybe I could win the spelling bee. Really, I don't know why I thought this. I became quite the little expert at pouring syrup on waffles just so, and I never did win a spelling bee. Perhaps all these years of advanced English courses were just a way to make up for it. Not to mention all these years of waffles. I still can't get enough. And now I like syrup all over the plate. I'm sure my therapist would find this healthy.

And so now having a cup of black currant tea with just enough sugar and cream seems a fine way to start a work morning—and I don't care if I even spill a little cream. It's not like I'm afraid it will affect my day, even. And then there's Dennis with his compulsion for frothy latte drinks inexplicably sprinkled with powdered sugar, which finds its way all over our shared office. Dennis's powdered drug of choice, Jackie calls it. While I like to find myself reading the paper on-line during my tea, and reviewing my e-mail, Dennis does do that thing where he searches his papers over and over. I guess it makes me feel good, as if I were the winner in the mental-health-in-the-morning-ritual department. I never much search for anything that's gone lost. I have this feeling that if I've lost something I've written—ad copy, promotional materials, whatever—it probably needed to be rewritten. A copywriter's subconscious at work, or maybe I'm just rationalizing.

Dennis starts searching. Powdered sugar goes flying.

"You know," I start, "this place is going to attract ants with all that sugar."

Dennis looks up from his riffling through papers, several of which fall to the ground, causing him to knock into his drink, all of which is fairly funny in that helpless male way, and might even make me laugh, but I notice it's beginning to take on a certain grace. A modern dance of frothy drink and confusion.

"I'm looking for something," Dennis says, a little agitated. He grabs his drink before it can fall to the floor.

"I noticed that," I say. "Can I help? Would I know where it is? Would you like help devising a filing system so you don't have to do this?"

"Do what?" Dennis says. He grabs a piece of paper and holds it up triumphantly. "Aha," he says.

"Do that," I say. "The thing where you look for something every morning and juggle your café au lait."

"I never juggle," Dennis says, "and it's a choco-latte, low-fat. And," he continues, "it's not like I haven't seen you doing your morning thing every day."

"I don't have a morning thing," I say. "I have a cup of tea."

"Uh huh," Dennis says, "you have a cup of tea with two packets of sugar and a drop of half-and-half that you pour for two seconds—I've heard you count."

"I count?" I say. This is bad, I think, something I may need to tell Claire the Therapist about. Counting while pouring. I wonder what it could mean.

"Well, maybe you were just talking to yourself," Dennis admits.

Good, I think, something I don't have to tell my therapist about, or at least I think I don't.

"But then," Dennis says, getting excited about this, "you always take a wooden stirrer, never a spoon."

"The spoons have to be washed," I say, getting defensive. "Wooden stirrers are more time efficient."

"And you never use the plastic stirrers," Dennis says.

"We have plastic stirrers?" I ask.

"You take a wooden stirrer from the left side of the stirrer holder and stir three times," Dennis says, a "so there" implied in his voice.

"Well, frankly, I'm not sure you've at all established that even if I do this, even if it's a habit, it's anything near the obsession you're aiming for," I say.

"Oh," Dennis says, disappointed. "I think I was going for compulsion, though, rather than obsession."

"I always get the two confused," I admit. "But I think *you* may have more of an obsession and/or compulsion if you've stood there counting how long I do that than I have actually doing it."

"It does have a certain charm, the way you stir," Dennis says, trying to make up, I think.

I find it interesting that Dennis has been watching me pour and stir, even if he's just amused by it, although I still feel I have to stand up for my sanity.

"You just bring this up to avoid talking about your terrible filing system," I say, reminding myself that I really

should have the upper hand here as my tea-stirring procliv-
ities don't affect anyone else, and I always recycle my stirrers.

"I don't like to file," Dennis says, which I already know.
Dennis has huge files in his drawer that say A, B, C, and so
on down the alphabet, but it's not always clear why he'll put
something under B, say, over D. And most of his work tends
to end up under A, which I've asked him about.

"Why is this radio copy about cowboy boots in the
drawer under A?" I remember asking.

"A for advertising," Dennis said automatically.

Since we work in an advertising agency, you can imagine
how thick the A file is getting.

"My system works for me," Dennis says.

"Sure, everything is under A!" I say.

"And how can that not work?" Dennis asks.

Maybe it's gender related. Maybe there's just no way we
can learn to file together, I have to think sometimes.

"What happens if you're not here, and I need something
from your files?"

"Where would I be?" Dennis asks, although I think this
is beside the point.

"You could be at the beach," I say.

Dennis holds up his cell phone.

"We'll always be fiber-optically connected," Dennis says,
"if not digitally so."

"My cell phone is missing," I say, not willing to put it in
the active voice by saying "I lost my cell phone, again."

"Your Barbie one?" Dennis says, a little sad.

"Not Barbie," I say. "Just pink."

"Sure not Barbie. My sister had one just like it when she
was ten," Dennis says. "It would connect you with Midge
and Skipper, but if you dialed Ken, you got a message that
he was out."

"At the beach, no doubt," I say.

Dennis shrugs.

"Without his cell phone," I try to make the point.

"Gee, no one's ever compared me with a Ken doll," Dennis says, somewhat shyly rubbing his beard. Dennis doesn't have the strongest self-image despite many ex-girlfriends, and I'm not about to tell him he looks just fine. I'm not sure having a conceited officemate would be much fun, and I know it wouldn't help with the filing one bit.

"You could be at the dentist, you know," I continue, "mouth full, unable to talk when I need to find something."

"In which case I think it would be a comfort to know you could check the A file first," Dennis says. He pulls out the A file and places his newfound papers inside, then puts the file away.

"A for advertisement," Dennis says.

"A for A creature of habit," I say.

Dennis shrugs and knocks his drink completely on the floor. It's not like it hasn't happened before. Yesterday, actually.

"Do you notice I never get to finish them?" he asks me, then sighs.

I don't bother to tell him I have.

After Dennis's elaborate morning rituals, followed by our discussing them or just bickering innocently but ritualistically about something, we often sit down to a staff meeting. Staff meetings here at Persephonia! aren't always daily or weekly, although we used to have a schedule where we held them on Tuesdays and Thursdays, with an optional Wednesday if any of our clients had made news. Wednesdays are usually pretty quiet, though.

We don't have a fancy conference room here in our offices. I often run across people I went to college with and hear them talk about their glamorous offices in downtown L.A., swanky Century City. They often mention the word "plush" when talking about Century City offices, as in plush carpet, plush couches, plush wall coverings, although I admit I have no idea what a plush wall covering is, nor do I much like the idea. And too much plush is just a haven for dust mites, anyway, I figure.

That's not to say we're not in our own enviable position here. Our Persephonia! office is located in a converted warehouse in Venice, only a few blocks from actual shoreline. It's valuable property, no doubt, or at least it would be, if anyone ever fixed the place up. Outside, the building is gray and graying, but fortunately not that noticeable from the street, as we're hidden by a hedge of something that grows green all year round but is very scratchy if you catch your arm on it when you walk by, which I tend to do. Inside, the building has been divided into smaller offices, or compartments. Our office is surrounded by other creative and semicreative businesses, including a prop company (we love it there, although Dennis doesn't like to try on wigs quite as much as I do), an antiques refurbisher, a floral arrangement office (worth a visit for good smells, not to mention the discounts they give us on flowers), and an iron welder (a bit of a throwback to the days when this really was a warehouse). The walls inside our office are all white, and as I mentioned are supposedly stuffed with straw, but no one knows for sure. It's a bright white in here and catches the reflections off the skylights, and sometimes makes you feel you need to wear sunglasses indoors. Our office space is not big, no lunchroom for us, just the storeroom where we have a coffeepot and a potted plant, which I admit most people water by putting their cold coffee into, but it must be one of those heavily bred palms, and it does just fine. There's also an old checkerboard table to eat on and twelve remaining checkers, just for the challenge. The office can be too bright and too cold, but I love it here. Anyone would. If you're not looking for plush, that is.

Out in the hallway shared by all the former warehouse's offices, you can find four old-fashioned, coin-operated rides. They are a palomino horsey ride, an elephant, a yellow car for two, and a petite merry-go-round for three. Although the rides have signs attached to them that say "Out of Order, Do Not Touch," intended no doubt for visitors to the building, those of us who work here know these rides work just fine. I have no idea who owns them, let alone keeps them in such good working order, but I have taken my share of rides, and I do know that Dennis is as fond of the elephant as I am of the palomino. I've yet to sit in the yellow car for two. I don't want to have to ride it all alone.

Dennis and I gather at a table that sits outside Perri's office in our tiny conference area, a table made out of steel that's always a little cold to the touch and looks like it came out of some restaurant, and I can picture chefs dressed in tall white hats creating pastries of delicious fluffiness. I can't quite explain it, but sitting here always makes me crave sweets. I'm always deeply indebted to anyone who thought ahead enough to bring in donuts for the meeting, but few of us ever do. I choose a seat on the side away from Perri's office and next to Dennis, who likes to write notes to me on his yellow pad while people are talking, even if only four or five of us are at the meeting, which is about all of us anyway. So you couldn't exactly call them secret notes. I often answer his questions with doodles of pastries. I guess my mother is right. I really should eat breakfast.

Joining us this morning is Josie, the twenty-three-year-old office secretary/administrative assistant. She's really not the kind of person who fusses over her title, which is refreshing, not to mention a lucky thing, as Perri isn't fond of handing out titles. Josie lives a little in awe of Perri, often changing her hair color—she has short boyish hair that looks adorable on her but would make me want to wear a hat every day. Her regular color is a great dark blonde, but this week it's deep brown with reddish highlights, to accompany Perri's new do. Perri, rather than buckling at being copied, seems to have begun to feel it's a requirement from her assistant. I love Josie, as she always provides us with little jokes (she seems to have found an AM radio station that tells actual funny jokes in the morning, another thing I have to admire, although I prefer my mornings quiet), and she's unswervingly upbeat, even though she does let Perri walk all over her. Plus, this morning she's the one who has brought donuts.

"They're the low-fat kind," Josie tells us, opening up the box.

"It's not possible," Dennis replies, not hesitating, though, to take one that looks to be stuffed with some very high-fat jelly, if jelly can be high-fat.

"No, no," Josie insists. "These are not your mother's donuts."

"Not my mother's," I say. My mom believes in bran flakes. She was bran before bran was cool.

"They're made by a special process that extracts oils and fats, and are sweetened by natural fruit juices. Plus, they're made from rice flour. They're called Ronuts," Josie adds.

Dennis takes a bite. I grab a chocolate one, since I believe Josie, or I want to believe her. Aren't young people always up on this stuff?

"Each Ronut is carefully extracted of all extraneous oils and fats, then sweetened to a delicate taste by fruit juice," Dennis says, "followed by deep frying in enough oil to block a thousand arteries." Dennis lets his copywriting skills take over.

"Maybe," Josie admits, "but at least there's none of those artificial sweeteners."

I take a bite. "Mine tastes funny."

"Too much natural rice flour?" Dennis asks.

"It's carob, not chocolate," Josie says. "Better for you."

My spirits sink. "But chocolate means so much to me," I say, "especially in the morning."

"There's some cocoa puffs in the storeroom," Dennis says.

"Too crackly," I say like the little kid I've become.

"Plus they're about three years old," Dennis says, "although I think that just adds interest to them."

Josie makes a note to herself, probably to clean out the storeroom. I happen to know there's also a box of tapioca pudding in there for no good reason.

Dennis turns to Josie, "See what your health food has wrought? What good is a depressed copywriter in need of chocolate and given nothing better than a carob Ronut?"

Josie seems truly sorry. "I only meant the best," she says.

"It's okay," I say. "I can get used to it." I scrape a little carob off my Ronut and taste it on a finger. Dennis leans over toward my Ronut and scrapes at it too, and since it isn't really chocolate and I don't care about it, I don't even ask him if his hands are clean.

"Kind of like chocolaty chalk," he says. Josie lowers her head.

"But in the best-meant way," I tell her. She seems a little uplifted.

Malcolm comes in. He looks at the Ronuts. "Did you save a skim milk low-fat blueberry and rice bran muffin for Perri?" he asks.

Josie pulls one out of her lap.

"Sweetened by natural apple juice?" Dennis asks.

"Actually," Josie tells us, "if I give her the no-fat one, she tends to get grumpy by noon."

"Versus giving her the high-fat one, where she doesn't get grumpy till 12:30?" Dennis asks.

"No," Josie says, "they have a mid-level muffin. Low-fat

with organic sugar." Josie nods her head. Malcolm seems impressed.

"But no chocolate," Dennis says to me. He goes back to our cubicle, an entire fifteen feet away. I hear him rummaging.

Malcolm stands over the Ronut box, his hair in his eyes. Perri will have a fit. She prefers Malcolm, her twenty-two-year-old progeny, and a very nice boy, to have his hair carefully tended by a salon up the street called Ringlets. They do straight hair, too, which is where Malcolm would fit, with his brown straight locks that generally tend to fall into his eyes. For all of Perri's outrageousness in dress and behavior, Malcolm is calm, studied, and a bit shy. Josie likes to bolster him, as do we all, well, except for maybe Dennis, who just likes to tease him.

"Have a Ronut, Malcolm," I say. He could actually use a real donut, I think. Really, he's far too skinny. Jackie always likes to say that Malcolm hasn't grown into himself yet, like a little Labrador puppy.

"Big-paws potential, though," she has said, meaning perhaps Malcolm will grow up someday.

Malcolm looks in the box for a long time. I notice these Ronuts don't particularly smell, not like that good whoosh of butter, sugar, flour, you get when you walk into an old-fashioned donut shop, which I admit I like to do, even if I'm just window-shopping. These must be health food store donuts after all.

"I could just have half," Malcolm says, cutting one open with a knife. I think it's stuffed with oranges, which seems inappropriate to a donut to me, and I don't care how healthy it's meant to be.

"Live dangerously," Dennis says to Malcolm, having returned from our cubicle. "Try a whole one."

"Take this carob one if you really want to live dangerously," I say. I've been trying to scrape the carob stuff off my tongue with my teeth, discreetly that is, not that our group hasn't seen me do this kind of thing before.

Dennis pokes me in the ribs, and under the table he hands me a small jar of Quick chocolate powder. "For you," he says quietly.

He sprinkles some on my Ronut, and despite that it looks slightly disgusting, it does help a lot.

"My hero," I say, really impressed. I sneak my almost-empty teacup into my lap, and Dennis pours in some Quick. I stir and swallow. You'd think it wouldn't taste good with tea, but taste is a relative thing.

"Ready to face the day," I say to him.

"The copywriter's Tang," Dennis says, directly putting a spoonful of Quick into his mouth. He spills a little.

"Remember Tang?" I say. Josie and Malcolm shake their heads no.

"I was very young at the time, of course," I say.

"Plus it was probably all unnatural," Dennis says. "But it had taste." We both look at my healthy carob Ronut, unloved and tastefree, at least good-taste free.

Perri approaches. Malcolm takes the rest of my carob Ronut and seems to swallow it in one gulp. Dennis looks impressed in that big-brother way. I'm just glad Malcolm didn't choke and that he probably didn't have time to taste the carob all that much.

"Good morning, people," Perri announces. "Let's not dawdle talking all day around the donut box," she says, and it occurs to me that we really would do something like that, if they were real donuts at least, but I don't think Perri realizes it. I think it's her stab at a joke.

"Actually, they're Ronuts," says Dennis, the only one brave enough some days to take on Perri. "The R is for rice flour," he adds.

"Or revolting," Perri says. Josie passes her the muffin.

Perri eyes it suspiciously, then takes a small crumb of it in her fingers and rolls it around.

"Not nonfat, right?" Perri asks Josie.

Josie looks horrified at the thought. "Good," Perri says.

Our boss, the leader of Persephonia!, is the kind of woman you just have to look at, whether you think she's attractive or not. And sometimes it's hard to decide this, too, as Perri likes to change her look (she'd be very popular at Billie's, my mother's beauty salon client, no doubt a Frequent Flyer, as Billie likes to refer to her clients with standing appointments). Perri often refers to herself as fortysomething plus as she doesn't believe that it enables women to tell their exact ages.

"Revealing one's age only gives credence to the mythologies supporting ageism and sexism," she has said, although I'm not certain I follow. But then, I'm never fond of telling my age, either, although I can't really explain why in such pithy terms. At least Perri has a philosophy, I figure, even if it is slightly undecipherable. After all, such things never seem to hurt elected officials much.

Perri is joined by our art director, David—although Perri still insists on doing some of the art herself, that is, criticizing what David does. David is about my age, a few years older maybe, and eternally sleepy and calm, despite owlish glasses that make him look constantly surprised and alert. I've asked him if he really needs the glasses, as I noticed once that the prescription seemed awfully mild (I'm near-blind without my only slightly blue-tinted contact lenses).

"I've found them to be useful around here," David has said of his glasses. "Although what I really want the world to develop is some sort of automatically tinting glasses."

"They have those," I told him.

"Yes," David said, "but I want them to tint based on my mood," he said. David is gay, our only gay staff member, which he laments constantly to anyone who'll listen, usually me. You just can't ruffle him, and Perri really has tried, it seems.

"At the very least," he said, "I want glasses to begin tinting when certain people enter the room." We were listening at the time to Perri harass Malcolm about his clothes over her intercom, although it seemed like the kind of mother-son talk they might have had face to face, not to mention in private. It's pretty small in here for that kind of thing.

David waves off our offer of Ronuts and takes out a Tab. I didn't know they still made Tab.

"So, Claire," Perri starts. "Tell us about the new boys."

"Well," I begin, "it's true, we do have a new group of boy singers." Everyone applauds, all five of them.

"New blood," Dennis says.

"New male blood," David and Perri say together.

Perri looks at some photos of the boy group. "But really, Heartthrobs?"

"The name is gone," I say. "They're now Montana."

"Montana," everyone mutters, sounding it out.

Dennis holds his hands like a megaphone. "Ladies and gentlemen, Montana," he says loudly. It echoes a little through the office.

"Rugged sounding, but not too country," David says.

"Kind of like Santana," Josie says, almost a question.

"But more like with an M," Dennis says.

"That would be Mantana," Josie says.

"Something entirely different," I say.

"They'd have to be Boytana, anyway," David says. "Which is really not what you want."

Perri waves the conversation away like some cigarette smoke. "Montana. I like the sound of it," Perri says, although her eyes are still glued to the picture of the boys. It's not that great a photo, and the boys aren't posed very well, but there's still something about it, about them. Even Josie is trying to get a look.

"Exactly how old a group of 'boys' are we talking about?" David wants to know. I give him a raised eyebrow look. "For art direction purposes, of course," he says. Actually, Josie seems to want to know, too, and I notice Perri has raised her eyes as well.

"Over twenty-one," I say, "but just barely."

There seems to be a group hmmm. Dennis looks at the picture. "Those clothes have got to go," he says of the group's mismatched T-shirts, even though his clothes are not exactly fancy, let alone colors you'd choose to wear together, although faded denim does tend to go with so much. Dennis's jeans are quickly becoming kneeless, and his shirt used to be maroon, as I recall. I pinch the fabric of his shirt and shrug my question at him.

"I didn't say *I* should be the one to get them new outfits," he says, and I like the way he says the word "outfit."

"Costumes," I correct him. "Outfits are for little kids."

Dennis directs my eyes back to the photo. They do look kind of young.

"I'm sure Claire can think of some appropriate attire," Perri says, "something twenty-one-plus but with a flavor that suggests a little more worldliness."

"So the teenyboppers' moms can have reason to listen in on their daughters' CDs," Malcolm whispers to me, although he's been pretty quiet till now. He seems unimpressed with the Montana boys. All the guys at the table seem a little grumpy, I notice.

"Claire," Perri announces. "It's your call—you can take Montana and run with them. Sort of a personal project."

This is new, really, because we usually all work together, writing copy or doing art for any of the clients as needs arise. I'm not sure I'm ready to handle the boys myself.

"We could split the boys up," I suggest, but even I know it isn't a great idea.

"I think you're ready," Perri says.

"A toast to Claire and the boy band," David says, raising a Ronut. Everyone grabs one for the toast, but David only takes a teeny bite. Not a health food enthusiast.

"It doesn't mean we won't help you," Malcolm says. Josie nods helpfully, brimming with good intentions.

"Of course," Dennis adds. "But we should probably hear them in person. I mean, I know they're cute."

"You think?" I ask him.

"Well, I can tell you think they're cute," he says, looking around the room, and Josie blushes a little as clearly she thinks they're awfully cute.

"But with better clothes," Josie starts.

"Or maybe fewer clothes," Perri suggests. "Just keep it in mind." She studies the picture again.

"They're playing Saturday night at the Grange," I say. "You can hear them in person."

"I thought it was the Grangey," Malcolm says. Honestly, we don't think Malcolm ever much leaves his studio apartment, not that I actually go out very much and almost never to anyplace like the Grange, which tends to have those slippery kind of floors that make you wonder what you're walking on.

"The Grange," says Dennis. "I used to go there when I was a college kid."

"Kind of a smelly place," Josie says.

"Still, it's part of our job," I say.

"Consider it a fringe benefit. I'll pay," Perri says. "You kids go," she says, looking to Dennis and me, and Malcolm and Josie, even though Malcolm seems like he'd like to hide under the table right now. David is just shaking his head no. David has higher standards of dives then the rest of us, I know. Or maybe just different standards.

"Consider it research," Dennis says to me.

"Take notes," Perri says to Josie, who nods, empowered by a sudden role in all this.

"Josie can be my assistant for The Montana Project," I say.

"Gee, it's gone from Montana to The Montana Project," David says.

"That means the art has to be even better," I say.

"Believe me, just wait till you see the bus boards. These guys splayed across the big blue bus," David says.

"Now you're thinking," Perri says, closing the meeting by standing up and twirling a long maroon skirt behind her.

"The Grangey?" I ask Malcolm.

"Maybe it was just a descriptive term we used," he says.

"We used to call it The Grunge," Dennis says.

"I'll pack a notebook," Josie says.

"And petty cash," Dennis says.

We sit at the table looking at one another, Dennis and I on one side, Malcolm and Josie on the other. It's a date, I guess, although an employer-sponsored one, which is new for me, and I thought I'd seen every kind of date there was. This one feels a little more like a game of foursquare than a typical double date. Not to mention that I think my date Saturday night is really Josie, who's the most excited about the whole thing.

"The sign outside won't say Heartthrobs, will it?" Malcolm asks.

"Don't worry," Dennis says. "We'll buy you a Heartthrobs T-shirt with petty cash."

Malcolm unhappily slinks away.

"Do you really think they have Heartthrob T-shirts?" Josie asks, very interested.

Chapter 6

Mommy and Me in the New Millennium

I sometimes think about the stages we daughters go though with our moms, especially when I drive by the Mommy and Me classes at the local park, where you can see those shapely but new moms exercising with their babies on their calves. It seems like everyone's having fun, despite the occasional infant crying and the occasional mom huffing. I guess no one said bouncing an infant on your legs would be too easy, or maybe I just haven't read that kind of self-help book yet. I know my own mom probably wishes I'd hurry up and get to those kinds of books. I've seen them in the store.

Next after Mommy and Me, I guess, comes the going-shopping-with-mommy stage of life, once you're old enough to be a walking daughter but right before you become the kind of daughter who says things like, "Mother, I would never wear that in a million years." The term of endearment "Mommy" seems to vanish, as I remember, remaining only on old artwork and scribbles long since stored away in the attic, if your mom happens to have an attic. Mine does. This stage of mother-daughterhood, I believe, just precedes the one where you learn to take a bus with a friend to the mall. No self-help books required, just a city map will do. It's not a very good stage for anyone, really, except maybe the transit system.

But on this Saturday morning, well, at 11:45, the last bits of morning but as early as I can manage to be very sociable, I'm meeting my mother for lunch. It's breakfast for me as well, unless you count three cups of coffee, which I usually do. I always add soy milk when I can, so somehow I figure it's somewhat of a healthy meal, but I could just be kidding myself. I admit it's not the kind of thing I'd tell a nutritionist, if I were the kind of girl who knew a nutritionist. Besides, I have Claire the Therapist, who tries to watch out for my nutritional needs as well emotional ones, and all for one low cost. She's all in favor of soy milk.

Since Jackie isn't coming with me this morning, and I know how helpful a buffer can be, a point of interest to boost the mother-daughter brunch, I bring along a stack of garden and seed catalogs that I get in the mail every so often, growing seasons maybe. I'm not a gardener, although I do love having my little pots of mint, geraniums, and whatever else will grow without much thought or tending. And I admit I like to look at the catalogs. The bright colors and flowers blowing in the wind can be soothing, I find. Maybe that's why people order the catalogs to begin with. Well, maybe a few people. I'm not sure how the catalog companies got my name, and I wonder if they know about their product's calming effect. I guess it's the advertising copywriter in me that makes me want to call them up and tell them how relaxing their brochures really are. Although I don't order anything, so maybe I wouldn't sound very convincing. There is also the possibility that my mom has the catalogs sent to me. I just haven't asked.

I meet my mom near her home, which is now in a fairly trendy neighborhood of Los Angeles, although when I was growing up, it was still miles to the east of trendy. But as the shops and haircutting salons and, to my mother's regret, piercing salons became crowded off of Melrose, they started heading Mom's direction to the east. So now my mother, if she wanted to, could walk down the street from her small house with that crooked stairway—it's something about the old houses in L.A., and I don't think it has to do with the earthquakes, but the stairways somehow look like they've been all shaken up—anyhow, she can walk (briskly, everyone walks briskly now, I notice) down to La Brea, which is lined with cappuccino stores and CD shops, eyewear (the expensive kind, and I notice no one calls them glasses anymore), and even a fly-fishing expert's store. And, of course, piercing salons. Some of the piercing places look fancy, from the outside at least, and it sometimes seems as if a piercing salon in need of a bookkeeper might fit right in with Mom's line of work. Mom says she just has to draw the line, though.

We meet at an old-fashioned malt shoppe, or at least a new take on the old-fashioned malt shoppe. It's called Shakes on Skates. The servers still wear roller skates like the days of old and roll around on what look like concrete floors. I've never seen anyone take a tumble on those floors, but they look cold and painful to me. What's new, I guess, is that the servers aren't short-skirted girls on skates, but white-T-shirt-clad boys on skates, or blades, actually. And by boys, again, I mean that under twenty-three or so kind of boy. The kind of boy just off-limits enough so that you tip well because you mean it, as opposed to trying to make a good impression, or any kind of impression, really.

Eleanor awaits me at a table for four, the kind of table that has become fashionable again, with a Formica top and metal rim around it, and four heavily padded vinyl chairs. If there were a course entitled Malt Shoppe 101, as there no doubt is in some social science institution across the country, this table and chairs would be discussed somewhere around Lecture One: The Basic Attributes of the Malt Shoppe, circa 1955. The boys on skates notwithstanding, of course.

But really all that matters to me is that the chairs are very comfy and that I'm sure I can get an old-fashioned malted, especially since I've had my healthy supply of soy milk for the day. Nestled atop one of the cushy chairs sits Eleanor, looking, well, pretty. My mom, I have to admit, is pretty. And not just for a woman with an admittedly thirty-year-old daughter. A pretty mom. But not in an intimidating way, even to her daughter, who I don't think most people consider pretty, although I have heard myself described as "cute," a description which even at thirty doesn't much bother me, despite all those Hallmark cards that still say "To a Cute Girl" and are intended for six-year-olds. In fact, Dennis gave me one of these for my last birthday, and again, I didn't mind a bit. But my mom is definitely pretty, even before noon.

"Hi, Mom." I sit down across from her on some ample padding.

"Oh, I'm so glad to see you wearing that nice flowery dress," my mom says. It's her way of saying hi.

I am wearing a flowery dress today, although I'm not usually one to wear more than an old white T-shirt, and not necessarily even a clean one, on a Saturday such as this. I usually bottom out the T with a pair of loose-legged pants, the cotton kind that are light and flowy. I've noticed a lot of women lately wearing these kind of pants low across their hips, with a little stomach showing. It's not really my intention when I get dressed in the morning to leave my stomach out, although sometimes my pants do slip down a bit, especially since I don't like to wear them too tight. I may be trendy without knowing it. But very little skin ever shows anywhere near my stomach if I have any say in it, although one time, Dennis did point at me and yell "Skin" when it happened in the office, an accident of course. It was just teasing, but even David came out to look.

"You should wear them that way all the time," David tried to convince me.

"I should get a supply of safety pins at my desk," I say.

"It's stylish," David said.

"It's embarrassing," I replied, pulling at my stretchy-waisted pants. Dennis just continued to point and say "Skin!" as if he'd never seen any.

"You need to get out more," David said to Dennis.

I have jeans, too, but sometimes they feel so restrictive. We're all pretty thin in my family and get to wear just about any style, but I still like things that don't poke at my body and remind me they're there. I admit the flowery dress was one of the few things that was clean (it's Saturday, after all). I like to think I'm not the kind of girl who dresses to please her mom, but I admit it may have crossed my mind that not only was the dress clean, but Mom might like it. It's possible she gave it to me, come to think of it.

Mom dresses in an all-periwinkle outfit, a more age-appropriate set of cotton pants than I usually go for (we so love drawstrings in this family) and a matching three-quarter-sleeved cotton top.

"You'll find you pretty much give up on short sleeves after fifty," she's told Jackie and me. Although really, I don't know too many women my age nearly as fit as my mom, who I know likes to work out to videos at home early in the morning. She's told me she finds gyms too smelly.

"Plus," Mom has confided, "I believe certain kinds of grunts and groans should be kept between you and your DVD player, should you happen to have one," she adds. She's been bugging me to get a DVD player for some time. I guess Mom's moved up from workout videos to workout DVDs, although I'm not sure the advantage in sound would please her much, given her feelings about the grunting and groaning we've come to know as modern exercise.

"I like your outfit, too, Mom," I say. The periwinkle seems a nice contrast with the red-vinyl interior of the diner, although

I wouldn't have really thought the two colors would be very complementary, had anyone asked earlier.

"Is there a special occasion for today, Mom?" I ask, as my mom was a little cagey on the phone when she invited me. Plus, this place doesn't exactly seem like the right setting for my mom. Not that she isn't upbeat, but Mom seems to me much more the afternoon tea type, rather than the just-before-noon-chocolate-milkshake type. But maybe that's not something a daughter is the best judge of.

"I thought it'd be fun to try this place," Mom says. "Live a little dangerously."

"Even if it's just a chocolate shake?" I ask.

"Well, one person's chocolate shake is another person's, well, cosmopolitan, shall we say?" Mom says somewhat cryptically.

"Mom, have you ever really had a cosmopolitan?" I refuse to confess I haven't. I'm hoping she won't ask.

"Oh, Claire," Mom teases. "You wouldn't want me to tell you *everything*, would you?" I'd have to think about this.

A young waiter in a very fancy pair of roller blades (I have tried those—I work near Venice Beach, don't forget) glides over to our table with menus.

"We'll need four," Mom says, as if it's the most natural thing in the world. He places four shiny menus on our table and glides away. Those skates are sure quiet.

"Is someone joining us?" I ask, realizing it's a dumb question. "I mean, who is joining us?"

"Well—" Mom starts, arranging the menus just so on the table. I notice they have a pretty strong plastic smell, but I don't say anything. I'm planning to drown out the smell with the alluring scent of chocolate shake, so this is a good excuse. "I just happened to invite some people I thought might make a fun foursome," Mom says. "Not that it isn't always fun to have girl talk, just the two of us."

"A foursome?" I say. I don't much like the sound of it.

"I think it's important for women to be brave, challenge their worlds, open themselves up for new experiences, new ideas," Mom says.

"They're men, aren't they," I say. It's not even a question.

"Well, naturally," Mom says.

"Ugh," I say, or something that sounds much like this. "You didn't even tell me."

"But see, you're all pretty in a dress anyway," Mom says.

"Not intentionally!" I say, wishing I'd worn my faded brown hemp drawstring pants, the comfy ones with the holes at the hems (they're too long). So what if they were a little dirty. They're brown anyway.

"I don't want someone thinking I dressed up for him," I say.

"And what would be wrong with that, theoretically speaking?" Mom asks, moving the menus aside for a moment. "Let's analyze this, since the fellows aren't due for a few minutes anyway."

"Uh-uh," I say. "I pay a perfectly good therapist for that."

"Oh, that woman," Mom just shakes her head. "But come on," Mom says. "Let's have that little bit of girl talk you were hoping for," Mom says.

I wasn't really hoping for the girl talk plus I'm probably not going to get to use my stack of gardening catalogs. And I'm starting to wonder if I'll get the milkshake I really was hoping for. Where is our roller blader anyway?

"What's wrong, from a working-woman, feminist perspective, of course," Mom begins, staring off into space a little, which gives her the opportunity to totally ignore my shaking my head No vehemently. "What's wrong with preparing oneself to look her best at any time and especially when meeting someone new, be they male or female, to show a certain quality of respect for that new person about to be met?"

I won't give in. "Who's the guy, Mom?"

"Oh, okay, philosophical party pooper you," she says. Just then, our roller blader, whose name tag says "Tucker on Wheels," zips up to offer us drinks.

"No, we'll wait," Mom says.

"Chocolate milkshake," I say.

"Would that be with soy protein, whey protein, or wheat grass?" Tucker on Wheels asks us. "I recommend the soy."

"I'll have mine with extra chocolate," I say.

Tucker on Wheels inhales his disapproval deeply.

"She's on a bit of a blind date," Mom tells him. "A little nervous," she adds. He seems to understand.

"Say no more," Tucker says. "I'll bring a few cherries on the side to nibble on while you wait."

My mind perks up a bit at the idea of maraschino cherries.

"They're all natural," Tucker says, bursting my dreams. Really, this isn't going my way. I smile at him in a less-than-friendly way as he takes off. I remember when I first learned how to scowl that way, although I think I learned it from my mom, come to think of it.

"Mom, I think the term *blind date* went out with the seventies, except for reality TV."

"Really," she says, interested. "I want to be up on these things. Fix-up? Meet-and-greet?"

"I prefer forcible torture by one who's supposed to love and support you."

"You're only talking that way because you crave sweets and sustenance," she says. "You'll see. And how about a little faith in the one who loves and supports you, and of course knows the best way to torture you?"

"Who's the guy, Mom?"

"I was on-line," she starts excitedly.

"Ugh," I say again. "Is this e-dating? Ugh." I'm feeling a little creeped out.

"Lots of girls are doing it," Mom says.

"You always told me not to fall for that line! 'Just 'cause lots of girls are doing it,' you used to say. 'Would you follow them off a bridge or something?' " I start.

"Lots of perfectly intelligent, modern women are logging in to converse with interesting people, some of them of the opposite gender," she says, as if she hadn't just started using the computer two months ago.

"They could be in prison, these men," I say.

"Well, then I highly doubt they'd be able to make it out for a quick milkshake and veggie burger," she says.

"Eew, now you're telling me they serve veggie burgers here?"

"You love tofu," Mom says. "Don't give me that."

"We are so off the subject," I say, and fortunately, Tucker on Wheels arrives soundlessly (I wonder how much he practices) with my shake and a large bowl of cherries for the middle of the table. The cherries are not bright and red, but dull and somewhat opaque. My shake also is a funny brown color.

"No pits in the cherries," Tucker says. Mom smiles her approval at him. "I know a little about dating," he says.

"Yes," Mom tells him. "The last thing you want is to have to spit out a pit in the middle of the conversation." He nods.

"Depends entirely," I say somewhat fiercely, "on who's talking and how the conversation is going."

"Now, now," Mom says. "Drink your shake, dear."

"It looks a little funny," I say to Tucker. Really, I hate to be one of those people who complains to waiters. But I do find it hard to believe that a shake-on-skates shoppe couldn't find it in their heart to stock maraschinos.

"I made it carob instead of the chocolate."

"That is so gracious of you," Mom says. I think my mom is flirting a bit.

"I have enough carob in my life," I say disappointed. "I'm

an adult. I think I should be able to decide on my vices by myself."

Mom pats Tucker on the hand as he looks a little alarmed. "You're wonderful," she tells him. "I'm Eleanor, and this is my daughter, Claire. We're on a blind double date," she tells him.

"Is it a blind double date or a double blind date?" I ask.

"It depends entirely on if they pick up the bill," Tucker says. "Wait and see."

Tucker pats Mom on the shoulder. I think he gets the clear impression she'll be the one tipping. He's right, of course. He glides off.

"What is it with carob, anyway?" I say. I take a sip. It's okay, but it's not the kind of taste to turn your day around, although maybe that's asking too much from a beverage, a nonalcoholic one, at least.

"Claire," Mom starts, "don't you know this is a healthy malt shoppe. This is the new La Brea Boulevard, remember?"

"I grew up around here. I've had malts before."

"It's a low-fat soy shake with carob," she says. "They do have strawberry, though." I think she's trying to make up.

"It's carob that's at the bottom of the degeneration of our society," I say. "Modern social science will prove me right, you just wait and see."

"I can only hope I live that long, dear," Mom says appeasingly. "I'm going to order the carrot and strawberry wheatgrass shake, though. I'll take my chances with the degeneration of society. You forget, I came of age in the nineteen-sixties."

My mother suddenly gets a different look on her face, and I turn behind me to spot a man coming in the door. There are certain women in the world who brighten when a man walks into the room, and we all know these women, and I'm happy to say that Mom isn't really one of them. She pays just as much attention to women—maybe more— given that all her bookkeeping clients are women. I do think, though, that my dad's walking into the room could make my mom brighten completely, but it had to be that special guy, my special Dad. To see her demeanor change, even just a little, when another man walks into the room does a little something to me, something confusing, something that may warrant a session with Claire the Therapist, not to mention a shelf full of self-help books. Maybe there are special chat rooms for these feelings somewhere, daughters across the nation or across the world in search of some sort of closure with their dads. Or daughters just missing their dads. There could be entire Web sites devoted to the subject. It wouldn't surprise me a bit.

But the man isn't Mr. Right (and where was his sidekick for me, I'd just started to wonder, not that I was looking forward to one), and instead he takes a seat at the counter, his red vinyl barstool making a little whoosh sound we can hear all the way over at our table. My mom takes a deep breath, what I think they call a "refreshing" breath in exercise class. In through the nose, out through the mouth. Wait for the next man.

Tucker on Wheels looks over at my mom. She just shrugs at him. He nods. That my mother has a sudden rapport with a young waiter on wheels isn't a surprise any longer, and I'm starting to take comfort in it.

"Tell me about this arrangement, Mom," I say more gently. "Who are we meeting, where did you meet them, what's the deal?"

"Okay, here it is," Mom starts excitedly. "I'd been wandering through different Web sites appropriate to a woman my age, give or take a few years. Not that I'm afraid to admit to fifty-three. I think fifty-three in today's society is still a young woman, still fit, still vital."

"Good," I say. I know Claire the Therapist would be proud of me. She says "good" a lot, I notice.

"And I'm a fit woman, I take care of my skin, which you should really start to do now, you know, dear."

"Good, go on," I say, trying to keep a smile on.

"Oh, all right. There's a site called fiftyandfabulous," Mom says.

"Is it dot-com or dot-org?" I ask. "Dennis and I were wondering about this stuff."

"Hmm," Mom says. "I'd have to check my computer. You and Dennis have been joining chat rooms together?"

"No," I say. "Can you do that together? And why would we?"

"Just wondering, Claire, about what you two get up to in that little office you share."

"We work very hard and try not to spill things on one another. That takes up most of the day, Mom. The subject of chat rooms just happened to arise. Dennis takes an interest in your personal life, what can I say?"

"That's sweet of him, actually," Mom stops to think.

"So, fifty and fabulous?" I try to get her back on track. Plus, saying it helps me remember. Fifty and fabulous. Dennis will want to know, although I'm not sure why.

"Yes, but run it all together: fiftyandfabulous, dot whatever," Mom says.

"Good, go on."

"And I started chatting with a gentleman."

"And he fit the bill fiftyandfabulous, one, two, or three words?" I ask.

"His name is Dalton. He owns a restaurant out by the marina."

"Not that place with the bad shrimp that time?" I ask, horrified. Some things you never forget, not that I'll go into details.

"That's been closed for years," Mom says. "Dalton owns a rib house."

"Meat," I say. I'm not big on meat.

"Many studies indicate that a little bit of meat won't hurt you," Mom says. "And his restaurant serves only free-range animals."

"I thought it was just free-range chickens. Are pigs free-range now?"

"There might be another term for it," Mom says. "I can't recall."

"Free-roam, free-pig, roaming pig?" The English major in me wants to know.

"I'm not sure that detail is key here, Claire."

"Oh, right," I say, thinking about happy pigs. I always had a thing for little piglets.

"He's been divorced for many years, has a son about your age who also just happens to be single, attractive, and work in advertising, just like you."

"He works in advertising?"

"Yes, one of those big firms on Wilshire."

"Oh," I say. "Those guys can be a little sharky."

"He's thinking about going back to law school, though."

"Oh," I say, wondering if that's an improvement. A sharky ad guy vs. a sharky lawyer. Hmm. Such wonderful dating choices.

"And becoming a public defender," Mom adds, reading my mind. Just like a mom.

"Okay, I guess. And he agreed to come with his dad on a double date?"

"Well, the father, Dalton, who actually goes by Dalt—"

"Dalt?" I say. I mean, really, Dalt?

"Please, dear, we don't make fun of names."

"Especially since they were given to us by our parents," I say.

"That's right." Mom says. "I believe Dalt was going to persuade his son to accompany him on a little Saturday morning trip."

"Much like you tricked me, you mean?" I ask.

"Just parents looking out for their young ones, perfectly natural. You'll see when you have grown children."

"Grown children who've been dating for fifteen years."

"It's never too late to lend a helping hand," Mom kind of whispers.

Tucker on Wheels comes over.

"I'll have that carrot shake now please, Tucker," Mom says.

"They're late, aren't they, Eleanor," he says. I can tell it really bothers him, as if they were late to meet him. Young Tucker is starting to sound a little paternal toward my mom.

"Yes, isn't it awful?" Mom asks.

"You deserve so much better," Tucker says, looking at Mom, but he nods my way also. "I just hate to see this. It gives the malt shoppe a bad feel." He revs one of his skates on the cement floor. I don't know why. Maybe he's going to go out and chase down our dates on the sidewalk. "Would you ladies like some onion rings on the house? Baked, not fried," Tucker says.

"That is so sweet," Mom says. "Now why can't you meet such a sweet guy," Mom says to me. Tucker looks at me inquisitively, wondering, I guess, what's wrong with me that I can't meet a sweet guy, and maybe bring an extra along for my nice mother. I admit I'm beginning to wonder this myself.

"Why can't we both meet such a sweet guy?" I ask, waving my watch around. The men are half an hour late.

Mom looks at her watch. "Thirty minutes," she says, to be exact. "How long do you young people wait for your dates these days?" She turns to Tucker. "It's my first time back in the dating game, so to speak," she says.

"Well," Tucker says, and Mom and I both lean in to hear. "In my experience, if a date doesn't show up within thirty minutes, or within forty minutes with a very large bouquet of flowers, you should just consider yourself saved from having to eat with a horrible, horrible person. And order something slinky for dessert."

"What do you recommend?" I ask, unsure what a slinky dessert might be but interested all the same.

Tucker smiles. "First the onion rings," he says. "You need to go slow about this, Eleanor. One step at a time, even when you're on wheels. I'll take care of dessert."

"Your Mom must be so proud of you," Mom actually says to Tucker. He seems to like it and wheels off toward the kitchen in a hurry.

"So we've been stood up?" I ask.

"By total strangers, at least," Mom says.

"Horrible men, if you take Tucker's word for it."

"And I think I will," my mom says. "Yes, dear, unless we see some very large bouquets—and they'd better be filled with roses," Mom says, then takes a breath to look out the window, where no one passes by, "I'm afraid we'll just have to have that girl talk by ourselves after all."

I nod. Although I don't care at all that my date won't happen, and I'm relieved, frankly, I feel for my mom. This was her first venture out there, and I know she's missed my dad badly. Her first date, and although she'd be delighted if I got a date out of it no doubt, I know I'm really here for support. Her first date, and stood up. A mother-daughter stand-up. It's a new avenue for our relationship, I admit, and not exactly a step forward for anyone. Hopefully something to look back on, something to laugh over tea and tell Jackie about some time. But right now, it's just really sad.

"I'm sorry, Mom," I say. "This must have been hard."

"It's a risk, that's all," Mom answers, sighing. "If you don't take them, you just wonder and drive yourself crazy with what-ifs. This isn't too much better than what-ifs, but at least I'm out of the house on a Saturday morning. It's not like I have to let it wreck my whole day. And it's not like it might have been all that better if they'd shown up."

"Besides," I say, "if they'd shown, would we have had the nerve to order slinky desserts?" I ask.

"I am so glad to see you've learned to look on the bright side," Mom says, taking a deep breath as if trying to cheer herself up, as Tucker arrives with her shake and our onion rings—a platter big enough for four but one Tucker has intended for just the two of us.

"Baked, huh?" I say. Not my first choice.

"Sometimes you just have to try new things," Mom says. We try them. It's true, they're not fried, but they're not bad at all. Mom lifts her healthy shake to me, and I clunk it with my carob drink, which I'm starting to like, actually, now that I slipped a few sugar packets in it when she wasn't looking.

"Excuse me," Tucker says, delighted that we like the onion rings, "while I slip into something slinky."

I think I'm starting to like him.

Chapter 7

Saturday Night Fever

Sometimes when I tell people I work in advertising, they get this look in their eyes not exactly of admiration or anything, but maybe of a certain tiny bit of envy. I can see they think it's glamorous or fascinating, maybe more amusing, more influential, more of a kind of job that would have better perks than their own legal/medical/retail jobs, any of which, as my mother would point out, probably has much more secure health benefits. Ours are always getting changed as Perri discovers something to save Persephonia! money. I'll admit there are times when I try to give these impressions of glamour/perks/influence in my job, especially, say, if I run into someone from high school who would normally not associate me with glamour or perks, and certainly not influence. I'm not above letting them think I'm an influential advertising executive, although I'm pleased to say I've never actually used the word "executive" to describe myself, at least not without seriously laughing afterward or maybe choking on something trying not to laugh. I'm just not the executive type.

And so maybe our little world at Persephonia! fits me, or

maybe I'm just trying it on for a while until I outgrow it. Either way, Saturday night finds me at a spot that shouldn't surprise me given the status of some of our clients. You wouldn't exactly call it a hotspot, and you might not call it a nightclub, which does bring up all those images of chic people holding martinis in those fragile, triangular-shaped glasses. Drinks in shades of sheer pink, glasses held just so, murmurs of important and somehow seductive conversations inching their way around the place. The place to be seen, the place to be not quite heard. The place to whisper into someone else's ear, someone else dangling a glass just so and dressed in that casual way you know requires a lot of money. Not to mention ironing.

You couldn't really say any one of these descriptions applies to the place we find ourselves tonight. We're in the Valley, where a lot of bands seem get their start and where no one dresses all that chic, let alone irons his or her clothes, all of which suits me pretty well. Saturday night brings us out to hear our Heartthrobs, not quite renamed Montana as they couldn't get the sign changed in time.

"We still have all these posters," Brendan said to me on the phone, in a three-way conversation with Dennis. "Although the guys really like the name Montana, even though not one of us has ever been to the state."

"I hear it's clean," I said. I've never been there, either.

"Mountainy," Dennis said, although it sounded a little funny when he said it. "It reminds you of big burly guys, enjoying a little outdoor time."

"We're all still a little pale," Brendan admitted.

"You guys may need a little outdoor time," Dennis suggested. "Lifting something heavy, getting those muscles in shape."

"And clean fresh shirts wouldn't hurt," I suggested. "No offense."

"No, no," Brendan said. "We know. New name, new look."

"Good-bye Heartthrobs," Dennis said. "Welcome to Montana."

But as I said, it's still Welcome to the Valley for us tonight. A trip to Montana might actually be nice about now, especially this time of year, late summer, when the Valley is kind of steamy, and not in the way you'd like. Not clean, not fresh, not mountainy.

"The drinks are pretty," Josie says. Dennis and I are seated at the Grange, a little club in the Valley that caters to kids eighteen and under. What we might call "real" drinks aren't served here. What they call drinks come in bright colors—neon pinks, blues, and greens—made from food colorings that might be as bad for you as whatever alcohol you'd choose to have in your real drinks, but might not leave you feeling dizzy the next day. Or maybe I underestimate the power of food coloring.

"My drink has a cherry in it," Josie says, admiringly. Josie, Malcolm, Dennis and I sit at a small table wet from the bottom of our drinks, or maybe it's just permanently that way.

"I haven't had a drink with a cherry in it since I was eight," Dennis says, looking at Josie's glass.

"It's delicious," Josie says.

"And yet it still doesn't fill me with that sense of nostalgic longing," Dennis says, lifting Josie's glass and looking closely. "No sense of loss whatsoever," he says.

"Maybe you never liked it to start with," I say. "I can just picture you, the boy who didn't like his Roy Rogers drink."

"I always liked Shirley Temples. Were Roy Rogers the same drinks?" Josie asks.

"I wasn't allowed to order a Shirley Temple," Malcolm says.

"They could be the very same," Dennis says, "and yet no boy I know was ever allowed to order a Shirley Temple."

"Shouldn't it be the other way?" Josie asks. "Boys get Shirleys, girls get Roys?"

We all think about this a moment.

"I'll just stick with Coke," Dennis says. "I'm too old to start switching the gender of my drinks."

"You're just feeling imprinted," I say.

"In the Valley, yet," Dennis says.

"You can order root beer," Malcolm says. It sounds like he wasn't allowed to order this as a child, either.

"It's not bad with cherries in it," I say. I've tried it.

"You'd probably drink Tang with cherries in it, wouldn't you?" Dennis teases.

"Which flavor?" I ask.

"There's more than one flavor of Tang?" Josie asks.

"I don't think I was allowed to drink Tang," Malcolm says.

"You need nachos," Dennis tells him. Malcolm nods.

"Hey, cheer up," I say, waving to a passing waiter that we'd like nachos like the next table has. I think it's a waiter, or maybe it's just someone in a white T-shirt who looks like a waiter. I guess we'll have to see. I turn back to Malcolm. "It's Saturday night, you're here to have fun. It's all paid for," I say.

"All the Roy Rogers you can drink, so to speak," Dennis says. "Relive your childhood, or mine, if you like."

"Where are our boys?" Josie asks, a little nervous. She has a large accordion file with her that she's labeled "Montana."

"You could be a travel agent with that thing," Dennis tells her. Josie looks a little hurt.

"Just because it's Saturday night," she says, "doesn't mean I'm not thinking about Montana's future."

"Those girls are staring at you," Malcolm says to Dennis. There's a group of four, maybe sixteen-year-olds, and they are looking Dennis's way.

"Maybe they're looking at you," Dennis tells him, trying to bolster Malcolm's confidence a little, which I think is nice. Malcolm is looking particularly thin and pale tonight. "Maybe they just looked at me when you looked at them so you wouldn't catch on," Dennis says.

"I'm getting confused," Josie says.

"All four are staring straight at you," Malcolm says to Dennis, who turns a little red on the parts of his face you can see beyond the beard. His neck, too. His neck is always a dead giveaway.

"You're blushing," Josie tells him. "That's sweet."

"Those are very young girls," I tell Dennis. "Just your type."

Dennis gives me a look. "They're not full grown yet," he says. "Besides, there are laws."

"Even in the Valley?" Malcolm asks.

"Especially in the Valley," I say. "So Josie, what are you going to put in the accordion file?"

"Anything we think of for the boys. Impressions, thoughts, feelings," she says. "Directions to go in."

"What are you going to write on?" Malcolm asks. We don't see any paper.

"Oh!" Josie says.

"It's okay," Dennis says. "You can use cocktail napkins."

"Are they cocktail napkins," I say, "if all you can order is Coke or a Shirley?"

"It's a fair question," Dennis admits. "They're small and square and paper. You wouldn't call them dinner napkins. Napkin scraps really doesn't have that ring to it."

"Weren't many great novels written on cocktail napkins?" Malcolm asks. He wasn't an English major.

"A common misperception," Dennis says. "Most cocktail napkins disintegrate before you get home."

"Especially if what you've been drinking is a little stronger than a Shirley," I say.

"Well," Josie says, bolstering herself, "I plan to use them anyhow and keep them in my file. Nothing will disintegrate in this." She taps the hard-cased file. It may even be fire-proof.

"Okay," I start. "Any impressions, thoughts, what-have-yous for Josie's file?"

"If they don't play soon," Malcolm says, "I may fall asleep. It's the ABBA."

It's true, the Grange has been playing ABBA music while we wait for the boys to perform. I hadn't really noticed before.

"This puts you to sleep?" Dennis asks him. "It's more annoying than soothing."

"Depending on your age," I say. The girls at the next table seem to be bobbing their heads and shoulders. "Notice younger folk find the sounds invigorating," I say.

"Present company excepted," Dennis says, as Malcolm rests his head on his hands.

"Beer would make all the difference," Dennis whispers to me, nodding toward Malcolm.

"Yes," I whisper back. "It would probably knock him out entirely."

"Beer makes me cranky," Malcolm says, hearing us.

"What a surprise," Dennis says. He pats Malcolm on the shoulder anyway.

"So, no ABBA," Josie says, writing on a napkin with a pink pen she took from her purse. It's one of those half-size pens I thought were for small children. But then, it's a small purse.

"No ABBA," Malcolm echoes.

"Too bad," I say. "I have an ABBA tape in my desk at work." It was a gag gift, but I don't add this.

"It might be good to use if we want Malcolm to give up something, like smoking. We could play it every time he smokes. Behavior modification," Dennis says.

"I don't smoke," Malcolm says.

"Don't miss the bigger picture," Dennis tells him. Malcolm doesn't smile.

The ABBA comes to a stop midsong, which makes the girls at the next table moan.

"They seemed to like it," Dennis says to Josie, who looks over toward them. She crosses out her words on the napkin, then files it in her file. "Sorry," she mouths to Malcolm, who barely registers it. Really, he should be having a much better time, even for Malcolm.

"I hope she put it under A," Dennis says to me quietly.

"Then we'll be able to find it easily," I say, as if any of us will ever forget the ABBA music anyhow.

"Hi." It's Jackie, who has come to share this evening's entertainment with us. We are all glad for the interruption as she pulls up a small table to ours and joins us, sitting beside me. Behind her stands a slightly smirking person who must be her date and client, Theo. Something about him says politician, and it's not just the fancy haircut that accentuates the gray around his ears to make him look not older, and not really wiser, but somehow still better than the next guy. I didn't know a haircut could do this, and it's something I'll have to talk to Billie, my mother's hairdressing client, about. I feel the need to understand.

"Everybody, this is Theo," Jackie says nonchalantly. "Theo, this is my best friend, Claire, and her office partner, Dennis, and their coworkers Josie and Malcolm," Jackie says diplomatically. She knows everyone well enough, having sat around our office with us and even helped us write some of our ad copy. She's good with ambiguity, which the ads for some of our clients require in their wording, especially for the ones who really don't sing that well.

Theo shakes hands with everyone, even with us girls, but with us he does that thing where he puts his left hand on top of the shaking hands as well. Kind of a shake-pat-shake. Dennis stares at this suspiciously.

"Theo is running for Congress in the beach neighborhoods," Jackie says to us.

"Jackie is a fine strategist," Theo says, then starts to look around the room.

"Feeling a little out of your district?" Dennis asks him.

"My daughter likes to come to these little clubs. Good for the kids to have a safe place to listen to music. No alcohol, you know," Theo says.

"Boy do we," Dennis says, handing me the cherry that arrived in his last drink.

"Is your daughter here now?" I ask before I put the cherry in my mouth. It'll keep me busy for a bit.

"You have a daughter?" Josie says, but actually, Jackie looks like she was formulating this question as well. I look at her. She shrugs almost imperceptibly, that is if you haven't known her for almost half your life.

"Two," Theo admits. "They're with their mom in Big Bear tonight," Theo says, taking one last look around. "It's good to check out these places firsthand, though," he says. "Know what the young people are up to."

"That's what we were thinking," says our twenty-three-year-old Josie. Theo looks at her approvingly.

A voice comes over a speaker in the corner, but we can't see the announcer. "Ladies and gentlemen," says the male voice, and I start to wonder if it's a recording, "please greet the Heartthrobs!"

The girls at the table scream, causing us all to turn to them in fear that something has gone wrong, but no, they're just excited about the boys.

"I feel really old," I confide to Jackie, who nods.

"You just haven't screamed that way for a while," she says.

"Not for anything without chocolate," I say.

The boys take the stage, and not quickly, either. It takes them a while to get to their instruments, although not one girl in the place seems to mind, as each boy is better looking than the next. I feel fairly confident that I've learned the names for each player: Besides Brendan (twenty-three), there's Scott, the drummer (twenty-two), who is blonde and what used to be called a surfer type but is probably now called a snowboard type, not that I can keep up; Kyle the bass player (twenty-two), with red hair; Eric, a guitarist and Scott's little brother (twenty-one, which is pretty close in age, or maybe they're twins and I've got it wrong), who has little gold glasses and brown hair, but in every other way looks just like Scott; and Jeremy, who has some Hawaiian ancestry and soft-looking dark hair, and at twenty-two plays not only piano but the harp, I'm told. It's really hard to pick the cutest, but if the girls at the next table have anything to say about it, I think Brendan would win. That's where most of the staring is going, anyhow.

"Wow," Josie says, looking at the boys and tossing her file to the ground. Malcolm sort of snorts in reply and starts crunching the nachos we've ordered, which I don't think are covered in real cheese, but I haven't said anything.

"Shh," Josie tells him. I look at Dennis and give him a "here goes" look. He scratches his beard. We're out of place.

"Think of us as chaperones," I tell him. "You be Malcolm's, I'll be Josie's."

"Maybe so," Dennis whispers back. "But who's going to keep an eye on Theo?"

Jackie seems to be keeping a close eye on him. I'm not sure how I feel about this. Dating a politician isn't exactly what you might want for your best friend. Dating a married and/or separated politician, that is. It just doesn't have the sound to it you'd hope for, even if he's a local politician.

Still, "It's Jackie's job," I tell him. "She's a professional, after all," I say, trying to convince myself as well. Jackie has her eyes on Theo in a way that Dennis doesn't seem to care for. "She's over twenty-one," I say.

"He's way over that," Dennis says. "But I'm not sure he's entirely willing to admit it." Someone places a Shirley Temple in Theo's hand, and Theo stares at it a bit. Dennis laughs quietly.

"Anything for a new constituency," Dennis tells me.

The boys on stage hit the mikes a few times, and not gracefully, but then they greet the crowd.

"Thanks for coming, everyone," Brendan says, and girls across the room scream again, causing Theo to almost lose his grip on Shirley, I notice. Dennis notices, too.

"Here we go," Brendan says, and although it's a bit cheesy of a way to open, when the band begins to play, no one can complain. "This one is for Claire," Brendan says, and everyone looks around to see who Claire is. I look, too, pretending it isn't me. After all, even I know more than one Claire.

"Wow!" Josie says again. "I guess I didn't know you knew him all that well."

"Shh," I say. "Pretend it's not me."

"You've always been our little heartthrob, anyway," Dennis says. Jackie raises an eyebrow at me. I just shake my head violently.

"Brendan's just being nice," I say. "Shh."

"I'm sure it's just a crush," Dennis says, but then he looks back to Brendan and stops smiling.

Brendan and the boys start to play, which fortunately grabs everyone's attention. Because although each boy is what can only be described as cute (although I'd wager someone at the next table might go for extra-cute or whatever the trendier version of cute is these days—it used to be awesome, but I really can't say), and while this place is beginning to smell of spilled grenadine, the soon-to-be-Montana boys are good. Brendan's voice comes right at us, not too loud, not too rock and roll, but direct, clear, resounding. The guitars are good, the drums soft but persuasive, the keyboardist, whose head lolls from side to side, enthusiastic.

"They're good," Malcolm says, surprised and with nachos hanging from his fingers.

"Wow," Josie says softly. "This is going to be fun."

Dennis and I look at each other and shrug.

"What did you expect from your first big client?" he says to me.

"I don't know about big," I say.

"I guess that'll be up to you," he says.

We listen as Montana-to-be finish their song, something original, although I know they play covers, too.

"That was for you, Claire, for everything you mean to, well, to all of us, really, for believing in us," Brendan says, directing his words right at my right eye, or somewhere about there, not that I can tell exactly as it's a little dark in here. All the boys join in with a cheer in my general direction. Then they start another number.

"You certainly are a lucky girl," Theo says to me.

"Yeah," Josie says, looking down into her glass of melted ice and pink liquid, but not in a particularly happy way.

"You know," Dennis says to me, "there are five of them. You should learn to share."

"Here," I say, sticking a nacho in his mouth.

"Yum," he says, although it may be more of an "Imm," what with the fake cheese in his mouth. He swallows.

"That's a good start," he says, but I notice Josie looking at me with a question.

"We have a lot of work to do," I tell her, and she snaps out of it and looks ready again, hopeful, then goes back to watching the boys.

"Maybe when she grows up," Dennis whispers about Josie, "she can be a copywriter with a boy band all her own, too."

"It's nice to have career goals," I say.

"Not to mention," Dennis says, "I think your job description has just changed."

I ignore him and listen to the boys. Brendan was right in his description of them as somewhat rock, somewhat rocka- billy, somewhat a little something that defies the categories we know and love. Something that would be really enticing even if they didn't look as good as each of them does. Brendan doesn't exactly look twenty-three. Maybe he could look a few years older, especially in this light, even if I know better. I close my eyes to check, imagining their sound on the radio, imagining it playing from CDs across the nation. Imagining Brendan's voice just about anywhere. I try to snap myself out of it. I think I've had too many cherries. They can affect you this way—you don't always need rum. I don't, at least.

I turn to Jackie. "They sound good even if you close your eyes," I tell her.

"Which you don't actually need to do from the looks of them," she says.

Brendan finishes another song and looks my way, then smiles. Girls across the room scream for the smile, trying to wish it their way.

"And you think you never get any good perks," Jackie says to me.

Chapter 8

Heaven Can't Wait

I'm sitting at my desk admiring a pair of new cowboy boots, the words, "Ooh, cowboy boots," escaping my lips every few minutes. They're pink leather with little jeweled pink hearts.

"Aren't they cowgirl boots?" Dennis asks, examining them. "No self-respecting cowboy would stick a toe in one of these," he says.

"No self-respecting cowboy could fit a toe in one of these," I say, not that I have a particularly small foot. Still, I like to think it is.

One of the clients I write ads for is a place known to us as the cowboy store, named Jeds Round Em Up (no apostrophe anywhere—I know, I've begged for one repeatedly). It's a Western wear store, or at least that's what it's listed as in the yellow pages. Jeds is a big warehouse of a store in Culver City, near the edge of Venice and not far from us, and Jeds often plays appropriate cowboy music in the store, sometimes even by one of our clients. Jed himself is one of Perri's oldest clients. At Jeds you can get boots, Western shirts with long white fringes, big silver belt buckles with or without turquoise, and those little bolo ties. I'd like to see Dennis in a bolo tie, but he's declined the offer. Repeatedly.

Jeds Round Em Up likes to advertise on the country station (okay, we call it the cowboy station, but as a term of endearment). That leaves me to write the lines the announcers
say in between the special jingle Jed has commissioned for
his store, a catchy theme where you can hear a cowboy crack-
ing his whip, against what I really don't want to imagine. I'm
the copywriter for most of these ads, and sometimes I think
Jed thinks that's all I do, write ads for boots, which are often
on sale, as they're very, very expensive. Especially the pink ones.
I know, I've priced them. Jed is being very generous gracing
me with a pair, but he's a big, generous, fatherly type anyway.

"What's this week's ad say?" Dennis asks me, pulling the
pair of boots on to his desk and tracing the hearts with his
finger. They're not real jewels, but I still like them. Dennis
puts one boot on each hand and walks them across his desk,
whistling some eternal cowboy whistle that reminds me of
Bonanza or maybe an old Clint Eastwood movie. Although
why the pink boots would bring to mind either of these is
anyone's guess. Probably, Dennis is just avoiding his own
work, but since he seems interested in mine, and isn't
scratching the boots on anything, it's okay with me.

"Wrangle on over to Jeds Round Em Up," I read from
my copy, which I'm fairly proud of. Perri took it upon herself early on to teach me how to match the lingo to the
client. I really like doing it, and I wish I'd written some of
my English papers this way in college, although really, they
weren't paying me enough.

I continue: "And 'rustle up a pair of all-leather cowboy
boots at twenty-five percent off."

"I like it," Dennis says.

"I'm not finished with it yet. I'm working on every variation of rustle. Rassle. Wrangle. You know."

"Is it rassle with an *r* or wrassle with a *w?*" Dennis asks.
He grabs Merriam-Webster, its cover ripped and half
falling off.

"I've noticed that if I write it with a *w*, then the announcer pronounces it funny," I say. "I use an apostrophe *r.*"

"But Jed hates apostrophes," Dennis says.

"He puts up with me," I say, trying to pull a pink boot off Dennis's hand. He holds on, so I just get a touch of it. The leather is very, very soft.

"Aren't you going to model them?" Dennis asks, one eyebrow raised. There is something oddly sexy about pink boots, little jewels or not.

"A little early in the day," I say. Dennis sighs.

Our art director, David, stops by and hands us some photos of another client, Elvissa, the girl Elvis singer, who's better than her name sounds. He stands and looks at Dennis, gloved in pink leather boots. Dennis does a little dance with them on the desk, some sort of odd do-si-do.

"Your day can really only improve from here," David tells Dennis. "Not that the pink hearts aren't you."

"My clients never send me presents," Dennis says. "At least not the kind you can kick someone and injure them with." The toes are kind of pointy, and they have that potentially dangerous metal on them.

"It's nice to have something to hope for, though," David says. "And if they ever do send you those boots in your size, please let me know. I'll want to get a peek."

"I'll see what I can arrange," I say.

"And if they have any of the navy eel ones," David says, "size eleven and a half? You can think of me, you know."

"You have a problem with the pink?" Dennis says.

"Not so much me," David says, "but I think everyone else would." He leaves.

Dennis thinks for a second then pulls his hands out of the boots quickly. "These aren't eel, are they?"

"No, just old-fashioned dead cows, studded with pink hearts, of course," I say.

"And you call yourself a vegetarian," Dennis says.

"You're just jealous," I say. "Besides, hemp boots just don't hold up the same."

"Tell me you haven't tried them."

I shrug. There's a natural clothing store down off Main here in Venice. I've tried the hemp boots. They smell funny and don't really cling to your feet. They seem to head in different directions as if they have a bad attitude, especially for a fiber you're not even allowed to grow around here.

"I love cows," I say. "You know that."

"I do," Dennis says. He knows a few things about me, like how I moo at cows along I-5 up to the north. It's just my natural reaction to them. I don't expect them to moo back, but of course if you wait long enough, they're bound to. In my experience, at least. Dennis takes off the boots again and hands them to me. They smell wonderful. I hug them to me. As a kid I always wanted pink cowgirl boots, and I've only had to wait about twenty-five years and write a little rustle-'em-up copy to get them. I think this cow has had my name on it for a long, long time.

"I'll eat tofu for a month," I say. "Just to try to make up for these."

"Not that you wouldn't eat it anyway," Dennis says.

"Then you eat tofu for a month," I suggest, "and I'll try to get Jed to send over one of those fringed shirts."

"Hmm," Dennis says, picturing himself in fringe, I can just tell. It wouldn't suit him at all, but I sometimes hate to interrupt his fantasies, so I let him consider for a while. He'd never eat tofu for a month anyhow.

It seems like Dennis's day isn't really about to improve after all, at least not from his point of view. From the space we share at the back of Persephonia!'s offices, we can hear the front door open (it takes all your weight to open it, so we often hear a little grunt of effort as well). We can hear Josie greet whoever enters, if we want to, but we've learned to drown this out. I think the hay-filled walls help to absorb sounds, but sometimes it is fun to listen to the UPS guys try to pick up Josie. She has an endless supply of gentle ways to decline any invitation. Really, she could write a book. But as we hear Josie quietly greet the visitor, Dennis's face changes slightly (you can only see so much under the beard, but I've learned to read what little flesh you can see). He starts clearing things on his desk busily. He sighs deeply. I look at him.

"Your client is here," I say.

"Ughruh," Dennis mumbles. I think it's ughruh.

It's not that we all split up the clients as we do a lot of work jointly, as in our promotions for Elvissa, but while I get to work on Jeds Round Em Up myself these days, Dennis has somehow managed to write all the promotional materials for another of our clients. Her name is Heaven. And it's her real name.

I would like to say straight off that Heaven has never posed for *Playboy* or any other publication that mothers everywhere would find offensive, despite the fact that many, many people have asked me if she has. I don't know why I tend to defend her, exactly. Because when you see Heaven, well, when I see Heaven, it's really hard not to just be amazed. I'm told that those of a certain persuasion find it a religious experience.

"The reason so many men ever bother going to church, I'm sure," David has said. "What they'd all hoped to live to see."

Except for Dennis, I sometimes think. Dennis, who is brave and kind—he is unafraid to scoop up the countless spiders in our office with his bare hands and take them all the way out to the planter boxes by the parking lot—Dennis who is not intimidated by our overbearing boss, Perri. Dennis with all the older sisters and girl cousins who no doubt adored yet teased him. And Dennis with his past— which I know about in detail, as we've talked about it, especially once when I got Dennis really drunk on this terrible champagne Perri gave us for Christmas one year. And maybe it's this past that keeps Dennis shy of Heaven if not just shy around her. The past's name is Annie. And like the rest of the strange things that happen in life, despite L.A. being a huge place, Dennis tends to run into Annie, or mentions of her, all the time. We all do. Annie and Dennis lived together for five years, a long time in our book (and in most women-who-love-men and men-who-love-women books, it seems).

"Five years," Jackie said when I told her, since she's the only one I gossip to, and she tells no one anything (even me, sometimes). I'm sure Dennis wouldn't be disappointed that I told Jackie. If you know me, you have to expect me to pass your info on to Jackie. After all—as my mother would be happy to point out at any time—it's not like I have a husband to share the good secrets with.

But Annie, well, Dennis doesn't talk about her in detail, except for that one champagne-induced time. I of course have met her. Annie is exotic and beautiful, long dark straight hair, a touch of Asian in her ancestry, and utterly serious. Annie is an important lawyer, managing to attract top Fortune 500 companies (I admit I don't really know what it entails to be a Fortune 500 company, and neither does Dennis, which no doubt was part of the problem). She also does a good share of volunteer work. I know they call it pro bono, but that sounds so conceited to me to have your own term for it. A volunteer is a volunteer, or should be, no matter how much you could be billing per hour, but maybe I'm just jealous. It's this volunteer work that tends to get her name, not to mention picture, in the papers. Jackie and I often evaluate these pictures of Annie in as nonjudgmental a way as possible, we try to think. Annie looks powerful. Annie looks in control, and from what (little) I've heard, she always was.

"It's important to her," I remember Dennis saying, "taking control of your life, not letting things just happen." He said it a little like he was trying to convince himself of its truth. It's really not the way he's ever lived, not that I'm criticizing, especially since I'm the same way. It is at the heart of their breakup, I've come to know.

"But don't you lose that fun sense of seeing what will happen next?" I asked Dennis.

"You mean," he said, "that fun sense of wondering how you'll pay the bills?"

"Well, that's one way of looking at it," I said.

"Yes, you lose that," he agreed. "Plus that wonderful feeling you get when you have no idea what's in the fridge." He meant this seriously. Dennis is constantly delighted at finding anything at all in his fridge, I know. And my fridge.

"I'd miss the surprise of that," I agreed, although I got the clear impression Annie wouldn't have thought such a surprise very valuable. Not that this is that bad a quality of hers. Not that it isn't a quality I could use a little more of maybe. And Dennis too, not that I'd tell him so. I'm sure Annie was appalled at Dennis's lack of organization. She probably didn't even like his spilling things. He won't really talk about this much, but I know it had to be a problem.

I've always been a little in awe of Annie, the organized and moving-up-the-ladder girl my mother might have wanted, maybe. I sometimes am in awe of just the pictures we see of her in various newspapers and glossy upscale magazines featuring local attractive executives. Dennis looks at the pictures, too, quickly but closely. He'll hand the newspaper or magazine back to me after a moment, or if I wave it off, he'll dump it in the trash can. As Dennis is usually happy to recy-

cle, I have to think this means something. I don't really know
how much it's related, but Dennis hasn't much dated since
Annie. He rebuffs offers from the various interns we sometimes employ, all young and female. And Dennis remains
terribly awkward around Heaven, not that she resembles
Annie or even asks for much. Maybe he's afraid she will.

Josie, though, seems to share my soft spot for Heaven,
although I'm not certain that all women feel this way toward her, or that, say, if Josie had never met Heaven and
passed her by on the street, she wouldn't sneer at her as I've
seen so many women do. Although Josie is cute-as-a-button
cute, with her freckles and light brown a-shade-below-
blonde hair, Heaven is, well, perfect. Baby blonde straight,
long hair. Blue, blue eyes never in need of contact lenses.
And that figure. Not too thin, not too curvaceous, not too
busty so that it's overbearing, but plenty busty nonetheless.

"Now there's a healthy girl," David always says.

"And they're real," Perri tells us. Perri is close friends
with Heaven's parents and has known Heaven all her life, as
if this qualifies Perri to judge another woman's cup size and
its contents with authority.

"I'm taking Perri's word for it," is all Dennis has said.

"Chicken," Malcolm has taunted Dennis, which is an odd
reversal, young Malcolm teasing Dennis for a change. Only
over Heaven. Not that Malcolm finds much to say to Heaven,
whom he's also known all his life.

My mom has checked in, too: "I think it's unfair to judge
a young woman harshly just because she's naturally beautiful," she's said.

"Especially because she's naturally beautiful," Jackie has
said, although a little distrustfully. Face it, it's odd to see
such a naturally beautiful person, at least here in L.A. Most
of us don't know how to respond.

So this morning, which so far has been filled with thoughts
of cowgirls and just where to wear soft leather boots with

what David refers to as "kick-ass toes," we find ourselves face to face with a little natural beauty. Heaven walks back to our cubicle. Dennis rises and shakes her hand. Intimidation brings out the professionalism in him. At least, I think it's intimidation.

"Hi, Claire, hi, Dennis," Heaven says, shaking Dennis's hand sweetly. Heaven is twenty years old, an unseemly young age to have so much talent, it seems, because besides the obvious that you notice when she enters the room, Heaven can sing. Heaven can belt. She could knock Dennis flat back into his chair, if not onto the floor, if she wanted to, although she might not be old enough to realize her true powers. Yet.

"What can we do for you?" Dennis says.

"Not that we're not always glad for a visit, even just to catch up," I say. Okay, so I like to see Dennis squirm. A better office-mate might leave the two together, but a better officemate might miss a lot. And Heaven never seems to mind my presence anyhow. I think most people are afraid to talk to her, and she seems to like coming by as only Dennis is afraid, and really only a little.

"I want you to help me change my image," Heaven says. Dennis looks to me as if I should translate what this means. Although Dennis is a very fine copywriter, he's not usually asked about image consulting. Plus he's wearing the same shirt as yesterday.

I think of Claire the Therapist and how she might respond to this. "What is it about your image that you feel should change?" I say, long-windedly but with therapeutical correctness.

"Well," Heaven begins, bringing out a flyer handed out at her last appearance, which was, unfortunately I have to think, at a county fair a few counties to the east. Which means not only was the weather hot, but there were pigs squealing in the distance. It was pretty uncomfortable, and I didn't even have to sing in a small arena decorated to look like a barnyard. As I've mentioned, I have a problem with hay, and it didn't seem to do Heaven's voice much good, either.

"Not that anyone would have noticed how she sounded," David said to me, and even Dennis had to nod. Heaven wore a little red bandana kind of halter-top, intricately tied by Perri. She may have come to the wrong place for image consulting, I have to think.

"I don't really like the photo we're using and some of the writing used to describe me. No offense," Heaven says to Dennis. He takes the flyer with a shrug. Heaven goes on: "I'm tired of this look, what would you call it?" Heaven asks.

"Sexy?" I say. "Provocative?"

Heaven wiggles her nose in disapproval and adds a slight shake of her blonde head.

"It's a nice photo," Dennis says. "Maybe we should call in David. He's the art director."

David appears without much delay. It's a small office, and eavesdropping isn't considered rude, exactly. More of a perk.

"It's a lovely photo," David says. "And as I recall, it needed no touching up."

"But it's a look I'm not comfortable with," Heaven says. "That's not who I am, and it's not how I sing."

"You sing love songs," Dennis says. "Doesn't that tie in?"

"How do you want to look?" I ask Heaven. "Just you, not what you think people want you to look like, just how you want to appear." I wonder if Heaven has had therapy of her own and recognizes my adopted tone. Then again, she may just be too young. Have barely twentysomethings even begun to read self-help books yet? I'm not sure the *What Color Is Your Parachute* book would really apply to Heaven, anyway.

Heaven looks over at the doorway for a second, thinking about her inner self, I imagine, and how to convey it in a small black-and-white photo. Josie comes by with a tray of cookies for us all, like a good assistant. I make a mental note to say something positive about her to Perri. I didn't know we had cookies.

"I want to look like Josie," the perfect Heaven says. Josie nearly drops the tray, which David rescues gracefully (he was once a waiter—more than once, actually).

"Like me?" Josie says.

"You have a great look," Heaven says. "You're pulled together but you don't look like it took you forever to get that way. A great haircut. You look comfortable in your clothes. Not too tight," Heaven says. We look back at her photo on the flyer. She is wearing an awfully tight sweater that only accentuates her already incredible figure. Maybe too much for Heaven's taste. We all compare them: Heaven with her long blonde hair, Josie with hers short and semi-red, semi-blonde, semi-brown today, mirroring the last look I saw on our boss, Perri, as Josie usually does. Today, Heaven wears a close-fitting pink T-shirt with a ladybug on the front, and pink low-rise capris. Josie's wearing a black T-shirt (not snug, and probably organic cotton from the store down the street) and khakis. In fact, Heaven is the only one in the cubicle not wearing khakis.

"You two look nothing alike," Dennis says.

"No offense to either," I add, diplomatically.

"You're both gorgeous," David says. "Who could compare?"

"It's okay," Josie says, a little confused. "I can take a compliment. Have an extra cookie, Heaven."

"I'm not allowed to eat cookies. Fat," she says.

"Oh, dear," David says.

"You're not fat," both Josie and I echo.

"But it's out there," Heaven says. "Fat. It's just waiting for us."

"They're organic oat cookies sweetened with blackberry juice," Josie says. "They can't hurt you—they're from the health food store."

Heaven takes a cookie and looks at it somewhat lovingly. And these are really ugly cookies. Almost everything in the health food store up the way is sort of ugly and doesn't really resemble what you think it should or what you were hoping for. This is more of an oat bar than a cookie, I think. I take one anyway. Dennis declines.

"Not fear of fat?" I tease him.

"Hey," Dennis says. "Bugs are organic, too. Would you eat those?"

"Bugs?" Heaven says, holding her oat bar away from her for a minute.

"It's just an analogy," Dennis says. "Okay, new flyers. New copy about Heaven and her singing. New pictures." He looks over to David, who nods.

"A whole new you," David says to Heaven, "although you're already too good for us the way you look now."

"I don't want to be too good," Heaven says. "Can you help, Dennis?" It's her most direct appeal to Dennis, and it's a little obvious, and just then I choke slightly, a small part of cookie stuck in my throat for a second. Healthy cookies can be so dry. Josie looks at me, a sense of concern written across her face, if not loyalty, although really I'm not exactly sure why. It's just a cookie stuck in my throat is all. I sip from my cup of lukewarm tea. It seems to take a while for the cookie part to melt down my throat, or maybe it just seems like an hour, since four people are watching me.

"I'm fine," I croak.

"So you'll work on it?" Heaven asks Dennis, and I feel the rest of us somehow evaporate from the room. I imagine just the two of them talking, and it's as if Heaven has moved inches closer to Dennis, which can't really be, as she's still seated on our recently fixed extra blue chair. I drink some more tea and try to clear my throat, not to mention my head. I don't really feel well.

"We can meet to talk more," Heaven says. "You should get to know me before you write new things about me." It's an awful lot of confidence from a twenty-year-old, although she seems sincere. Is it just because she's so (naturally) blond that I'm questioning her motives? And why should I care about her motives, I ask myself in my therapist's voice. I like Heaven, I remind myself a couple of times.

"I'll get to work on it," Dennis says and rises, extending his hand to shake good-bye. Heaven rises and hugs him instead. Dennis doesn't look at any of us. David giggles slightly and leaves the room, waving off Josie's offer of more oat bars.

"I have Mystic Mints," David says over his shoulder, a general invitation.

"I'll be right over," Dennis says, evacuating himself from Heaven. She smiles and sort of hops out of the cubicle, waving her good-byes, invigorated, it seems. The little Energizer bunny comes to mind, perky and pink, although I'm sure I'm being overly judgmental. I take another oat bar. Josie and I stand close to one another, not talking, but not chewing oat bars. Josie looks at me. I shrug.

When the coast is clear and Josie has gone to see Heaven out, Dennis pops back into our office.

"I brought you a Mystic Mint," Dennis says. "To get the bad taste out." I take the real cookie and place it in the center of my desk.

"It isn't that bad," I say to Dennis, a little defensively.

Just then Malcolm comes by our doorway, delivering two reams of paper for the printer Dennis and I share.

"Did I miss anything?" Malcolm asks.

"Just bonding with our clients," I tell him. Malcolm misses a lot of the good stuff running errands. Although I'm not sure if what just happened can be called the good stuff.

"Are we allowed to bond with the clients?" Malcolm asks. "Aren't we supposed to keep a certain distance?"

"I think that just applies to doctors or other people equipped with sharp implements," I say. "Is it possible for a copywriter with extended job duties to become overly attached to his or her client?" I ask. I glance to the side of my desk, where I have a CD by the Heartthrobs-turned-Montana band. All five boys smile from the cover, Brendan in the lead, and not just because his smile is the best.

Dennis doesn't answer my question. He turns to his computer and starts typing. He waits a second, and a large picture of Heaven appears on his screen.

I eat my Mystic Mint. It tastes just a little too sweet.

Chapter 9

I Have an Entourage

At least, it looks like I have an entourage, albeit a pretty small one. Actually, I feel a little as if I'm being followed. On this clear, clear Los Angeles day with a slight wind blowing all the pollutants out over the ocean, we're walking along trendy Beverly Boulevard. I'm in the lead, not that it's a race or anything.

Josie follows a bit behind me, looking efficient with a clipboard, and not just the old brown kind but one that's see-through and has "Josie" hand-painted on it. It looks hand-painted, at least. Walking somewhat shyly between us, with that slumpy shoulder thing that mothers just hate, is Brendan, the former Heartthrob, who at least for today is all mine. And Josie's, of course. We're in search of a new haircut for Brendan, and on company time, too.

"I have to write three new ads for Elvissa," Dennis said to me before I left the office, envious of my assignment, sort of. "While you get to stroll through West Hollywood, no doubt stopping in at all the leather stores."

"Oh, yes," I said, "and maybe I'll get something pierced." It's a joke around here—I never even had my ears pierced. I'm not very brave.

"Maybe you'll get lots of things pierced," Dennis taunted.

"I'm going to get Brendan a haircut," I said. "It's really not quite as thrilling as it sounds."

"Maybe Brendan and Josie and you can all get matching haircuts," Dennis suggested.

"Kind of a Beatles thing?"

"Except that you and Josie aren't in the group," Dennis said. "More like groupies."

"Well, I prefer 'trendsetters.' We probably don't have enough piercings between us to be groupies," I said.

"Do we know this for sure about Josie?" Dennis asked, interested. What is it with men and the idea of piercing, anyway?

"You never know," I said. "Maybe even Malcolm has a few piercings we don't know about." Malcolm had poked his head in, delivering a box of pencils, one to each of us. Dennis and I each grabbed one. We each lifted a box to our nose and inhaled slowly. We love pencils. It's a thing with us.

"Jeez," Malcolm said about the pencils, "you'd think they were expensive cigars or something."

"Our drug of choice," Dennis said. "And cheap."

"You haven't been to Staples recently," Malcolm said. "I think you could get pharmaceuticals cheaper."

"But they wouldn't smell as good," Dennis said. "Or so I'm told."

"I'm taking Brendan for a haircut," I said to Malcolm. "Want to come?"

"I'd rather clean out all the ashtrays," Malcolm said. "No offense."

"We don't have any ashtrays," I said.

"It's a metaphorical statement, even though you're probably all going to stop for a long lunch," Malcolm whined.

"A field trip to the outside world," Dennis said, enviously. "With optional piercings."

Malcolm looked a little frightened.

"Details at the next staff meeting," I said.

"No thanks," said Malcolm.

"Take the digital cam," Dennis said.

"So I can show before and after pictures," I said.

Malcolm looked a bit faint and left the cubicle.

"I don't think he has any piercings, either," Dennis said.

Brendan walks beside me now, and I have to admit I can almost feel some kind of jitteriness coming from him, some combination of nerves and blood pumping that's, well, literally attractive, that makes me think of one of those old horseshoe-shaped magnets you use in grammar school. Magnetic is a word that's so overused, but to actually feel like you're being pulled toward someone, well, that's not so common, not for me at least, and generally not to someone who has recently turned twenty-three. I think Josie feels it too as she has tripped down the street a couple of times while keeping her eyes on him. I can tell we are both a little protective of Brendan, although I may be projecting. It did seem the other night, at the Heartthrobs' last performance as the Heartthrobs, that Brendan might be becoming more attached to me than I'd intended. So I'm trying to keep some kind of mental distance if not physical distance, despite the magnet imagery running through my mind and despite the fact that we're walking close enough to be holding hands. Which we are not doing. If Brendan has been looking at me in any funny kind of way—and I do get that feeling—I've been looking straight ahead. And I haven't tripped once.

We have an appointment for Brendan at a shop called The Split End on Beverly. Dennis giggled when I told him the shop's name, which is worth saying a few times just to hear Dennis giggle, but it actually took several weeks to get the appointment. There's a Split End on Beverly and a Split End on Melrose, and although they're pretty much just a few blocks away from one another, they have very different reputations. Both are booked solid.

"The Split End on Beverly is where musicians go," Josie tells Brendan and me on our stroll. "The one on Melrose is for television actors." She says it a little disdainfully.

"We're definitely headed for the right one," I tell Brendan. He looks hopeful. His hair is long and shaggy and looks suspiciously like he's been cutting it himself, although not recently. It has a nice curl to it and is very thick and deep brown, now that I really look at it. His hair does something nice with his light brown eyes—the color of those light brown M&Ms. They've always been my favorites.

"Don't worry," Josie says knowledgeably to Brendan. "They don't just have one musician's haircut. They individualize. I sent them a copy of your CD. They like to cut to fit the voice, or so they tell me." I'm interested to see what this means. I've given Josie control over arranging for the haircut. She's risen to it.

"That's good, because I wouldn't want to have to sing in the shop or anything," Brendan says.

"No, no," Josie says. "They have to listen to you on your CD before they agree to the appointment. They turned down one of the guys from The Clash recently." We consider this.

"So you know you must be good," I tell him.

"Wow, my strangest audition yet," Brendan says. "I win a haircut."

"You still have to pay," Josie says.

"Oh," Brendan says.

"Didn't there used to be a Split End on Sunset?" I ask Josie. She seems to know.

"Yes," she says, "but it had a very difficult parking lot. Only Cher went there."

We think about this.

"She had a driver and didn't have to use the lot," Josie says.

I wonder what has happened to all the haircutters from the Sunset shop, whether they've disbanded or been sent to other Split End shops. Maybe they went to work for Cher.

We walk by Billie's, my mother's client's beauty salon, which is the prettiest shop on the street by far. Even Brendan has to stop and look at the pink awning with little yellow flowers painted on it, the display of fresh flowers outside by the door. Billie's doesn't smell like other hair salons I've visited. There's none of that awful acidic nail salon smell—I don't know what those chemicals are, but they don't smell healthy. Billie's smells of coconut and mango, somehow. Even outside the shop. It's enticing. We all stop outside the door and inhale a moment. Like Hansel and Gretel, Brendan and Josie find themselves drawn inside, entering the shop slowly, shoulder to shoulder, and noses first.

"Ooh," they both murmur. It's just a hair salon, I have to think, but I do know what they mean. I've been amazed at Billie's for years, so I'm a little jaded, but I'm still always surprised at what the scent of mango can do to your senses. It reaches in and meets some deeply held desire that you didn't quite know you had. It does this to me, anyway. Hansel and Gretel seem similarly affected. Lured by fragrance into this pretty, pretty place.

Billie greets us herself, a great-looking fiftysomething woman with salt-and-pepper hair. Billie is tall and broad-shouldered while still looking feminine, a quality I admire, even though I never have to worry about being tall, let alone broad-shouldered. I've worn a lot of shoulder pads in my day.

"Welcome, guys," Billie says casually. She gives me a hug. She's one of those people who could say "I've known you since you were a little baby" but is classy enough not to. I can feel it in her nod, but not in a bad way.

"Hi, Billie," I say. "This is Josie, who works with me, and

Brendan, who's a musician. We're getting Brendan a haircut down the street for his new image." Billie usually limits her clients to women, so I know she won't mind.

"Oh, The Split End?" Billie asks.

"On Beverly," Josie answers.

"Have you thought about what kind of cut?" Billie looks at Brendan, then at me. Josie seems confused—she clearly hasn't thought about it, and it bothers her. I, on the other hand, haven't thought about it either, but I'm not bothered at all. Brendan looks a little intimidated to be in a ladies' hair salon. I think he may have thought it was a smoothie shop, what with the mango smell and all. He's scrunching down into his very old brown Gap jacket a little.

"I thought they'd know what to do," Brendan almost asks.

"They do all the rock stars," Josie explains.

"Oh, I didn't mean for you to worry," Billie says. "Let's just take a look at the hair." She leads Brendan over to a chair by some mirrors and begins rumpling his hair in a way mothers do. Billie has three boys, all older than Brendan. This is a treat for her.

"You have great hair," Billie says. Several other hairdressers gather around. They seem to agree, based on the oohing, and maybe it's the sounds or maybe it's the momness of them, but Brendan seems to relax. I love it here, and not just because everyone here has always agreed I should let my hair grow as long as I like. Not one of the hairdressers has ever tried one of those "You'd be so pretty if you'd get rid of that long hair" lines on me, which I'm grateful for, even if my hair has made my own mother sigh more than a few times.

Josie checks her watch. "Ten minutes," she says. "They're pretty strict about check-in time."

"Good curls," says one hairdresser nearby, Babette, a close

friend of Billie's. Babette did my hair for the prom, and although I don't usually like thinking about that day, my hair smelled nice. That's about my best memory of it all, though.

"Thanks," Brendan says. "I have my mom's hair."

Billie's ladies seem to like this remark. I hear lots of "What a nice boy" murmured in our direction. Josie writes something on her clipboard and comes up to whisper to me.

"He does have a certain way with older ladies," she says. I shrug—there are a couple women in their forties here, which doesn't qualify them for older status as far as I'm concerned, but I know what Josie means. Brendan could reach past the eighteen-to thirty-five demographics. Into the thirty-six-to-forty-five. And beyond. Different radio stations, different commercials. Maybe they can all fall for the boy from the boy group.

"I think short but not too short," Billie says. "Let that wave show. All the girls love waves," she says. The hairdressers and women wearing blue robes all voice their agreement.

"What do you think, Claire?" Brendan asks me. He's been whooshed into a chair and is surrounded by women. He looks very relaxed now. All eyes turn to me.

"I'm with Billie," I say. "She's managed my curls, and sometimes lack of them, for years." It's true, she's even made Jackie's super-straight red hair appealing to Jackie, who's so critical. The rest of us always envy her head of deep red hair.

"Claire's in charge," Brendan says. "She's remaking our band. I have faith in her."

The ladies pat me on the back. Josie looks a little hurt but stands tall, assuming her junior advertising executive role. Not that I'm the senior executive, but I guess it makes her feel better to think so.

"With this head of hair," Billie says, smoothing Brendan's very messed-up hair, "I'm not sure there could be a bad cut, don't you agree ladies?" Other hairdressers—and they're all women here—begin to touch Brendan's hair, just to check. They nod in agreement. Brendan looks at me and shrugs, as if to make it clear this wasn't his idea. Or maybe he's inviting me to try it. But I keep my distance as I'm not a hair-care professional, although this isn't my only reason. I'll admit I half felt myself moving forward at the invitation. But nobody else needs to know this. And Josie's watching me carefully, clipboard in hand, which makes me wonder who she's taking notes on, exactly, not to mention who she's taking notes for.

We move on to The Split End, right on time. Brendan's salonist—that's what they call them, although I'm pretty sure Webster's wouldn't approve—is named Shaunnaya, which Josie jots down. I'm finally grateful that Josie's taking notes as I'd have no idea how to spell this in case we need to know later. I'm not sure why we'd need to know, but I'm sure we can file the info away somewhere. Josie likes to file.

"I've heard the tapes," Shaunnaya tells Brendan.

"We sent a CD," Josie corrects her. Shaunnaya, a woman about my age but dressed all in black—it almost looks like one piece but is a two-piece shirt and pants in a an ultra-clingy and sparkly black—walks by Josie so closely that it almost seems as if she doesn't realize Josie is right there. I see Josie's self-esteem take one giant step back, along with Josie herself. Shaunnaya takes several minutes—in utter silence—to observe Brendan's hair from various angles. Brendan sits very still in his chair and breathes deeply. I lean against a shiny marble column in Shaunnaya's cubicle and wonder whether Dennis has spilled anything on my newspaper (I didn't get to read it). Josie watches the floor, which is spotless.

"I think short but not too short," Shaunnaya finally announces. "Let that wave show," she says, echoing Billie's words exactly. Brendan smiles at me in a mirror. I hear a slight "humph" from Josie, who writes something down and marches out of the cubicle, head held high.

"Great," I say. "A trim." Brendan looks relieved. "How can you improve on perfection?" I ask him in the mirror, and he looks grateful. Shaunnaya, who I notice has no sense of humor, clearly thinks she can.

It's a nice haircut, hardly worth the fuss of having to get here at ten-thirty on a workday. I still think as if I'm in school—some activities should only occur after three-thirty, like haircuts and dentist's appointments, things that aren't worth dragging you away from pre-algebra for but that you wouldn't want to waste your Saturday morning on. Some feelings just stay with you, even postgrad. Billie, no doubt, could have done this haircut in her sleep, and she charges a lot less. Plus, she has better magazines to read. Josie and I had to settle for old *Vogue*s and *GQ*'s, none of which has the slightest thing to do with my life. Josie seemed to have read them all before, so she wasn't happy, either.

"It's a nice cut," I tell Brendan. "Your mom will like it," I say. He likes this.

"Girls everywhere will like it," Josie says. "That's the important thing."

"You haven't met my mom yet," Brendan says, "but thanks."

"Let's get an expensive lunch on Perri," I say, "and let's show Billie Brendan's head." He seems very up for this, so we backtrack to Billie's.

My mother greets us at the front desk, not that she works the front desk. She's clearly dropping off some bookkeeping, and she and Billie are laughing as we come through the door. My mother's wearing very uncreased linen pants with a pink boxy sweater that looks both age-appropriate and great with her blondish hair, done no doubt by Billie, as always. My mother looks businesslike, I can't help thinking. But healthy and pink, too.

"It looks just darling!" Billie says about Brendan's hair as if Brendan were eight years old, but still not in an insulting way. And he's not insulted but instead goes and hugs her. Billie pats his back.

"Who is this boy?" my mother asks, charmed.

"Hello Ms. Duncan," Josie says to Mom. They've met lots of times.

"Josie," Mom says. "Good to see you out of that overly white office and in some natural sunshine." Like me, Mom finds the bright white of our office hard on the eyes.

"Not to mention the skin tone," she's not forgotten to mention.

"Hi, Mom," I say.

"Working hard, dear?" Mom says, greeting me and motioning delightedly toward Brendan. Mom wants the lowdown, I can just see it in her eyes.

"Mom, this is Brendan, our new client, the leader of our new band, Montana."

"Formerly known as the Heartthrobs," Brendan says, shaking Mom's hand. "Claire is reshaping our band—new name, new haircut."

"And new jacket?" Mom suggests, fingering Brendan's jacket and actually causing him to blush. "Not that you kids don't have your own way with those well-worn garments you all seem to like. Grunge, is that it?"

Brendan nods, a little embarrassed.

"I'm just wondering what a little denim work shirt wouldn't do with that haircut," Mom says. "You could wash it many times, soften it up, give it that inviting feel," she says, a little suggestively for someone's mom. For my mom.

"I know," Brendan says. "Everyone hates the jacket." He moves his head from side to side, kind of like one of those little bobblehead dolls. Josie has moved in close. I don't think she hates the jacket. "Claire's going to do something about it, Mrs. Duncan."

"You have to call me Eleanor," Mom tells Brendan. "And you'll have to follow Claire's advice very closely—"

"Oh, I will," Brendan says.

"—because I'll be happy to consult with her if she has any questions. You know, fashion questions. Motherly advice. I have a long-standing subscription to *Glamour.*"

"Do's and don'ts?" I suggest.

"That's what mothers are for," Eleanor says. "To give advice on what styles you'd never dare to wear but really should, and which clothes are ready for Goodwill."

"Is that where my purple sweater has gone?" I ask, teasingly.

"No, I borrowed that one." Mom raises an eyebrow. It's a very tight-fitting purple sweater, a little too tight for my comfort. She gave it to me, too. And clearly isn't ashamed to wear it, unlike me.

"Good," I say, "such slinkiness is wasted on me."

"I don't know where she got this self-image," Mom says to Billie.

"You girls today," Billie says. "So skinny and yet so many layers."

"It's just a waste," Mom agrees with her. I look at my outfit, a cotton T covered by an aging black linen jacket (not as old as Brendan's jacket, but I can see there'll come a day when someone—Eleanor—will find it that way). Plus there are my really baggy cotton and hemp capris I know my mom finds too loose, not to mention itchy. Still, I really like my clothes.

"Clare always looks amazing," Brendan says, seeing through my clothes, it feels like. My mother smiles. Josie doesn't, really.

"We should get lunch?" Josie suggests, pointing at her watch, one of those little gold ones that are too small to read, it seems to me.

"I'll take all the advice I can get," Brendan says to my mom.

"Be careful what you wish for," Eleanor says back, and I have to admit, I was thinking the exact same thing. Mom looks at me and seems to know what I was thinking again, in that annoyingly psychic way mothers seem to have.

We both smile an awfully similar smile at Brendan. He smiles back, and on some kind of impulse, he and my mom shake hands, as if agreeing to something.

Josie starts to make a note on her clipboard then stops, as if not entirely sure what she wants to say.

Chapter 10

Sex and the Married Politician

"Theo's numbers are up," Jackie tells me.

"I'm not sure how you mean that," I reply. We're sitting at the little Café Bob's near my office, a beachy place where the tables are laminated, and underneath you can look at old ads for suntan oils from bygone eras but none for sunscreen, I notice. We're on the Venice Boardwalk, a place where you can see things you hadn't dreamed of, not in a good dream at least. We're watching a very young woman with purple hair stand on one foot in roller skates while drawing a mural of what looks to be the Mona Lisa. She's using pastel chalk, the kind little kids use for hopscotch, and she seems to be drawing it from memory. It's going fairly well.

We like it here, and despite the soaring values of property and the trendsetters who've taken over, Café Bob's (not to be confused with Roberto's Café up the boardwalk, which charges seven dollars for an undersized coffee and extra for steamed milk) is cheap and a five minute walk from my office. Which also makes us feel as if we've exercised, although not enough to make us tired or cranky. Just enough to earn a chicken burger on a whole-wheat bun, slightly toasted, and a view of the Pacific. For only $4.95, no tip, as no one here at Café Bob's would dream of serving you. Pick it up or lose it, I believe, is Bob's credo.

Jackie is wearing a pair of clunky black glasses that could make anyone with less of a fine bone structure than Jackie's seem unattractive. On Jackie, they just magnify her perfect little face, freckles and all. You can always tell Jackie's mood by the glasses she wears. She usually puts in contacts, so when I see the thick black glasses, I know I'd better order extra fries and maybe try to tempt her with a little dessert, which in Café Bob's case means freshly baked brownies I wish someone had given my mother the recipe for way back when. If I ever have a daughter, I'll try to cheer her up with Bob's brownie recipe whenever life lets her down, but for now I'm working on Jackie.

"So the campaign is going okay?" I ask. Theo is Jackie's candidate for our congressional district, a candidate she has failed to maintain a professional distance from, as the newspapers like to say.

"He's a wonderful candidate," Jackie says dreamily. "Really sincere opinions about educational reform, an understanding of teachers' needs, and the intricacies of assessment, the pros and cons."

"I've never dated a man who's prematurely gray," I say. I don't have kids, so educational assessment just doesn't hold my interest yet, I guess. Not the way thick hair styled just right would, for example.

"It does help his image, that presentation of seriousness," Jackie says. "He's a head above anyone else we've done demographics for," she says, shredding the lettuce that comes on the side of her chicken burger into careful strips.

"Jackie, is he still married?"

Jackie shrugs. "Separated."

"I don't really know what separated means anymore. Living apart and headed for divorce? Considering getting back together? Checking out the options?"

"It is a changeable concept, you have to admit," Jackie says, dipping a fry in ketchup from Bob's little packages, which we've spilled out onto one of the cardboard boats Bob's gives you for such purposes. Jackie double-dips but with such great focus upon the ketchup, as if it has some answers, that I don't say anything.

"Have you met his wife?" I ask.

"She appeared at a fund-raiser we had last month."

"And?"

"Very educated, health-care manager, very liberal. Hair dyed a chestnut but natural looking."

"And does anyone talk about their being apart, or is it secret for the campaign?"

"Well, technically," Jackie stops here and sucks out the inside of a French fry, leaving the outside on her little paper plate (Bob's recycles). This is kind of tacky eating, but I do it, too. "They're not really that far apart."

"They live nearby one another?" I ask.

"They share a house," Jackie admits.

"Eww," I say. "Yuck." I know they're junior high words, but I really mean them.

"I know," Jackie says. "But Theo says it's easier."

"Does he say this when he's staying at your house, for instance?"

"Ugh," Jackie moans. "Let's talk about something else."

"No way," I say, pouring more fries onto her plate. She starts shredding them, too. I hate to see a fry wasted, but I can tell this is a time of need. "I'm the best friend," I say. "I'm the one who gets to ask the tough questions."

"Since I don't tell my therapist anymore, you mean," Jackie says.

"Right," I say. "Let me use my own years of expensive therapy experience here. No charge."

"I bought lunch," Jackie says.

"Okay, then," I say, "I'll just have to give you fifteen dollars' worth of therapeutic advice." I think for a minute. "What does he mean to you, really?"

"You mean have I slept with him," Jackie says.

"Jackie, you're wearing horn-rims. You're shredding your food. The answer is obvious."

"True," she says.

"How did it start?"

"Dinners to discuss demographics." Jackie shrugs. "Statistics can be sexier than you think."

I hadn't thought much about this. I failed my statistics class in college. Although the professor was cute, come to think of it.

"Dinners," I say. "You've done dinners with clients before."

"Not clients with soft, soft hair," Jackie says.

"Not to mention an understanding of class struggle and educational uproar," I add. Jackie nods again.

"An attractive, educated, interesting man," Jackie says. "Even if he had bad hair," she takes a minute. "It may have made for more than a few dinners."

"Okay, so more than a few dinners. Then?"

"Then a review of statistical regression at my house," Jackie says.

"So to speak," I say. She nods.

"Sex with a political candidate," I say. "You could write an article."

"But not a very professional one," Jackie says.

"Okay, professional, unprofessional, put all that aside," I say. In an effort to do so, we slide the remnants of our chicken sandwiches away and place the brownies in front of us. Getting down to business.

"Right," Jackie says, taking a big bite. We're old friends. We don't care about talking with our mouths full. And this is chocolate, so rules of etiquette don't apply anyway.

"He's still married, more or less, right?" I ask.

Jackie licks the frosting off the side of her brownie. Her glasses slide down her nose.

"It's so cliché," she says. "Sex and the married politician."

"Sex and the prematurely gray-haired married politician," I say. "That's got some originality."

"Face it, it's a *Cosmo* article," Jackie says. "But I still want to see him elected."

"And divorced? Do you want to see him divorced?"

She nods.

"And has he made any campaign promises in that direction?"

"Fairly convincing ones," Jackie says. "He says he's moving in with me after the election," Jackie says, starting to rub at her face. It's her habit, plus she may be a little allergic to something in the brownies. Walnuts, I think.

"How is his believability rating?" I ask. I may have the jargon wrong, but Jackie seems to know what I mean.

"He usually gets nine on a scale of ten in terms of credibility."

I can tell it's that one point that worries her, statistician that she is.

"So there's just that one point on the scale," I say, making it sound not so bad.

"Only if you don't count statistical error," she says.

It sounds like a dangerous move for a statistician, but I probably don't have to tell Jackie this. Instead, I order more brownies. I notice Jackie is staring at Mona Lisa, who now has a nice nose and that all-knowing smile. I can't say it's particularly helpful at this moment.

Walking back down the boardwalk toward my office, Jackie and I stop in at a health food place called Get a (Healthy) Life that sells the kind of coffee beans Jackie likes. Organic beans from Sweden, the label reads. I like a coffee bean that's traveled a little, too, if we're admitting things here. There's a café in the back we could have eaten at, but they don't serve fries. Café Bob's is our place. We're loyal that way. And besides, the brownies here are all made of carob, which everyone knows just isn't the same. Especially after fries.

Picking out Jackie's coffee seems to make her feel better. We're in the coffee bean aisle with its pungent smells—the place is alive with that semisweet smell, enough for some kind of coffee contact high, which I admit is one thing I like about this place. Sometimes, when no one is looking, Jackie likes to open up a large plastic bin and run her fingers through some beans. I know it isn't healthful, but I stand guard for her anyway. Touching the beans really doesn't do anything for me, but Jackie is more tactile.

"Feeling better?" I ask her.

Jackie picks up a packet of her Swedish beans and hugs it to her chest. "I can't really explain it," she says, "but yes." She smells the package. "It's my comfort food."

"Can there be a comfort beverage, or does it have to be a food?" I ask.

"Swedish coffee is the food of the gods," Jackie says.

"The Swedish gods," I say. "Who no doubt dress in warm woolens with stripes."

"Do gods need warm woolens?" Jackie asks, surreptitiously sticking her fingers into a bin of dark, dark beans, then removing them and smelling her bag again.

"Maybe just coffee and ambrosia," I say.

"Ambrosia," Jackie murmurs. "That would be the little milky froth on top."

"You people are way too obsessed with your coffee," I say, reaching for a bag of regular house beans. I'm on a budget.

"As if you don't like froth," Jackie says.

"I live for froth," I say. "Plus, I love the loud swooshy

sound of the hot milk machine." I'm a bit auditorily obsessed, the way Jackie is with her tactile need.

"That sound always makes me jumpy," Jackie admits. Just then we hear it, coming from the café, the whoosh of the steam, and its allure leads me back a few steps toward the café. Jackie, good friend that she is, follows, rubbing two beans between her hands. I motion to them.

"You can buy them by the bean," she says. "I am not the only one with these needs, I guess."

"I like a health food store that makes allowances for every kind of anxiety disorder," I say, and Jackie nods her agreement.

"All part of getting that parenthetical healthy life," she says.

We stop by the swooshing steam machine and see two people seated at one of the back tables, a couple that take us by surprise.

"Speaking of anxiety disorders," Jackie says.

Dennis sits at a table surrounded by papers that he's jotting things down on in a clockwise manner, one jot on the paper at two o'clock, one jot on the paper at four o'clock, and so on around the table. Seated to his right (at about three o'clock), we see Heaven. Dennis no doubt would see her too, were he ever to look up from his jottings.

"Copywriter at work," I say. "Warning."

"Copywriter at work with copywritee," Jackie says. She shakes her bag of beans to get their attention.

"No—" I say. Jackie just looks at me asking why. I'm not sure I have a reason, but I feel a little like slinking over to the tofu aisle. Get a (Healthy) Life has twelve kinds of tofu, not that this matters right now.

Heaven looks up. She's dressed in an oatmeal-colored sweater with matching oatmeal-colored jeans. Oatmeal-colored anything generally makes me look as if I've been ill for a few days and am just coming around, but barely. Heaven just looks fantastic, as if the color were invented for her. She waves.

"Hi, Claire," Heaven says. Discovered, I feel I have to lead Jackie over to their table. Dennis looks up and smiles, but just a little.

"Hi," Dennis says to us.

"Heaven," I say, "you remember my friend Jackie." They've met before.

"Great glasses," Heaven says to Jackie. Jackie stiffens a little. These aren't the glasses she wears when she's looking for compliments, especially not from thin, well-formed twenty-year-old blonde women. These are Jackie's in-your-face leave-me-alone glasses.

"Thank you," Jackie replies incredibly businesslike. She shoots Dennis a look that makes him turn away, something feministic and knowing that seems to go right to his stomach.

"I need to get a pair," Heaven says.

"Are you having trouble seeing?" I ask.

"No," Heaven replies. "I want people to take me more seriously, though. I think glasses like that would help." She seems sincere, but it's still a little offensive, at least to Jackie, who smiles, but I know that smile.

"People always take me seriously," Jackie says.

"You remember what it's like," Heaven says. "To be twenty and have people shrug off anything you say."

"I still have that problem sometimes," I say. "Like with salesladies."

Heaven just nods wildly in agreement.

"We just came from Bob's," I say, my way of asking what they're doing at this café, although from the papers it's pretty clear.

"Fries or brownies?" Dennis asks. Heaven's eyes light up a little at the mention of potentially healthless foods.

"Both," Jackie and I say.

"Such brave girls," Dennis teases us. He's got the remnants of something with sprouts on a plate in front of him. Bob's can't be bothered with sprouts.

"We're working on Heaven's personal history," Dennis says, looking at his notes.

"As told to Dennis Cooper?" Jackie says. Dennis ignores her.

"Not that I have all that much history," Heaven says. "I just want Dennis to put more of me into what's out there, the ads, the publicity. It just all seems to have been about someone else, not the real me."

"You can always make some history up," Jackie suggests.

"Jackie works in the world of politics," Dennis says. Heaven doesn't seem to know what this means, but she seems impressed. I forget how young she is sometimes.

"We need to put the real Heaven out there," I tell Jackie.

"Oh, okay," she says. "That should do it."

"Thanks," Heaven says.

"I've heard you sing, you know," Jackie says. "You're good."

"She is," Dennis agrees, which makes Heaven smile.

"Thanks," she says. "I just think we need to bring my image down a little, in a way."

"Down?" Jackie says.

"Less sexy," I say, braving the word we're all thinking, if not a few others.

"I know what you mean," Jackie says.

"Although I don't think we need to go as far as the glasses," Dennis says, "since you're not nearsighted. Not that they don't make a statement," he says to Jackie. "Eyewear as political proclamation."

"I just report the numbers," Jackie says. "I don't make the policy."

"Oh," Heaven says.

We stand there a minute.

"Well, you two get back to work now," I say.

"We will," Heaven says. She touches Dennis on the arm, which we can see from his face he's pretending he didn't notice. We all say good-byes.

Jackie and I walk off. "What's the deal?" she asks me. I head over to the low-carb counter. I think the whole low-carb thing is an unhealthy fad, but I like the power bars at snack time, which is anytime an hour or so after lunch and up to fifteen minutes before dinner. I refuse to eat a bar for dinner, though. It just doesn't seem right.

"Dennis has to redo Heaven," I say. "All new ads, copy, new photos. She wants it to be more her, but less her physically, if you know what I mean."

"You have to admit," Jackie says. "She wears a sweater well." I look back to their table. They're sitting close together, and this time Dennis is looking at Heaven, not his notes, pen poised to write something she's murmuring, if a twenty-year-old knows how to murmur.

"Heaven's okay," I say.

"I can tell you feel that way by the number of chocolate bars you're collecting," Jackie says. I've gotten five into my hands, although I didn't notice.

"They're power bars," I say.

Jackie shakes her head. "The things we women fool ourselves with."

I hug my (okay, chocolate) power bars and Jackie hugs her coffee. She pushes her glasses up one last time and looks back to the table behind us.

"Ask Claire the Therapist why we don't like that," she says of Dennis and Heaven. Not that I don't have the question myself.

Chapter 11

Miss Popularity

It's no secret that Claire the Therapist does yoga, or what Dennis refers to as heavy breathing with a twist. She is constantly yet gently reminding me to take care of my body and mind, not in too new-agey a way but quieter, the kind of soft reminding you get from someone who has nothing personal to gain from the situation and someone you suspect is probably right.

Yoga mats remind me of those mats we sat on in kindergarten, even though now the mats are thin and purple, and not really cushy or comfortable. I borrowed my mother's once to take to an outdoor concert, and it did not add much padding to the situation at all. Although at least the purple didn't show any grass stains. It's true—even my mother does yoga. She's offered to buy me a matching mat and take me to "Family Time" at her yoga studio, where mothers and daughters of all ages revive their spirits. Claire the Therapist would approve, but I'm a sedentary creature. I admit I like to walk around my neighborhood or at the beach nearby, which I know is supposed to burn more calories if you walk on the sand, which I try to do. That is, I think it counts for more calorie burning. If it doesn't, I may have to reevaluate my sand-walking, because I've ruined several pairs of sneakers by getting sand under the soles that I could never get out, not counting the particles that find their way into my socks. I don't know how they manage this.

All of this leads me to today, my latest session with Claire the Therapist. We meet once every two or three weeks, which I admit is unusual, but that's how long it takes me to build up what I want to talk about. And it's what I can afford. My therapist is very agreeable to the unusual timing, which she thinks lets me feel I have some control, something she's always advising me (yet gently) to take.

Not unlike my mother, my therapist believes I spend too much time indoors. Really, my mother would like my therapist a lot, given the opportunity to meet her, not that this is an opportunity I'd ever really want my mother to have. Today, Claire the Therapist has decided we should sit outside, which we do, on a soft multicolor blanket she smoothes onto the grass in the courtyard behind her office, a quiet area with a small rose garden. Since roses aren't one of the flowers I'm allergic to, I've agreed to sit out here. The blanket isn't very plush, but I don't want to complain.

"Let's start with some deep breathing," Clare the Therapist suggests.

"I don't really like the deep breathing exercises," I tell her. She's recommended some books, and I did look at them in the library. I tried a few of the exercises there in the stacks, although I think the air was a bit dusty for taking in such deep breaths. But I did try.

"Why not?" Claire the Therapist asks.

"It makes me nervous," I admit.

"It's supposed to do just the opposite," she says. "Maybe you're not doing it right."

"I think that's the part that makes me nervous," I say. "The idea that I'm not doing it right. I don't find it at all comforting that I might not be breathing properly. It seems at the very bottom of what I should be able to do for myself."

"But if you're breathing wrong, you can fix it," Clair the Therapist says. "You can take control." There it is again.

"I just don't find it comforting that there's a wrong way to breathe," I say.

"Well, deep breathing's just an idea," she says, a little dejected. "You don't have to," she tells me.

"Good," I say. "Isn't it enough that we're outside? The air kind of has to get in somehow, doesn't it?"

"True," she says, feeling a little better. I do notice that I'm comforting my therapist, although not all the time or anything.

"So," she continues, "we skip the breathing part." She looks like she's turning a few pages in her mind.

"We can just get to the talking part," I say. "It's okay."

"All right." Claire the Therapist perks up. "Why don't you tell me what's been worrying you."

"You can tell I've been worried?" I ask.

"No, I mean just general worry," she says. I'm always generally worried about something. She knows this about me. But I also don't like others to think of me as worried, which really only gives me more to worry about.

"Oh, okay," I say, getting started. I am in therapy. I was a scout. I do prepare. "Well, my mother wants me to join a book group."

"Oh," Claire the Therapist says, interested in the idea, as if maybe she would join, too. "What kind of book club? One of the by-mail kind?"

"One of the meeting kind, where you tear apart people's work," I say. I was an English major, after all. I took a few aggressive writers' workshops. I haven't discussed a book with anyone since.

"They're not all like that," Claire the Therapist says. "I belong to one, it's a group of Santa Monica therapists. We sit around and talk about recent fiction. Only macrobiotic foods are served as snacks," she says with a nod.

This doesn't much appeal to me, but I don't mention it. "This one is a mother-daughter group," I say.

"Awww, how sweet," she actually says.

"Well, it might be sweet if we were eight and reading Nancy Drew with our moms or something," I say. "But aren't I a little old for this?"

"Do you feel old for it?" she asks therapeutically.

I shrug. "They're starting with a book that has lots of sex in it, I skimmed," I say. Might as well take a look, after all. "My mother dropped it off for me one night, so there I was, just after work, finding a box just inside my door."

"Does your mother have a key?" Claire the Therapist tries to keep any judgment out of her voice.

"She's insisted," I say. "It makes her feel better. And she almost never uses it. Why, your mother doesn't have a key?"

"Well, my mother," Claire the Therapist starts, then waves it away with her hand. I guess her mother doesn't have a key. "But we're talking about Eleanor." She says the name softly. No hostility toward my mom there.

"But what was really weird, besides finding the book, was that inside the box was a stack of photos from my childhood."

"Does your mother often give you photos?" she asks.

"They were mostly of my dad," I say. "Some of all of us, on trips to Sea World, to the snow. Some with just me and my dad." They're happy pictures—no fighting on road trips in my family, none of the family bickering you see so much of in those made-for-TV movies and sitcoms. No getting lost and screaming from parent to parent in the front seat. Not with my dad. My dad was a circuit engineer, and he loved to sit quietly and put things together, or to teach me how to solve math problems. When I was little, he built me a set of what must have been hundreds of small blocks, different sizes, painted in bright purples and pinks. To this day when I see those exact dayglow colors, I feel a little tug for my smooth, smooth blocks. I had a happy childhood, I admit it. I don't think it necessarily adds much to my therapy sessions, and I don't even know if it prepared me all that much for what Jackie and I like to call "real life." But I had a happy childhood anyway.

"Were you glad to get the pictures?" Claire the Therapist asks.

"Sure," I say, "sort of. It's funny, looking at them, I feel like I remember all those events when I didn't think I did."

"And that's good?" Claire the Therapist asks.

"I think one real issue is why Eleanor dropped them off in the first place."

"Have you asked her?"

"No," I say. "But she left a note, the one that mentioned the reading group, and then it said she was 'cleaning out,' those were her words, and she had some extra snapshots—Mom used the word snapshots—for me."

Claire the Therapist nods her head.

"Actually they were all pictures with my dad," I say.

"You mentioned that," she says.

"Well," I say. "My mother packing up a boxful—even a small boxful—of pictures of my dad. Isn't it meaningful?" My therapist looks at me and opens her hands, palms up, as if waiting for me to fill them with the answer.

"It's meaningful to me," I say. She raises an eyebrow and nods.

I return home to my apartment and take out the photos. My dad has been gone almost two years, which sometimes takes me by surprise. His illness—cancer, like all the other parents falling around us, it sometimes seems—was surprising and then short. I hate when people say it's best this way.

Although I know they're probably right. It still doesn't help all that much.

But I hate to dwell on that part of our lives together, so the pictures take me back to happier yet still quiet times. I admit I'm feeling a little sappy tonight. I put on a record from my childhood (I still have a turntable attached to my stereo for such purposes, although most people laugh when they see it, not that I entertain all that much). I like the weight of an album, and the deep black and the shine. I take out my father's old Beatles albums, which my mother gave me when Dad died. She mostly listens to Celine Dion, all post-vinyl, and although I can take a little of Celine at a time, I don't think those torch songs help my mother's mood all that much. But maybe I just can't understand.

As I hum along with Paul (I don't have a good enough voice to sing even by myself, although I might be overly judgmental), I hear a knock at my door. I go to the door and check my peephole. Despite this, I open the door.

"Just a visit from the landlord," says Andy, who is indeed my landlord. He's also, of course, my last boyfriend of many years, which is a long story even Claire the Therapist hasn't heard the end of yet.

My relationship with Andy is one of those things in life that you wouldn't want to have to sit down and try to explain to an alien, say, not to mention your mother or your therapist. We met in college, at UCLA, and I swear it was one of those moments where our eyes met and something happened. Not that my heart skipped a beat or I got goose bumps even, just that something inside said *Yes*. It may not have been a voice I should have listened to, but I distinctly heard it say something that sounded positive. It was one of those moments when you're not thinking all that clearly, but you don't really care.

Andy was seated on a grassy hill looking like some kind of flawless Greek statue, but better because he had blonde hair blowing around slightly and one of those really good smiles that never needed orthodontic work, although I learned this about him later. He sat on the hill looking perfect, talking to a girl. A girl I barely noticed. Just a friend of his, really, he later told me. His eyes met mine. I kept walking. I don't think I stumbled. I tried hard not to.

The next day I saw him walking toward me in Powell Library. I was working on a paper for a graduate course in Shakespeare: "The Effect of Color and Light in *A Midsummer Night's Dream*." Although it was still winter and rainy out, our Shakespeare adviser was the optimistic type. Andy sat down across from me at one of the large tables where there aren't usually many vacant spots. We smiled. We rolled pens back and forth, as quietly as graduate students can do that sort of thing. Most people in Powell Library are kind of cranky studiers and like it quiet. Somehow in this quietness, we agreed to move to the student coffee house. A few months later, somehow equally quietly, I agreed to move to his apartment.

He had an apartment near the ocean and crystal blue eyes. I was twenty-three. He was twenty-three. What should I have done? He had blonde hair that curled in any kind of weather, curled itself right around my fingers. He had no roommates and a rooftop view. He was earning a business degree (something useful—Eleanor was impressed). He liked me because I didn't talk about business administration or economics. I liked him because he didn't talk about alliteration or allegory. I'm not sure what we talked about. But everything he ever said to me sounded perfect. For a while.

"Rent's paid up," I say.

"Nice music," Andy says tonight. He's not much for Beatles, although I still find this hard to believe. "I've brought some insurance papers you might want to have around for the apartment."

"Okay," I say. I let him in. I blame Paul.

Andy comes in and sits down on my couch, which isn't the couch we used to have together, which was frankly a much nicer couch. But this one is mine.

"I like what you've done here," Andy says. He picks something off his pants that probably came from my couch, which gets a little nubby, but in the softest way possible. He looks around at the fading pink-and-white couch's pillow back with a slightly pessimistic look on his face.

"Why are you in town?" I ask. I take the papers from him. I can't imagine why I need such papers, but okay.

"Conference," Andy says, knowing full well that I don't really understand what he does. He works in international insurance, or is it reinsurance, and I've never much understood the difference. He travels a lot and is based out of San Francisco now. Andy looks relatively unchanged in that way thirty-year-old guys have. They seem to change drastically at forty, I've noticed, as has Andy, and I know it worries him. The hair is still light and curly. Classic nose the same, classic cheekbones the same. Classic Andy.

"I'm on my way to Switzerland," he says.

"I hear it's very clean there," I say. I sit down in the fuzzy white chair by the couch and look at the table covered with pictures. George starts singing, which I admit isn't my favorite thing in the world, but then a lot of things in the room aren't my favorites at this point.

"Why don't you come with me?" Andy asks. I look at him. He has a small smile on his face but otherwise is impossible to read, which isn't surprising.

"Gee," I start, "thanks for the papers and all—"

"Just kidding," Andy says. "Keep these papers around somewhere just in case. Fire insurance and all."

Andy of course does own the apartment I'm living in, although I often think of it as my apartment. It isn't. It was a gift to Andy from his father at graduation (undergraduate) from UCLA. That's right, his father gave him an apartment on the Santa Monica/Venice border. And just for earning a bachelor's degree. If you go up to the roof, you can see the beach. That would make it what I think they call prime real estate, or at least just to the south of prime real estate. For graduation, my mother gave me a leather bag that doubled as a briefcase. I still use it. It's very nice. No one in my family would consider real estate a proper gift for a twenty-one-year-old. Which may be why none of us owns property at the beach. But still.

Andy and I lived together for about five years, some of which time I kept myself busy studying, some of which time I got busy at work, which helped keep part of my brain occupied, the part that might have otherwise wondered what Andy was keeping himself busy doing. I still thought our relationship was okay. I began to question it around the time of my dad's death, and although this sounds like bad timing, it felt right at the time. I didn't appreciate the way Andy didn't help much with my father's illness. He kept asking me what I wanted him to say, what I wanted him to do. I guess I wanted him to somehow intuit these answers himself, to know how to comfort me even if I didn't, or at least to try. I couldn't explain it to him. He never volunteered to help with my dad or volunteered affection or sympathy. He stayed out of the apartment a lot to give me space, he said, but I'm not sure this was at all what I needed. He kept such a distance, from me, from my family. Somehow, while my dad was sick and dying, I knew I wanted a better relationship. I wanted to share something emotional with someone I loved. Everything about my dad, and his getting sick, helped me see this, made me want to be with someone better than Andy. It makes perfect sense, except sometimes I wonder if I was just being rash, just upset at the world. I'm not always sure.

Andy blurted out to me one day that he was moving to the San Francisco headquarters, to a better position, although he did light candles at the dinner table before breaking the news. And he invited me to come, much in the way he just casually invited me to Switzerland. He thought I would come, I think, just like that. I know my mom always felt my relationship with Andy was a little bit too easy. "You kids are so casual these days, easygoing," she'd say, but not enviously. I know she just didn't love Andy. And ocean views don't really do that much for her.

I broke up with him. I would have even if he weren't moving to San Francisco. I'm fairly sure of this. I just didn't leave the apartment. It was close to work, I told myself, and told my mother and Jackie. My therapist hasn't ever asked why I still live here, since apparently ocean views really do a lot for her.

"Why all the pictures of your dad?" Andy asks. He starts picking them up.

"I don't really know," I say. "Mom dropped them off."

"You and your dad," Andy says. "Such a pair. It was always amazing to me to watch you two together."

I try to remember how Andy felt about my dad, and vice versa. I look at the pictures of my dad, of me. They're pre-Andy and don't help me think at all. I don't remember Andy liking my father that much. He comes from the more dysfunctional kind of family where you get little attention and little emotional contact but, let's say, extravagant gifts. Like real estate. And he seems to like it that way. It's much the way he treated me. I got lots of presents. They used to be enough, I'm often sorry to say, usually to my therapist.

"I didn't know you felt that way," I say.

"Your dad just doted on you. Girls and their dads," Andy says. "You can't compete with that."

"I guess not," I say. We look at a picture. It's me at my junior high school graduation. I'm wearing white eyelet (I was a little bit babyish still). My dad is grinning, I'm grinning. It's the same grin.

"Look how adorable you are," Andy says. He holds the

picture up for us both. Andy and I are sitting closer together now, although I'm not sure how this happened, as I don't think the furniture has moved any. "How could he not adore you?" Andy says.

I start crying. I don't know if I care that Andy's sitting here or not. It's not like it matters if I start to look bad or make snorting sounds. It's Andy, and Andy is over.

Which does not explain why I'm next to him on the couch crying into his chest. If my mother knew, she'd probably curse herself for dropping by the pictures in the first place, although this is beside the point at the moment. Still, the thought crosses my mind, although it's my last semi-sensible thought for a while. Andy strokes my back and makes cooing noises. He is so good at this. He lifts me up and carries me to my room, our old room. I still have the old bed. It's expensive to replace a bed on a copywriter's salary. I think I notice the bed is unmade (I wasn't expecting a visit from my mother or anyone this morning), but I don't know if Andy notices. Or cares. His kisses are gentle and familiar. They erase my thoughts, which seems like pretty much just what I need at this moment.

Although I'm sure Jackie would say I'm only fooling myself. She says this a lot.

It dawns on me, later that evening when I find myself alone again—Andy left, saying he had an early meeting before his flight—that it's only nine o'clock. An unfortunate day, I think to myself, and still a few more hours to go. What I really need are evening therapy sessions. "Wouldn't this be better for everyone?" I've asked Claire the Therapist. It's nighttime when you make the real mistakes, after all.

I make myself a huge bowl of popcorn. It's the extra-butter kind, which I save for special occasions. Or especially needy occasions.

There's a knock on my door. Miss Popularity, I hear my mother's voice say, but not in a way that would suggest I won the title in an honorable, let alone deserving, way.

Dennis stands behind my door, making a funny fish face into the peephole. I open the door.

"I didn't recognize you with your fish face on," I say.

"But you opened the door anyhow," he says, coming in, although unexpected and not that invited.

"I've let in worse," I say. I don't elaborate. "What's up?"

"I'm having problems with my life," Dennis says. "I thought I'd come over and listen to you complain about yours, rather than dwell," he says.

"Or try to fix what's wrong with yours," I say.

Dennis waves his hands in front of him. No way he'd do that, he admits silently.

"Ooh, family photos," he says. "You need one of those scrapbooks," my disorganized officemate says.

"What would you know about scrapbooking?" I say. Dennis sits down and pulls over the big bowl of popcorn, which nestles in his lap. He looks at me.

"I've seen them at Ralph's," he says. "They must be popular. They keep them right near the cash register, next to the Junior Mints." I'd really like some Junior Mints right now.

"They're the new impulse items," I say, sitting down close to the popcorn. "For when you get the urge to organize your childhood past."

Dennis makes a shuddering movement with his shoulders. "That explains why I've never bought one."

I pull up the big box my mother left with the photos. "That's why I have a box instead." I say.

"To put the past in its place?" Dennis says, mouthful of popcorn.

"I wouldn't go that far," I say, thinking of tonight, when I have not exactly put the past where it belongs. Dennis picks up a photo of me in about the fifth grade. I have a tan (undoubtedly the last one and undoubtedly the result of a really bad sunburn). I'm curtsying before the camera, my dad next to me taking a bow. We're in our pajamas. I can't really explain why.

"I love this one," he says. "I miss your dad."

Dennis really did like my dad, I remember. They used to sit around and chat—I don't really know about what—in low voices. Lots of nodding, which can somehow be more important than words, I guess. Agreement over something doesn't need to be loud.

"I miss my dad," I say. I put the photos in a box, except for the pajama photo, princess curtsying to the king. Dennis takes this one again.

"One of us has to frame this," he says.

Dennis grabs the remote and settles back comfortably in my couch. He puts on an old movie, something in black and white where everyone's wearing a hat, even the women in their tight suits. A woman screams for what seems longer than necessary. Dennis searches through the popcorn bowl and finds the butteriest piece. He holds it up for me to eat.

We go on this way for a while, watching old movies on TV through much of the night, eating buttered yet organic popcorn, and watching shady characters come to no good. It only happens in the movies.

Chapter 12

Fringe Benefits

You can call my couch both aging and unattractive, and many have, or maybe they've just thought it and kept it to themselves, but it's large enough for one regular-size person (that would be me) and one larger person (that would be Dennis) to sleep at opposite ends of it and actually not touch. Maybe toes touch, maybe once or twice, while dreaming of long-ago days when girls curtsied and in return were fed little bites of daintily buttered ambrosia. Those were my dreams, at least—confused, but not in a bad way.

In the morning I wake to find Dennis on what's known around here as his end of the couch. I've noticed that Dennis always sits on the left, which represents some kind of brain thing, no doubt, although we've had discussions where he claims he doesn't always sit there even when he's sitting there at the time. These are not productive conversations, I've found, but more the kind of debate you have when nothing good is on TV and your expectations for an evening's entertainment are low.

This morning I have that almost indescribable kind of hangover you get from too much buttered popcorn. It's not the same as a too-much-vodka kind of hangover, but it still

leaves a heavily coated taste in your mouth. Dennis and I
don't have the kind of relationship where I would have
wanted to brush my teeth before falling asleep or anything,
so this morning my mouth feels thick. I guess it's something
to focus on, rather than, say, anything else that might have
gone wrong last night. Plus, it's easily fixable with a tooth-
brush. That the hangover could be the kind you might also
associate with inappropriate sex is really more than I want
to think about, and I don't think toothpaste is going to help.

I kick Dennis awake. He opens his eyes and sees the bowl
of popcorn—the remnants, stale and unloved. He picks up
the bowl and begins eating.

"Breakfast?" He offers me the bowl. I wrinkle my nose at
it.

"Not the leftover type?" Dennis asks.

"I've been accused of worse," I say, going off to brush my
teeth. I hear Dennis crunching kernels slowly, and I'm overwhelmed by a sudden desire to make him banana pancakes.
I may even follow up on it.

I am low on powdered sugar, but if Dennis notices, he doesn't
say anything. He's what Jackie calls a nonconfrontational eater,
which she claims is the best kind of person to have a first
date with. Jackie is the expert on first dates, so I take her at
her word. My mother would just call Dennis A Joy to Feed,
and has. She hasn't exactly ever used these words to describe
me.

"I have to take Brendan shopping today," I say, although
I don't really feel so obligatory about the whole thing.

"Excuse me," Dennis says, requesting clarification and
almost laughing. "You have to take Brendan where?"

"I want to fix up the band a little," I say. "We're going to
Jeds."

"I love Jeds," Dennis says, enthused. It's true, Dennis

isn't the kind of man who hates to shop, although he doesn't exactly ever shop for himself. He loves to look at each item in a store, and I mean each and every item, and comment on it, not always in a positive way. Like most men I've met, though, he hates to try on anything. It accounts for why many of his shirts don't seem to fit right, I guess.

"Would you really want to be with a man who did want to try things on, perhaps model them for you?" Jackie has asked me. It's a conundrum. You want them stylish but not too stylish. And not vain, never vain. Shopping is that unspoken testing ground between men and women, although I wouldn't be surprised if there's a rack of self-help books on the subject, a rack never touched by men.

"I want to come," Dennis says. "Chaperone."

"You just want to play with the fringe shirts," I tell him. Jed has a complete line of Western wear.

"Like you don't," Dennis says. I like the feel of fringe. I've admitted it more than once.

After pancakes—Dennis washes up, which he's very persnickety about and likes to do by himself, I've noticed, although I don't know why and I've never bothered to press for an answer—we head to Jeds. Brendan is meeting me there. We find him standing in front of the shop, head down, humming.

"If he had a cup in his hand, he could make a few bucks," Dennis whispers to me. There are more than a few people with cups in this neighborhood, and many of them sing better than much of what I hear on the radio.

"Hi, Claire," Brendan says to me. "Oh, hi, Dennis." He seems surprised but not too upset by our chaperone.

"Dennis likes the fringed shirts," I say.

"Oh," Brendan says. "I'm not sure I could get the guys to go for those. Especially Kyle. He says he hates it when things get caught in his bass."

"No, no," I say. "No fringe."

"Not yet, anyway," Dennis says.

"Let's just look around," I say. "See what strikes us."

We go into Jeds. Banjo music plays on the loudspeakers—not in an annoying way, but in a way that makes you appreciate how hard it must be to get the instrument to sound that good. It makes me feel this way, at least.

"Wow," Brendan says of the vast store.

"It's true," Dennis says. "Jeds makes an impression." Jeds Round Em Up, one of Perri's first clients, has beautiful red floors with what housewives used to call no shiny wax buildup, just pure shine. There are blocks of hay in the corners that give me a hayride feel—there's a wagon tucked into the hay as well. I try to avoid the hay corner, of course. Allergies. There are plaid curtains—not too frilly, not too manly, somehow just right for Goldilocks to bring her perfect cowboy into the store and make him feel at home. Little girls try on pink boots, which makes me remember mine—I should have worn them. Large men pick out Levi's.

"Wow," Brendan says again. He sees a display of whips on the wall. Cowboy whips.

"Those are the real thing, kids," says the owner, Jed, a tall man with mostly gray hair and a dimpled face, which only adds to how much we all adore him. Jed is one of my favorite people, and I'm fussy. Or so my mother says.

"And he's particular who he sells them to," Dennis says to Brendan. "Right, Jed?"

Jed comes up and gives me a big hug. I wish I could tear him away and just hug him a while, in a very father-daughter way. Jed is no-nonsense about his hugs. He pats Dennis on the back and turns to Brendan.

"Really?" Brendan asks.

"You have to take lessons," Dennis says.

Brendan backs away a little, "I, I don't think—"

"He's just kidding you," Jed says. "They're just display.

Valuable antiques. Had a guy in last week wanted to give me thirty thousand dollars for the set."

"Wow," I say. I didn't know they were valuable. Scary, yes, but valuable, no.

"Just a little nest egg," Jed says, "for retirement days."

"You'll never retire," I tell Jed, kind of a command. Jed is in his late fifties, but really he's ageless, too. He has three of these stores, and for reasons we city kids don't really understand, they do very well.

"How's the Web site, Jed?" Dennis asks.

"You did a fine job," Jed tells him. "Everyone loves the bull's-eye."

"Bull's-eye?" I ask. I know Dennis designed a Web site for Jed, with David's help in the art area. I didn't know Dennis had this skill, but I do remember he and Jed laughing as Dennis showed it to him.

"Sure," Jed says. "After you place an order, you can play a little bull's-eye game."

"Virtual darts?" I ask. It doesn't much appeal to me.

"That's not a very sporty way to describe it," Dennis says.

"I'm not a very sporty girl," I say. I'm a little upset that Dennis never asked me to try it, anyhow. I do know there's a dartboard next door in the lunch place Jed also owns, not the kind with pointy darts, though. Insurance, Jed once explained to me.

"But I am an expert at darts," I say. Brendan looks surprised.

"We'll see," Dennis says.

"This is Brendan Baker," I tell Jed, and Jed claps Brendan on the shoulder, causing Brendan to almost lose his balance. Jed is big and tall yet trim, in a comforting sort of dadlike way, not that my dad was anywhere near that big. "Brendan's in a band called Montana that we're representing."

"I need new clothes," Brendan explains, as if his torn shirt, torn Levi's, and torn sneakers didn't say this for him. I didn't know you could tear Nikes, which tells me more about Brendan than I may have needed to know.

"But he doesn't want fringe," Dennis says. Dennis and Jed share a look and shake their heads, a shared too-bad between them.

"Plenty of other places to start," Jed says, waving an arm across the room.

"I thought maybe accessories," I say.

"Because you're a girl?" Dennis asks. He's forgotten even a belt today, not that he usually remembers.

"Accessories say you care," I joke.

"Accessories say you care about accessories," Dennis argues.

"Now, now," Jed says. "Let's take it slow." Brendan looks a little overwhelmed by the place. It could be all the flannel, which sometimes makes me feel a little sleepy.

"Montana, eh?" Jed says. "I like it."

"Here," I say, reaching for a CD of demos Brendan has given us. "You can listen."

"You just carry those in your purse?" Dennis asks.

"It's a big purse," I say.

"Wow, thanks," Brendan says, pleased.

"I'm going to put this on right now," Jed says. "No bad language, right? It's a family store."

"No, not at all," Brendan insists. "Some rock, a touch of rockabilly."

"But no banjo," I say.

"Not yet," Dennis kids.

"Sounds perfect," Jed says and takes off to put on the soundtrack to our shopping.

"Okay, Brendan," Dennis says, putting his hands on Brendan's shoulders and propelling him forward. "Let's take it one aisle at a time."

When I head off to touch the flannel—I can never resist—Dennis grabs me with one hand and leads me toward the boots. He knows I can get lost in the flannel for hours. We've shopped before.

Jed's voice comes over the loudspeaker. "Ladies and gentlemen, girls and boys, I give you the latest from Montana." He plays the CD, and the sounds of strumming lead into Brendan's clear young voice. We hear some murmuring around the room. The small crowd of shoppers seems pleased. Men in the Levi's department bob their heads. Girls in Belts giggle.

"Montana's lead singer is with us today, so feel free to clap," Jed says. Brendan turns a very pretty shade of pink, although I'm not sure he'd describe it that way. Dennis turns round and round, pointing at Brendan, who's trying to bury his head in bandanas, but Dennis won't let him.

"Is it you?" ask two girls, about fourteen, that odd combination of brave yet shy, pre-piercing and tattoos. Must be a school holiday today. Brendan nods.

"Cool," they say together, then smile and head to the checkout counter, holding matching bright-white button-down shirts.

We stand around and look at bandanas together, the soft music that's Brendan singing in the background. When the song ends, everyone in the store claps not just politely (everyone always does just as Jed says) but enthusiastically. I place a cowboy hat on Brendan's head, then tie a bandana around it. His brown curls peek out perfectly underneath. He stands a little taller.

"Well?" I ask Dennis.

"It's not a fringed shirt," he says, shrugging.

The girls look back at Brendan again, a look on each's face known well by boy bands everywhere, successful boy bands at least.

"It's Montana," I say. Dennis nods. Brendan smiles hesitantly, takes off his hat and looks at it, nods, and puts it back on.

"It's just the beginning," Dennis says as the little girl in pink boots begins tapping her feet to the next song.

Dennis goes off to Jed's office, murmuring something about fixing the Web page.

"Some kinks to work out," he says not very believably. I know they're going to play computer darts. You can tell.

"We'll get lunch next door," I say.

Dennis nods, but I don't know whether he'll be joining us. Somehow, I wish he would.

Jed waves good-bye to me and Brendan, and he and Dennis begin gesturing, then seat themselves behind the computer with a guylike concentration that can only mean group sports or computer games. Dennis looks behind once at Brendan, a little suspiciously, but he's overwhelmed by his desire to look at the computer screen.

Brendan and I, along with a large bag full of five cowboy hats and bandanas for the band, stare at each other. I lead him to the bar/lunch place next door, also owned by Jed, called simply Jeds Lunch Place. It's also a gold mine, Perri has informed us.

Jeds Lunch Place continues the theme of the Round Em Up, lots of cowboy motif but no whips. Jed doesn't want to attract the wrong crowd, he's told me, and as we're still in the outskirts of Venice, this could mean many things. I take Brendan over to the dartboard. Who needs a Web site?

"Darts?" I suggest.

"Okay," Brendan says after he orders lemonades. He's old enough to get beer, but lemonade works better for me after a morning of pancakes and shopping. It does make him seem young, though, not that he didn't seem that way before. Still, nothing wrong with playing an innocent game of darts with a client while drinking lemonade, I hear Jackie's voice telling me. Or is it Eleanor's?

I gather up the point-free darts and begin to throw. I like real darts better as these make me feel eight years old. Real darts can sail, which makes me look like a pro, and that's worth a few people getting poked now and then, if you ask me.

I surround the bull's-eye with the magnetic darts. They're as close to center as they can get, considering how clunky they are. Brendan is clearly impressed.

"That's amazing," he says. It's a little-known fact about me, but I spent some time in English bars in college. The kind of places where old British guys walk around and try to hit on you. But you can learn a lot about darts there.

"One of my hidden talents," I say. I offer him the darts but he waves them off and wants me to try it again. I do.

Brendan walks closer to me as if to take the darts I've gathered after my throw, inspired by my dart-master skills, I guess. But he kisses me, instead. That would be the second person kissing me in two days. Unexpectedly kissing me.

It seems to me a good thing the darts aren't pointy, as I have a handful at the moment and I'm not sure where I put my hands during the unexpected kiss. Can anybody ever be sure where her hands will end up? It's admittedly nice to have something to hold on to so your hands don't end up anywhere you'd regret later. And Brendan doesn't exactly say ouch or anything.

"Oh, Brendan," I say, not in an inviting way, exactly, more as a question, but Brendan leans in and kisses me again.

"It's just that you mean so much to me, Claire," he says. "I know you might think I'm younger, and the group has so far to go. But you seem to believe in us so much."

"You're talented, Brendan," I say, taking a step back. "I just want your group to do well."

"And you picked out the hats," he says.

"But you paid for them," I say. Perhaps mentioning a business relationship will get me off the hook. The kisses were very good, but it might be better not to think of that now.

Brendan steps closer again. I'm getting excessively close to the dartboard, so I take this opportunity to study it. Brendan turns my face to his, which I think is brave of him. You never really know what can happen when you touch someone else's face. He has very smooth hands.

"We have to think about this," I say. He kisses me again. That's three times, and I'm not even good at math. "I'm just your copywriter," I say.

"You're the cutest person ever," Brendan says. A twenty-something boy has just called me cute, and it doesn't hurt a bit. Not just cute, but the cutest. A cute thirty-year-old. I know this isn't in my job description, but then again neither is picking out cowboy hats. I let Brendan kiss me a fourth time, which goes on a bit. He tastes like lemonade, which makes me grateful he didn't order beer for us after all.

I stop him there, hand him the darts, and step back, letting him throw. I look up to see Dennis by the bar, holding a mug of root beer, scraping the frost off the side. I don't know how long he's been there, although clearly long enough to have ordered and received a mug of root beer, not to mention time to scrape off half the frost. Time enough.

I wave Dennis over. He comes, but not too quickly.

"Darts?" I ask.

"Darts?" he asks back.

"They're not the pointy kind, though," I say. Brendan looks up and hands the darts to Dennis.

"Must be a few good reasons for that," Dennis says. He tosses a dart. It lands in Brendan's mug of lemonade, a good foot from the dartboard.

"Funny," Dennis says to Brendan. "I'm much more accurate with the pointed ones."

Brendan takes the darts and stands back to throw. He gets a bull's-eye on the first try. "Hey, that's never happened before," Brendan says. "It must be my lucky day."

I notice Dennis smiling at me, the kind of smile that you plaster on your face without showing any teeth, the kind of smile that asks questions you wouldn't really know how to phrase properly if you were to, say, actually open your mouth and try.

"It might be enough darts for now," I say.

"Two out of three?" Dennis asks Brendan, then throws more skillfully. With great assurance, it seems to me.

Chapter 13

Running Low on Bon Ami

Jackie drops by the next Saturday morning with two low-fat cranberry muffins and a video.

"Videos in the morning?" I ask. No way would I criticize the muffin, although I'm skeptical as always about the low-fat business.

"It's called *Unleashing the Creative Flow: Working Women's Meditation for Morning,*" Jackie says.

"Coffee isn't enough for some people?" I ask.

"It's a top seller," Jackie says with a shrug. "I checked it out of the library instead of buying it, though."

"Good," I say. We sit with our backs sunk into the sofa, watching. We think it's best to watch first, to see if it's really worth your energy to actually get up and do anything suggested in the tape. Especially first thing in the morning. Often we use such exercise and awareness tapes just to pass the time, not to mention criticize what the Working Women are wearing.

We chew for a few minutes. The low-fat muffins always take a little extra chewing, I've noticed, although if you think of it as exercise it makes the effort feel more worthwhile.

"I'm a whore," I tell Jackie.

"I don't accept that word," Jackie tells me. "I think it has a solely negative connotation and is demeaning toward women and anything else it's chosen to describe."

"You've heard other things called whores?" I ask.

"Someone in the office told me the fountain out front looked whorish," she says.

"The one with the cute lily pads?" I ask. Jackie nods.

"It's a completely unacceptable description," she says. "It's an indication of a very lazy vocabulary."

"It was a guy, right?"

Jackie nods an "of course."

"I agree with you entirely, you know," I say. "I just think maybe it's okay to call yourself one, but no one else can."

"Oh," Jackie says, "one of those words. Like racial denigrations, you mean?"

"I guess," I say. "Plus it has that *h* sound that kind of relieves stress when you say it. "*H*," I say. "Like letting go of a breath in a yoga class."

"But you don't like yoga," Jackie says.

"Maybe I should try again," I say. "I think I need some deeper sense of self-understanding, plus some heavy breathing."

"So you won't be such a whore?" Jackie says.

"It does sound worse when you say it," I tell her.

"Then can you please now tell me in excruciating detail what's caused you to criticize yourself with what I consider socially if not politically unacceptable terminology?" I forget Jackie's sensitive to words you could never imagine a successful candidate saying, at least in public.

"I don't want you to lose all respect for me."

"That bad," Jackie says, intrigued.

"I slept with Andy," I say.

"Oh, that is bad. Bad, bad, bad. You should get off this soft couch and sit on the hard floor and meditate. Or worse, do sit-ups, maybe."

"You're being very judgmental," I say.

"That's what friends are for. Bad, bad, bad," Jackie says. "And don't think your therapist will tell you otherwise."

"I know," I say.

"Okay," Jackie says. "So why?"

"Why would I sleep with Andy?"

"Not to mention why you'd let him in the door. It was indoors, right?"

"Please," I say. "I'm over thirty."

"But just a little over," Jackie says. "I know people in their forties still doing it in cars."

"Eew," I say.

"They wait till the kids are asleep, then head to the car. But these are Mercedes," she says with a shrug. "In attached garages in front of pricey Westside real estate."

"Oh," I say. It doesn't sound too bad.

"Not to change the subject," she says.

"I was upset about my dad. Eleanor gave me some old photos. I think she's moving on. I think I'm not, so much," I say. "Andy came by, he was in town, he was on the couch—"

"He hates your couch," Jackie says.

"It wasn't really an issue," I say.

"Never sleep with a man who doesn't respect your couch," Jackie says.

"Even if you bought it half price at the outlet store because the entire underside is ripped away?"

"It's a good couch. Macy's sells it for sixteen hundred dollars."

"Don't tell Eleanor," I say. "She'll think I overpaid."

"It might mean something if he had sex with you on a couch he hated," Jackie says.

"Not on the couch. We moved to the bedroom," I say, putting my head down.

"Bad, bad, bad," Jackie says.

"Wait, now it's better to do it on the couch?"

"It might have meant he cared more about you than he hated the couch. A trade-off sort of thing where you'd win, sort of," Jackie says.

"I'm not sure I follow," I say.

"He took advantage," she says.

I shrug. I know.

"Where is he now?" Jackie says.

I shrug again. "Don't know, gone, meetings, back to San Francisco? Or Switzerland maybe. He didn't stay long. I didn't ask."

"Wait a minute," Jackie says, and tries to look in my eyes. "He didn't stay the night?"

"I actually think it was a plus," I say.

"Bad," Jackie says again.

"Dennis came over after that and we had popcorn."

"Did he stay on the couch?" she asks. "On his side, I mean?"

"Yes, all night." I say. "And he let me have the remote," I say. "Eventually."

"I don't think that qualifies you as whorish," Jackie says. "You lived with Andy for years. It's bad, but it's a slip."

"Then I went shopping and kissed Brendan from the boy band. Four times. Although technically he kissed me."

"Oh my," Jackie says. "This is getting good. How old is he again?"

"Twenty-three," I say.

"Still not whorish," Jackie says. "Kind of more sluttish."

"I can live with sluttish," I say. Jackie nods, understanding. "I think I'll just scour my bathroom for a while. That always makes me feel absolved or whatever."

"I know," Jackie says. "I have a very, very clean bathroom."

"It may be something about the shine that makes us feel better about ourselves," I say.

"It's just what we do," Jackie says.

"Although I'm running low on Bon Ami," I say.

"I know how that is," Jackie says.

We watch the tape a little more. The woman meditating wears a black tank top, and you can see orange bra straps on her shoulders. I've never seen an orange bra, but maybe I just haven't needed to look for one. Jackie points to it, making a mental note, too.

I return to work after my fun-filled weekend to see a large poster of Heaven on our white wall in the cubicle space I share with Dennis. Large doesn't really describe it. Life-size, maybe, but it seems even bigger than that. Larger-than-life Heaven. It curves around our walls, which curve anyhow around all that hay, no doubt. Actually, the curves in the office seem to accentuate Heaven's own curves. As if they needed accentuating.

Dennis comes into our office.

"I prefer Kandinsky," I say. "A nice Monet print. Even a bad Picasso's okay with me."

"It's the new bus art," Dennis says.

"Then perhaps it would look good on, say, a bus?" I ask. Dennis stands back and looks at the poster. Although you can't really stand back too far as we have a small office between us. There's a space cut out of Heaven's middle. She's leaning sideways, as you'd pretty much have to do to fit on the side of a bus, not that I've thought much about this, and our doorway has cut her right in the middle. And she still looks good.

David, our art director, pops his head in. "Cute," he says.

"Cute?" I say.

"Not too sexy, not too kitteny," David says.

"Kind of a kitteny pose," Dennis says.

"Why are grown women described as kitteny?" I ask.

"Meow," David says.

"No, really," I say. "Here's a pretty girl who can sing. Not that you can tell she can sing from this poster."

"You can intuit it," Dennis says. David nods.

"Well, from the guitar at her feet, I guess," I say.

"By the tight pink sweater," Dennis says. David nods.

"I thought Heaven didn't want tight anymore," I say. "I thought it was all agreed. A new Heaven."

"This is a different sweater," David says. "We had her try on three. This was the loosest. She liked it."

"This is loose?" I ask. It's not skintight, I admit. But there are curves under there. I like baggy, myself, and even if I do have little curves under there, I think it's a private thing you shouldn't know about me at first glance. Heaven clearly disagrees.

"It's cashmere," David says.

"Nice," Dennis says.

"It's a perfectly good photo," David says. They both look at me.

"Hiss," I say, then go to work at my desk. David leaves. Dennis stays and watches the poster.

"It's not going anywhere," I say.

"You can take it down," Dennis says.

"Good," I say.

"After a while," he says, then goes to his desk, opens a drawer, and knocks over his latte. Dennis sighs and looks around for paper towel. I throw him the roll I keep in my drawer, but I wait a few seconds before doing it. And I aim for his face.

I am in the storeroom searching for stirrers. I keep some in my desk, but they tend to smell funny after a while. It could be Dennis takes them and uses them, then puts them back in my drawer. This is extremely unhygienic and guylike, and I refuse to think about it. I dumped all my old stirrers.

We have a small storeroom where we keep paper goods, supplies, and a small coffee machine and cups. Sometimes even coffee to put in the coffee machine. If there isn't coffee, Malcolm gets yelled at, and he frequently gets yelled at. There's a small tree—someone once told me it is a ficus, but I've no idea what this means—that no one ever waters, but everyone does dump their cold coffee into it. The ficus seems to like it. Dennis named the tree the Coffee Pig. It's funny when he says it. I hadn't realized before that he was the kind of person who gives houseplants names.

I find the stirrers and fresh coffee (I've already finished my tea), which I pour into a recyclable cup, since I hate washing my mug. Malcolm comes in the storeroom carrying a box of those little balls you put on your antennae. Usually you only see them with the Jack in the Box clown's face. These have Heaven's face on them. She actually looks good in styrofoam.

"No, no," I say. It's all I can say.

"They're not my idea," Malcolm says. David comes in the storeroom as well. It's a small room.

"They're adorable," David says. "Everyone will want one. The guy who does the Jack in the Box voice will even want one."

Dennis comes in as well. It's getting pretty tight in here.

"Are you guys overfeeding Coffee Pig again?" Dennis asks, rubbing the ficus's leaves. Perri has begged him to take it out of here many times (there's barely room for us). Not that Dennis is the one who brought it. No one will admit to that.

"No," I say. "Look."

Dennis looks at the box of Heaven antennae toppers. "Oh, my," he says. He and David both reach in and pick out one.

"It's a whole new marketing approach," Dennis says.

"Isn't this in some way demeaning?" I ask.

"Probably," Dennis says. "But I've never seen a blonde-haired antennae topper before."

"We could put Jack out of business," David says.

"They got the blue eyes right," Malcolm says, which is fairly observant of him. They did get the blue right. All the guys lean in to look and nod approvingly.

"Are you responsible for this?" I ask Dennis. He and David look at each other and sort of grumble something. It's like the ficus. No one's taking responsibility.

"You should get docked for this," I say.

"Perri mentioned something about bonuses, actually," David says. Dennis just nods.

"I'm telling Jackie," I say to him, which scares him a little. "And here," I say, angrily pouring out my now-cold coffee into the Coffee Pig's pot.

"Now that's not nice," Dennis says. I humph and go refill my cup, although it's getting kind of soggy. The recyclable cups do that after a while, but we put up with it because we're Democrats.

"Plus those toppers aren't even recyclable," I say.

"No one's going to try to recycle these babies," David says.

"They'll be collector's items," Dennis says, scooping out some of the wet coffee dirt from around the ficus, which I think is going a little overboard. Nothing's ever hurt the ficus, even when Perri poured down an entire container of raspberry iced tea from the health food store. It really wasn't very delicious stuff. The ficus perked up, actually, for a ficus.

"You're just sorry you didn't think of it for your little Heartthrobs," Dennis says.

"Montana, thank you, and no thank you," I say. I start to leave.

"Get lunch at Bob's?" Malcolm asks Dennis, shorthand for "What are your lunch plans?"

"Um, no, I have to be somewhere," Dennis says.

"Date?" David asks suggestively.

"Well, kind of," Dennis says. I turn around. I can't help myself.

"You have a date for lunch?" I ask. We don't even go out of the office for lunch that much. Even though the ocean beckons, and as my mother always tells me, a little fresh air wouldn't hurt any of us.

"I met someone who has a lot of information about health food," Dennis says.

"In this neighborhood," David says. "What a surprise."

"What does she look like?" Malcolm asks. We all lean in to hear.

"No, no, nothing like that," Dennis says, but I don't think any one of us believes him much. "She's a nice person I met at Get a (Healthy) Life. We're meeting at the café in back, just to check out some of the new menu options. She was interested in the kale and cranberry salad, that's all."

"Sure," David says. "It always starts with the kale and cranberry salad. Then you get to a little tofutti for dessert. I've seen it a thousand times."

"You may have lived in Venice too long," Dennis tells him.

"Maybe," David agrees.

"It's just salad," Dennis says with a shrug. We all look a little lost at the idea.

"Why don't you take her an antennae topper?" I suggest. David takes a topper from the box and bounces it. It has a perfect little bounce.

"I don't think she's the topper type," Dennis says, then ducks out of the room, leaving us with the large box of toppers and a few unanswered questions.

"Enjoy your kale!" I yell after him. Dennis, I know, hates kale.

*   *   *

I'm not really any sort of snoop, and it's something I'm proud of. People should live their lives and not harm anyone, I truly believe, and then I really don't need to know any more about it.

"Let's go to the health food store and get tofu burgers," David suggests to me as I'm sitting at my desk, examining the container of chocolate yogurt I brought for lunch. The idea of chocolate combined with yogurt is unappealing, although I like each taste individually. It was an impulse item. If only the health food store would stock candy near the cash registers like a normal store, I wouldn't be stuck with this problem.

"I brought lunch," I say, showing him the container.

"Interesting," David says. "May I?" He reaches for my yogurt. I give it to him, and he carefully reads the label. "Hmm, chocolate yogurt," he says.

"At least it isn't carob," I say.

"So true," David says. Then he throws it in the trash. "Bring a coat," he says.

Chapter 14

It's a Small World After All

"**Y**ou don't even like tofu burgers," I tell David.

"Sometimes a tofu burger isn't just a tofu burger," David says. "If you know what I mean."

I'm not at all sure that I do. We walk down Main Street from our office toward Get a (Healthy) Life, which is two blocks down.

"I'm not going in the café part," I say.

"We don't have to," David says. "We can get our food from the coolers in front and semi-inadvertently peer into the café from behind the coffee machines."

"Not that you've done this before," I say.

"I've learned a few things about our boss this way," David says. "Good to stay in the loop, you know."

"I didn't know there was a loop," I say. "Only six people work in our office. How far out of the loop can you get?"

"You're so young," David says, although he's only a few years older than I am.

We are inside the store, and David shows me what he means about the six-or-so-inch gap between the coffee machines. You can get a clear view of anyone you want to see in the café. And a clear view of anyone you don't want to see.

"No, no," I say.

"Move your head," David says. "I can't see."

"No, no," I say again, but not really to David. More to the world at large or the God of your choice. What I mean, of course, is "No way," but I'm far too mature to say it.

"Could you elaborate?" David doesn't get it, and, of course, how could he?

I walk toward the café. I can't help it.

"Hi," I announce myself.

Dennis is seated with a fork in a kale and cranberry salad (it's really very good). He looks up.

"Hi, Claire," Dennis says, not all that surprised but a little pissy nonetheless.

"Hi, Claire," says Dennis's new friend, who also happens to be named Claire, I know. Although I like to call her Claire the Therapist, but not to her face, not that I really expected to be seeing her face at this very moment.

"Oh," Dennis says, "do you two know each other?" David stands behind me now, curious but silent.

"Well, yes—" I start.

"You're both named Claire," Dennis says, sort of excitedly, as if it has just occurred to him.

"Claire is my therapist," I tell Dennis.

"How are you, Claire?" asks Claire the Therapist.

"This is confusing," says David.

"It really is a small world," says Dennis, looking from one Claire to another, which makes that awful "Small World" song start up in my head. "And you two look a little alike," he adds.

It's not like Claire and I are identical, but we do look similar. Claire's hair is straighter, and neater, but the skin tones are similar, not to mention we're both wearing long-sleeved ballerina Ts and long skirts.

Still, we both answer him the same: "No, we don't." Like sisters fighting against the family inheritance of identical noses.

"Wow," Dennis says, "you're even both wearing black T-shirts."

"But who isn't?" David asks. He's right. Most of the people here are dressed in black T-shirts, although many are wearing tie-dyed harem pants, too. It's that Venice Beach-meets-New York look everyone out here seems to strive for.

"Claire, um, hi," I say to my therapist. "So you know Dennis, my officemate?" Obviously, she knows he's Dennis. They've had several bites of salad. They probably know each other's last names by this point in the conversation.

"I didn't realize," Claire the Therapist says.

"Your therapist has the same name as you?" David asks, catching on very slowly, I have to think.

I nod.

"Doesn't it get confusing?" David asks.

"Not really till now," I say. Claire the Therapist looks a little embarrassed and moves her kale salad around her plate. She hasn't eaten that much, so either she's been busy talking (or listening enrapt), or she doesn't like it. I love the kale salad.

"Wait," Dennis says looking at me, "you haven't talked about me with your therapist, have you?" He looks from one to the other of us Claires.

"I've talked about the office, of course," I say. Claire nods.

"This is really interesting," David says. "I never run into my therapist at all."

"Why are you in therapy, anyway?" Dennis asks.

"Oh," Claire the Therapist says, "we shouldn't really go into that."

"Especially since you haven't asked us to join you," David says. It's true, they haven't.

"I'm sorry," Dennis says. "Why are you here, anyhow?"

"We work up the street," I say, "you know?" I direct this last part to Claire the Therapist. Claire the suddenly quieter-than-usual therapist. "We wanted tofu burgers. It happens."

"This is a wonderful health food store," Claire the Therapist finally perks up. "I'd been meaning to try the café when I ran into Dennis the other day."

"The-Dennis-who-shares-an-office-with-me Dennis," I say.

"That would be one description," Claire the Therapist says.

"You don't like the tofu burgers here," Dennis says suspiciously. "You said they're too greasy."

"Can baked tofu really be greasy?" David asks.

"They're fine if you get them from the cooler in front," I say.

"But you said they have too much mayonnaise," Dennis says. "Don't pretend you didn't."

"I said you could scrape it off," I say.

"I don't find them greasy at all," says my therapist.

"And how's the kale?" I ask them.

"Very fresh," Dennis says. Dennis hates every green food, I happen to know. Claire the Therapist just moves her kale around a little more noncommittally.

"We should be going," I say, although David groans softly. "See you," I say.

"Yes, see you," my therapist says, but fortunately she doesn't name a date and hour, which is more than I want to think about at the moment.

"You have a little kale in your teeth," David says back at them, but not at either of them in particular. They both look away from each other and hide, putting pinkie fingers to teeth. A kale salad, like spinach, isn't really a good lunch date option. Still, it makes my stomach ache a bit to see that they both care about this.

"I'm too disgusted for tofu burgers," I say to David at the front of the store.

"Let's go to Bob's for fries," David says, for which I will love him eternally.

My therapist is dating my officemate. It dawns on me that I may need a second therapist to talk to about why this bothers me.

"Your therapist is much cuter than mine," David says.

I return to my office to find a vase filled with roses—very red ones—tied with a bandana around it. Josie pops her head in.

"Delivery," she says without much expression.

"Pretty," I say, not reaching for the card. I smile and sit down at my desk, pretending to get to work. Josie stands a moment, then takes a deep breath.

"Okay, then," she says, a little disappointed I think that I'm not reading the card, although it can't be too much of a surprise who they're from. Everyone around here has seen the hats tied with bandanas that I chose for Brendan and the Montana boys.

After Josie leaves, I take out the card. It says only "Thank you, Brendan," on it, which is kind of a relief. I'm not sure what I was expecting, but roses, it seems to me, often come with some sort of declaration. Not that this has happened to me personally, but I see a lot of movies.

I get busy, writing this week's Jeds Round Em Up copy. It seems Levi's are on sale. I'm sure Dennis needs some new ones, but I'm not about to tell him about the sale right now. Just then, Malcolm comes into the room with a ladder—a huge metal thing that is not quiet when he opens it, but I'm still grateful to see it coming. He begins to take down Heaven's bus panels, which fall to the ground with a *flump* sound, panel by panel. He starts to remove staples from my wall with one of those tiny staple jaws, standing on the ladder to get the staples at the top. I can imagine little piercings left by staples all over Heaven's four-color body. I wonder how she'd feel about this. When he's done, Malcolm says, "Voilà."

"Thanks," I say. "I didn't realize Heaven removal was in your job description."

"The advantages of nepotism," Malcolm says dryly.

"Maybe you should ask for a job description—another advantage of nepotism, not to mention working in the twenty-first century," I suggest.

Malcolm shrugs. He has finished rolling the panels and turns to fold the ladder, but it crashes to the floor. David next door to me lets out a scream but doesn't exactly come running. This happens a lot.

Perri, though, does come running. She's been in the conference room with her personal trainer, a guy named Ron who has many muscles and murmurs encouragement at her while she's exercising here in the office. For such a large person, Ron has a particularly soft voice. Otherwise, he'd be unbearable, as he looks a lot like that guy who used to pose for the covers of romance novels with half-clad women, or is it half unclad. He has blondish-brown hair that's a bit too long even for Venice standards, unless you're going for the true Venice hippy look, which we don't think Ron is. His looks are a little intimidating even to the bravest of women, even, it sometimes seems, to Perri. She actually does what he says—I've peeked at her training sessions. Sometimes I'll hear his instructions from my office ("Stretch deeper," "Hold that move,") and find myself doing this at my desk—stretching out a leg from under my chair or holding my pencil with great concentration. He's good at his job. Very motivating.

Perri, though, is displeased with the noise the rest of us are plain used to, despite David's practiced scream. "Malcolm," she starts, her voice rising, which can't be helping her endorphin level any, "you are too clumsy. Get that ladder out of here. I can hear you scraping it against the floors from one end of the office to the other."

"Sorry to interrupt your busy work schedule," Malcolm says to his mom, who's wearing her dress-up exercise clothes, as we call them—a black tunic-type thing over black leggings. It looks hot to exercise in, but I'm not about to say anything.

"Malcolm was nice enough to help me get the bus art down," I say. I don't trust myself on ladders.

"I want a quiet, positive environment," Perri says. "If you can't handle that, Malcolm, don't think you'll be able to function well in an office in the real world."

"This isn't the real world?" Malcolm says. I was wondering that, too.

"Not even close," Perri says. I hear David shifting uncomfortably in his cubicle next door. We all hate these fights almost as much as fighting with our own mothers.

"And another thing," Perri says, getting on a roll, even though Ron is following her with a blood-pressure-taking device and shaking his head in disapproval. He waves to me, and I wave back. Everyone likes Ron, and he tries to be an intermediary, even though I'm not sure that's part of being a personal trainer. Or maybe it's the biggest part. Perri starts leading Malcolm on a tour of all the things he's doing wrong around the office. It's a tour he knows well. Josie comes into my office and sits down against a wall.

"I hate this," she says. I nod.

"Why is the paper stacked this way?" I hear Perri yelling at Malcolm in the storeroom. Malcolm's pretty neat with the paper, which comes in easily stackable reams, but we do knock them over. It's a small room, after all. We lean against the reams a lot. They have a nice give. But they don't always respond the way you'd like.

I picture the ficus cowering, not to mention Malcolm.

"I'd never work with my mom," Josie says. I nod again. "And I like my mom," she adds.

"Some things you just have to learn the hard way," I say.

"Why doesn't he leave? Is it a guy thing?" Josie asks.

"Maybe," I say. "Or just a Malcolm thing."

"He can't like this," she says. "He could quit."

"It's a tough economy. And Perri does take a lot of vacation time off." Josie nods. She loves that time, too. We all do.

Perri stops ranting in the other room. I can hear Malcolm picking up reams of paper and putting them in the closet with that whoosh sound reams make when you throw them (we do this sometimes just for fun). The closet, I know, is fairly full. I hope the extra paper doesn't end up in my office, which is also fairly full.

Dennis returns from his lunch engagement and picks up a large box of Heaven topper balls that's now in our office.

"You missed all the excitement," Josie tells him.

"I think my life is pretty exciting," Dennis says to me. I just sort of sneer, although I'm not very good at sneering. It probably looks more like that face a cat makes when it smells something bad. Not an attractive face, I hear my mother's voice say.

"I'm going out distributing," Dennis says. He points to my flowers tied with a bandana and makes a little sneer back at me. He's better at it, I notice.

Malcolm brings a couple of reams of paper into our office. I point to the corner, where he can leave them. It's worth losing a little free space to restore peace in the family, so to speak.

"Thanks," Malcolm says.

"Come with me to distribute," Dennis says to Malcolm. Malcolm's eyes light up as he nods yes. Malcolm wouldn't mind a trip to the dentist right now, I know.

"What, are you going to stick those on people's cars?" I ask. "Stand at corners waving them? Stand at the car wash and put them on the shiny detailed vehicles?"

"We're professionals," Dennis says, and Malcolm nods, although a little surprised. "I've discussed these with the local record stores. Wherehouse is very interested." He waves a ball at me.

"No one goes to Wherehouse anymore!" I almost yell. "It's Tower or nothing," I say. I'm kind of making it up, but I think I might be right.

"Our next stop," Dennis says, taking Malcolm.

"They really bounce, too," I hear Dennis say to Malcolm.

"Do you think all workplaces are like this?" Josie asks me.

"It's Venice," I say. "I'm not sure anything we learn here will apply anywhere else."

This does not make Josie happy one bit. We hear Perri making deep sighing sounds as she exhales in the conference room area. It's a little creepy—she's much louder than the enormous Ron, the quietest breather I've ever heard. Josie likes to ask him to lift the water bottles into the Sparkletts machine, which could explain why she's hanging around listening to the breathing. She may have other reasons, too, but she's keeping them to herself. Finally, after a few more unappealing noises from Perri, Josie shudders and returns to her desk.

I put on a headset and turn on the lovely voice of Boy Brendan, as Jackie now refers to him, a sound that I'm beginning to find very soothing. I can't exactly explain what it's doing to my breathing, but I think Ron might approve.

"**H**ard at work?" a sort of sexy, drawly kind of voice asks me from just beyond my headset. I take it off and turn to see the source of the voice, although I'd know it anywhere.

"Bobby Henry!" I say like the fan I am. "I'm always hard at work."

"You smell wonderful," Bobby says. Bobby is one of our clients, a classically handsome country singer. If Bobby got any cuter—and there's the possibility, as he's my age and has the suggestion to his face that it's going to look even better creased—women would just die when they see him. I've seen them swoon, but no ambulances have been called yet. He looks, somehow, as cute as his name. Bobby Henry. He's really just at the beginning of his career—which explains why we represent him—opening for bigger acts, but he has a good voice and that alluring quality of making women in the audience feel that he's singing right to them.

"Thanks," I say. "You'd smell great too with a dozen roses on your desk."

"Let's have a smell," Bobby says. He comes over to my desk—he's been here a hundred times—and I hand him a rose. He inhales.

"American Beauty," he says approvingly.

"You know your roses," I say.

"Someone cared enough to send the very best," Bobby says. He hands me back the rose, and I stuff it in the vase. Bobby gets a lot of roses from his female fans, most of them older ladies. We've no idea why he attracts this demographic. He just does. Even Eleanor, who's actually toward the younger end of Bobby's fans, falls for him every time I take her to a concert.

Bobby goes and sits in the newly repaired blue chair we keep for visitors. We try to keep it near my desk in the same place, except for when it breaks. Even the cleaning crew knows to leave it there. Bobby is blind, so we don't like to change things.

"So what's the special occasion for the roses?" Bobby asks. "Not that I ever need a special occasion to send roses."

"Not that I ever get them," I say, "until now."

"I'll remember that," Bobby says.

"Just another of my clients madly in love with me, I guess," I say.

"So all of us are madly in love with you? I thought it was just me."

"I guess you should have thought of sending roses, then," I say.

"Okay," he says. "But it's kind of cliché. You know how I hate the cliché." It's true, Bobby has to fight the cliché blind singer routine at all times. We have to make sure none of his advertising falls into that kind of thing. He can be a pest about it, but he's right.

"You can send candy," I say.

"And perfume?"

"I don't like perfume," I say. "Unless it smells like chocolate."

"How about dinner?" Bobby asks.

"Yes, I like chocolate for dinner, too," I say. Bobby and I always fall into these kind of mindless conversations just for fun. Another office perk, and I feel like I really need one today.

"No," Bobby says. "I mean how about real dinner?"

"Oh," I say. Oh.

"Not tonight, I mean," Bobby says. "But some night. What would you think?"

"I never date clients," I say. Not exactly a lie, not yet at least.

"Another cliché," Bobby says.

"True," I say.

"Why don't you think about it?" he asks. Bobby's wearing one of Jed's special-skin blue boots. Not blue suede (another cliché), but something in a deep blue, something exotic. I don't really feel I need to know what animal it came off of, but I appreciate the Crayola Midnight Blue appeal. My favorite crayon of youth.

"I'm admiring your boots," I tell Bobby. We remember to tell him these things, although it's nice sometimes not to have to explain to someone that you're staring. Still, it's a courtesy.

"Jed, you know," Bobby says. Jed takes care of all of our clients. All of us, really.

"I know," I say.

"So dinner, you think about it, okay?" Bobby says.

"Wow," I say. "Just because one client sent roses?"

"I've been meaning to ask. I hope I didn't wait too long," Bobby says.

"Don't worry," I say.

"How many of them are there again?"

"A dozen," I say.

Bobby shakes his head. "Typical," he says. "You think about it." He waves and takes off.

I look back to my roses, then my headset, where I can just barely still hear Brendan's voice singing on low. I forgot to turn it off, and for some reason, I feel a little guilty.

Chapter 15

The Yoga Within

I call Jackie on the phone. I need to vent.

"Bobby Henry asked me out," I tell Jackie.

"Bobby Henry the blind country singer?" she says.

"That's terrible," I say. "You never say things like that."

"That was what *you* were thinking. I could hear it in your voice," she says. I can hear her at her desk at home, where she has one of those ancient adding machines that make a *ka-ching* kind of noise. She doesn't use it for work, exactly, more for relaxation. Jackie's most comfortable with numbers, not to mention a little noise.

"Meaning?" I ask.

"Meaning?" Jackie asks. "Let's break it down. Number one," Jackie says speaking in her numeric tongue, "how comfortable are you with dating a country singer?"

"Medium," I say. "I like all kinds of music. He doesn't twang much or anything."

"Number two, then," she continues survey style, although I think she may just be working too much. "How comfortable are you dating a blind person?"

I make a strange face squishing my lips together. Eleanor would tell me to stop. Jackie just waits.

"A very cute blind person?" I ask. "And why should I have a problem with this, anyhow?"

"It depends," Jackie says, weighing options. "Is it just dinner?"

"He only asked me about dinner," I say. "I think it's small-minded of me to say no."

"Would you say yes if he weren't blind?"

"Maybe," I say.

"Because it's been such a slow week?" Jackie kids. Andy was only a few nights ago. Andy who didn't call, not that I wanted him to, exactly.

"There may be too many men in the world right now," I say.

"What does Dennis think of your dating the clients?" Jackie says.

"One client, and only maybe," I remind her. "The other one just sent me flowers."

"And you didn't even have to put out," Jackie says, "as Eleanor might say."

"Eleanor hates that expression," I say.

"All women do," Jackie says.

"Dennis doesn't know about this, nor do I think he'd much care. He's busy dating my therapist," I tell her.

"Dennis is dating Claire the Therapist?" she asks.

"A lunch date, that I know of," I say.

"That's sick," she says.

"I don't think they knew who the other one was, although I'm still a little suspicious about Claire the Therapist. She knew I worked right near there, couldn't she guess that Dennis was Dennis?"

"Because there's only one guy in Venice named Dennis? Hey, I made a rhyme," Jackie says, pleased with herself.

"Rhyming in public isn't that great a quality," I tell her.

"Oh," she says. "You're the English major."

"And always will be," I say.

"Maybe she did know it was Dennis. Have you talked about him?"

"Maybe in a generic way," I say vaguely.

"Hmm," Jackie says. "She looks like you, you know."

"Who does?"

"Claire the Therapist, kind of."

"Only in a very basic way," I say.

"Oh," Jackie says, "right. Hair, clothes, lack of makeup."

"Her hair is straighter," I say. "I think she combs it."

"This is getting kind of soap opera-y," Jackie says. "Me and the politician, Dennis and your therapist, you and the country singer. Somebody's heading for a wedding or breakup, or maybe a hurricane."

"Or maybe amnesia," I say.

"I know I sometimes wish I were," Jackie says.

I am the kind of girl who would be perfectly happy to meet my mother each week at the same café, or coffee shop, or whatever they're called these days. I'd be happy to establish a routine, get to know the wait staff, order the usual. My mother, however, is not fond of repetition. So this week, and it's not like we meet every week, but more when we can, this week, Mom's got a different suggestion.

"Family yoga," Eleanor suggested succinctly.

"I don't know, Mom," I remember saying. "Yoga and I don't really get along. I fall over an awful lot."

"It's not that kind of yoga," Mom said.

I'm thirty, and I live in Venice, California, a place that prides itself on at least an attempt at being hip and now. I'm not exactly either of these things, but as a resident, I could not have gotten away with not trying yoga in my lifetime. I have never tried a yoga class where I didn't fall over. Sometimes on someone else, setting off a domino effect of fallen yoga positions. No one has appreciated this much. I once knocked over two other women who then tumbled into the instructor, who then fell into a small fountain gurgling in the room. Everyone had to throw towels over to keep the puddle from spreading across the room. I left not long after that.

"I didn't know there was another kind of yoga," I told my mom.

"There are several kinds," Eleanor said. "This is for families and partners, and you get to use one another for support, if need be."

"Can't I just stand against the wall?" I asked her.

"Of course you can, dear. This is a nonjudgmental form of energizing the body," she said.

This I have to see.

We meet at a yoga studio in my neighborhood. There are, to be exact, seventeen yoga studios in my neighborhood, and that's just in Venice. This one is called The Yoga Within. This sounds just new agey enough to be less than pleasant, but the storefront does have a nice sign that's a cross between a yin-yang symbol and a curled-up infant. The infant has a little smile on its face. I find it cute, which puts me in a much less resentful mood.

I'll admit that the last yoga I tried was at the Y, led by a large and much older woman named Lake. I'm not sure if it was her real name. All the women wore leotards, which made me wonder if they had all thought it was an aerobics class. I try never to wear a leotard as you have to spend way too much time pulling it to try to cover part of your body, sometimes even several different parts. It makes it hard to focus on the exercise, or maybe that is the exercise.

Mom meets me just outside The Yoga Within.

"You can't go in till the last class comes out," Eleanor tells me.

"How'd you find this place?" I ask her. It's on a side street not too far from my office, but definitely out of the way. They could have called it Out of the Way Yoga, but then I'm not sure they could have a little smiling baby on the sign.

"I've been hired to do their bookkeeping," Eleanor says matter-of-factly.

"Wow," I say. "Branching out."

"That's important for a woman," Mom reminds me.

When they're ready for us, we go in. The studio has a lovely warm floor—you have to leave your shoes outside, which makes me grateful we're on a side street, as I'm fond of the sneakers I brought, and Venice, as my mother would agree, isn't the best place to leave valuables lying around.

"It's good you brought old shoes," Mom tells me. She doesn't realize I like them broken in.

"But these have sentimental value," I say.

"A good arch beats sentimental value, I've found," Mom says. "Not that I'm meddling."

Mom lays down her purple mat. She's brought a matching one for me as I don't have my own. I still have one of those thick mats at home that you use for sit-ups. I can do many sit-ups, although mostly I only attempt them on New Year's Day.

"This mat is too thin," I tell her.

"You need to feel the floor," Mom says.

"I think that's part of the problem with yoga right there," I say. "I'm not the hardwood floor type."

"It builds character," Mom says.

"Sort of like, Feel the Burn in aerobics?" I say. "You know, they've proven that's not good for you, either."

"This isn't like aerobics at all," Mom says. "This is to balance your mind and body."

"Oh," I say.

"That's what the brochure says," Eleanor tells me,

straightening her ponytails. My mom, along with wearing a lovely purple knit top over purple stretchy capris, is wearing ponytails. They suit her, although I wouldn't have thought so. I'm dressed in a torn, off-white T-shirt and shorts. The T used to be white.

I look around the room and am a little alarmed.

"Mom," I say. "There are men here." Something about unisex exercise still freaks me out. Too much time spent in girls-only gym in junior high, or something I can't quite explain. Maybe too much time spent at the Y in a leotard I had to tug at continually. Not that I even like doing that in front of women.

"It's family yoga, I told you," Eleanor says. "Many people actually have men in their families, dear."

"Imagine," I say.

"Something to strive for, even," Eleanor says, looking around the room as she stretches on her mat.

"You're hunting," I accuse her, but lightly.

"Claire," Mom begins, "we're here to expand our horizons, become one with our imaginations. If we should happen to meet someone who shares those goals in his life, how could that be a problem?"

"I don't want to meet anyone when I'm sweaty," I say.

"I don't mind at all," Mom says and looks around the room again.

"Shocking," I tell her.

"Don't forget to open your mind as you exhale," Eleanor teases me.

What I didn't realize about family/partner yoga is that I wouldn't be able just to sit and stretch quietly on my mat, imagining breath going in and out, but that I'd be pushed and prodded into stretches by my partner, in this case, my mom. I'm not sure that in the mother-daughter relationship of the twenty-first century there's really a place for pulling your mom all the way onto your back, but maybe I haven't thought about it enough, or maybe I'm not doing the exercise right. Yoga's all about learning, I guess, experiencing thoughts and feelings. I do learn that my mother has very strong back muscles and that she's lighter than I would have thought.

"Ouch," I say a lot of the time, in response to our push-me-pull-you yoga stretches.

"Breathe in," Mom whispers.

"I can't breathe and say ouch at the same time," I tell her.

"You're just out of practice," she says, not that an ouch ever slips through her carefully parted mouth. My mother is good at this.

I do like the part where you lie quietly under a warm throw, but I have to wonder where the eye pillow has been before me. It makes me itch a little.

"Do you feel refreshed, enlightened?" Mom asks me after class.

"I like the soft blankets," I say, searching for the positive.

"They keep them very clean here, you know," Mom tells me. "Oh, look," she says, casually leading me over to the father-daughter pair she's had her eye on all class, although I'm not sure how she could focus on her breathing that way.

"Sam," my mother says toward the father of the pair.

"Hi," says the girl who must be Sam's daughter, a woman about twenty-five in a royal blue one-piece yoga suit. You have to admire a woman brave enough to wear a one-piece anything in public, or maybe I have to admire her. She's not very sweaty.

"I'm Tammy," she says to me.

"This is Tammy and her dad, Sam," my mother says. "My daughter, Claire," she tells them. Lots of hand-shaking follows. Mom even shakes with Sam. Both Sam and his daughter are shorter than my mother and I—we are both exactly five foot six, not giants, more what my mother calls "average but perfect," in her way.

"Why don't we all get tea next door?" Tammy asks, as of course there is a café next door. Actually, there's one on both sides of the yoga studio, this being part of Los Angeles, where there is some kind of requirement for several cafés per street. Tammy and Eleanor share an excited look. They seem to have hatched a plan.

"Well," Sam says, "I have some work."

"Oh," Eleanor says, fixing her ponytails, although they are perfect. "What is it that you do, Sam?"

"Tax attorney," Sam says, looking down, not that there's really anything to be ashamed of.

"Oh, how funny," Eleanor says. "I'm a bookkeeper."

"The same line of work," Tammy says. "I'll bet your mom was helpful when you had math homework," Tammy says to me.

"She still is," I say. My mom's done my taxes a few times. I'm not the kind of girl who has a lot of financial secrets to keep from her family. I don't have a lot of financial anything, really.

"Just a cup of tea, Dad," Tammy says, trying to persuade.

"Maybe a little coffee cake," Eleanor says. "For sustenance."

"Feeding the mind and the body," Tammy says.

"All on a Saturday morn," I say, completing some kind of odd nursery rhyme. Eleanor and Tammy nod excitingly and say, "Yes." Sam grabs his mat and comes along.

We find a table at the café, called The First Café, no doubt so named because they just knew someone would open another café up the street, which is called Coffee All the Time. I've been to both, and in their striving to attract customers, they've somehow managed to become almost exactly the same. We all smile at one another and sip Calming Tea, although

I really would have liked a mocha latte right now. Peer pressure, once again, has forced me to abandon my desire for something frothy. Mom gets a plate of low-cal cinnamon biscotti, although I'm pretty sure she promised coffee cake.

"How long have you two been doing yoga?" Eleanor asks the other pair.

Tammy stuffs biscotti in her mouth and looks to her dad, no doubt to try to get him to take the question. I guess biscotti have a purpose after all.

"Tammy's got me doing it," Sam says, after taking a sip of tea. He pours in another sugar pack, clearly not pleased by the subtle infusion. I kind of agree, not one for weak tea. "We've been coming for about six months."

"After Mom died," Tammy says, "I wanted Dad to get some exercise, get out a little." Sam nods, although I can tell his heart isn't exactly in this, any of it, really. I feel for him, but I'm a little resentful, too, mostly because after an hour and a quarter of strenuous stretching, my mother looks absolutely radiant, ponytails and all. All of which seems lost on Sam.

"Before we take the yoga class," Tammy continues, "we bicycle along the beach. Two miles," she adds.

"Wow," Mom and I echo. We both tend to find bike seats unacceptably uncomfortable, although I like the thick padded ones on stationary bikes a little.

"That's impressive," Mom says, and we both check Sam out a little. He's very fit for his age, upper fifties, slightly graying, prominent cheekbones for a man but not in a bad way.

"We try to stay fit," Tammy says. "Right, Dad?"

"The bicycling is productive," Sam says.

One of those silences ensues. We use it to sip our drinks slowly. I focus on breathing in and out, après-yoga style, although it still doesn't quite fill the silent space.

"Claire is in advertising," Mom says.

"So I can only try to stay fit on the weekend," I say. Tammy and Eleanor laugh. Sam nods.

"You young women need to take care of yourselves," Sam says.

"It's so true." Eleanor says.

"It goes fast," Sam says. I don't think the yoga is helping his mood, much. And maybe he should have ordered the Excitement Tea. Calming Tea may not be the right speed. He doesn't really seem open to the suggestion, though.

"Well," I say, "maybe we should get going." Eleanor looks at me at first unhappily, but then when Sam doesn't much look up, she seems to agree.

"So much to do on our day," she says.

"Oh, yes," Tammy says, agreeing to I'm not sure what. Agreeing to general conversation, basically, which her father clearly hasn't regained an interest in. It might be best to get Eleanor out of here, before she returns to this state herself. She's passed it, and now I realize how glad I am. It is painful to watch on anyone, and I see a familiar look on Tammy's face. The daughter wondering what she can say to her parent after the other parent is gone. Gone but not forgotten. I don't want to go back to wearing that look, and I don't want Eleanor going back to any of it.

"Well," Eleanor says, "maybe we can do it again next week." She looks at me. I can't imagine another push-me-pull-you session, but I can tell by her look that she'd prefer I keep this to myself.

"I'm not sure yoga is really for me," Sam says. My mother looks out toward the window. So much for my mother's second attempt at a twist on double-dating, I think a little sadly. Tammy pats her dad's hand, then turns to me with a little smile. I smile back at her and nod. We are so unpracticed at fixing up our parents. I have to admire her attempt.

I take a deep breath, exhale by pulling my belly button in, just as I've been instructed repeatedly throughout the morning.

"I'm thinking of getting my own mat," I say, and my mother smiles at me with appreciation.

Chapter 16

The Best Bachelor

The phones are ringing. There's a wave of activity in our usually quiet, somewhat stark office. Chairs are squawking as they move across the floor. People are calling to one another. It sounds like twenty or thirty people work here, when really it's just us six. David plops a *Billboard* magazine in front of me.

"Welcome to the big time," he says.

Dennis scoots over my way, nearly knocking his coffee over again. We have not been too friendly to one another this morning, mostly just nodding in the other's direction.

"Keep that coffee out of here," I say. "Can't you just drink hot water or something for a change? Something that doesn't stain?"

"You should just buy more brown hemp clothes up the street," Dennis says. "You can't tell if they get stained."

"Children, please," says David, drawing our attention back to *Billboard*.

"I can never make this magazine out," I say.

"Is it a magazine or a newspaper?" Dennis asks. I've never figured that out, either. "It's not bound like a magazine, and it's too big," he says. Dennis is whiny today, but then so am I. My back still hurts a little from yoga. I don't know what Dennis's excuse is. He's not the yoga type.

"We're number thirty!" David says. "Would you please stop bickering and look?"

"Wow," I say. Brendan and Montana have skyrocketed—and there's really no other word for it, or at least that's the one I've always heard people use, as I've never had a client on the list before—with their new CD, the self-titled *Montana*. Montana has hit the big time.

"Wow," Dennis echoes. Really, we've never much dealt with success before.

"So spill your coffee all you want," David says. "I'm getting champagne. And charging it to Perri."

Josie appears at our doorway, flustered. We don't have an intercom, but then, we've never much needed one.

"*The Best Bachelor* has been calling," she says.

"And what would he want with Claire?" Dennis asks nastily.

I sneer at him.

"It's a new show," Josie says.

"Is there a *Worst Bachelor?*" Dennis asks.

"No," Josie insists. "It's prime time—don't you guys watch TV?"

Dennis and I mumble. We watch way too much TV, but we both tend to watch shows that are nearly as old as we are. Cable gives you that choice, for which we've often expressed our gratitude.

"Why, exactly, would I be watching a show about bachelors?" Dennis asks.

"To watch the bachelorettes?" David says.

"Oh, yeah," Dennis says.

"Because you don't have enough bachelorettes in your own life?" I ask, not really wanting an answer. I notice there's a small version of Heaven's bus board on Dennis's desk.

"To watch skimpily clad bachelorettes?" David suggests.

"Because you don't have enough of those in your own office?" I ask, pointing to the bus board picture. Dennis picks it up and waves it.

"You mean this?" Dennis says. "This is fine art," he says.

"I designed it," David says proudly.

"What's next, T-shirts with her picture on them?" I ask.

"Well, yes, actually," David says.

"It's sexist," I say.

"It's a girl and her guitar," Dennis says. "I'll take an extra large," Dennis says to David, who nods.

"I told them you'll call back," Josie says.

"Who?" Dennis and I both say.

"*The Best Bachelor,*" she says.

"Is this *The Bachelor?*" I ask.

"*The Bachelor* is over," Dennis says.

"They ran out?" David asks.

"Maybe of good ones," I say.

"Oh, they never really had good ones," Josie says authoritatively. "And no, it's not *The Bachelor.* It's *The Best Bachelor.* It's NBC."

"Oh," I say.

"What's on up against it?" Dennis asks. Josie seems to know these things.

"It's up against *You Bet Your Lawsuit,*" Josie says.

"I cannot keep up with these reality shows," I say. I didn't know there was a show about lawsuits.

"Is that like *Cops?*" David asks.

"No, no," Josie says. "It's the show where they have troops of people running around town looking for places to sue." No wonder I've missed it.

"At least that's not as bad as the show where they do plastic surgery on people," David says.

"But the ratings aren't as good, either," Josie says. "I've checked. *The Best Bachelor* is in the top ten."

"And they're calling Claire?" Dennis says. I was wondering this myself.

"I don't want to go on any *Best Bachelor* show." I'm hoping my mother would applaud this decision. Then again, maybe she'd like to meet a best bachelor, if they have one over fifty, that is. *Best Older Bachelor*, maybe.

"How do they decide who the best bachelor is?" Dennis asks. "Wait, I don't think I really want to know this."

"They don't want Claire," Josie says. "They want Brendan."

"Brendan the Montana boy Brendan?" Dennis asks, as if we have more than one client named Brendan. We do have two clients named Pete, but they wouldn't qualify as best bachelors for any number of reasons.

"Brendan on a show called *The Best Bachelor?*" I ask.

"He's like what," Dennis says, "twenty-three?" Something seems unfair here to Dennis.

"It's in the top ten," Josie says.

"Would he sing?" I ask.

"You should call them back," Josie says, and hands me one of those little yellow message slips with a phone number. Josie loves those little slips. She keeps a file of them, I know.

"Whatever happened to *American Bandstand?*" Dennis wants to know. "That was respectable."

"*The Best Bachelor* is respectable," Josie says. "They just don't always wear their shirts much of the time."

Dennis groans and goes back to his desk. I think about quiet Brendan taking his shirt off in front of millions of Americans. Maybe wearing his cowboy hat and bandana. It is easier to imagine than I might have thought.

"I don't see why it's such a problem," Josie says, clearly also having no trouble with the imagery.

* * *

I spend much of the morning returning phone calls from radio stations and newspapers. Everyone wants details on Brendan and the boys in Montana. Dennis spends the morning slamming his desk drawers shut.

"You're just jealous because no one's calling to make Heaven the Best Bachelorette," I say, although I don't think that show exists.

"Not yet," Dennis says. "Not that I can think of a better candidate," he says.

"Really," I say.

"Why not? Heaven is sweet, young, pretty, motivated, intelligent—"

"Blonde," I say.

"So you hold that against her?" Dennis asks. "She can't help it that she's blonde."

"She could darken her hair to look more like the rest of us," I say, although it's a little ridiculous.

"Heaven is pretty and attends college," Dennis says. "She's a good role model."

"For Barbie," I say under my breath, although I'm being a little unfair.

"Now who's jealous?" Dennis says.

"Like I want to be on the side of a bus," I say. "Or have my picture in a tight pink sweater lying across people's desks."

"It's not tight," Dennis says, "it's cashmere."

"Cashmere makes me itch," I say.

"I rest my case," Dennis says, then slams another drawer. He only has four drawers, so I can't imagine how he's managing to make so much noise.

"You could keep it down a little," I say.

"I'm reorganizing," Dennis says.

"No wonder you're in such a bad mood," I say. It's not his favorite activity, I happen to know.

"I need more space for Heaven's account."

"Goody," I say. "I guess I need more room for Brendan's account, now that he's going to be the Best Bachelor."

"You've put him on that show?" Dennis asks.

"Yep," I say. "He'll be great."

"Does he have to do something to get to be the Best Bachelor, or does he start out that way and have no where to go but down?" Dennis asks.

I don't really know. I've only set up a meeting, but I don't want to admit it.

"Do you really have to ask?" I say, managing to make Dennis feel bad and avoid the question at the same time. Ambiguity has its good points. Dennis starts to leave the room.

Malcolm sticks his head in the room. "Conference room," he says, then disappears, commanding us to the conference room in his way.

"Oh, and I think you'll like the wallpaper now in the conference room," Dennis says.

"We don't have wallpaper," I say, following him to the conference room, which is really just an area with a big table surrounded by what are usually white walls but now are covered with Heaven bus art. It's everywhere. We enter the room.

"Ladies and gentlemen," our boss, Perri, announces, "I give you the top thirty artist Brendan Baker of Montana." She puts her arm around Brendan, who's standing in our conference room. Brendan looks at me happily.

"Hi, Claire," he says.

"Wow, congratulations on the chart," I say. "You're my first client on the chart," I say, kind of amazed.

"Isn't it the top twenty that counts?" Dennis says. Brendan just shrugs.

"That'll be tomorrow," Perri says. "You just wait." Perri removes her arm from across Brendan's shoulder and begins patting his arm, but not in a particularly motherly way. Malcolm looks a little uncomfortable, but not compared to Josie, who looks ready to jump out of her seat.

"Creepy," Malcolm whispers. David shudders.

"We are going to make a very big star out of you," Perri says to Brendan. "Our Best Bachelor. Right Claire?"

"We're working on the TV show," I say to Brendan.

"Do you think it's a good move?" Brendan asks me.

"Let's look it over," I say.

"Exposure," Perri says seductively.

"That means you take your shirt off a lot," Dennis says.

"I think that's mostly on *Survivor*," I say.

"I don't want to go on *Survivor*," Brendan says.

"But the hat fits right in," Dennis says of Brendan's cowboy hat, not that Brendan's wearing it at the moment.

"It's a good hat," I say. "Jed approved it."

"It's a fine hat," Dennis says. "I'm just saying."

"*Survivor* is passé," Perri says. "We can do better than that." Perri goes to the table and raises a filled champagne glass. I don't remember hearing a pop earlier. Maybe Dennis was distracting me by slamming something.

"To Brendan, our *Billboard* artist with a bullet," Perri says.

We all drink, and the small group crowds around Brendan congratulating him. I'm not usually one for champagne, but I think Perri has splurged and bought good stuff, although I doubt it's sulfite-free like the bottles at the health food store. I doubt that stuff really tastes this good anyway. Perri hangs off Brendan's elbow as if acting as his escort for the morning. Josie shakes Brendan's hand (the one not hampered by Perri) professionally. Malcolm just nods at him and starts to leave.

"No champagne for you?" Dennis asks him.

"Heavy lifting," Malcolm says and goes.

I drink another cup of champagne, then start to leave as well, but Perri stops me.

"This means a little something extra, bonus-wise, you realize, Claire," Perri says.

"Maybe my own office would be nice," I say. Dennis just stares at me, then turns to Perri defiantly.

"It's a great idea," he says.

"I'm not sure how we'd arrange it," Perri says.

"I'm sure we can think of something," Dennis says.

"Dennis could maybe work in the conference room, since he likes the artwork so much," I suggest.

"I'll have Malcolm help me move my desk," Dennis says. I hear Malcolm groan from the other side of the office. Dennis's desk doesn't look light.

"Good thing Malcolm passed on the champagne," Josie says to me, but not very happily. None of us looks particularly happy, including Perri, from whom Brendan has managed to slip away.

"Excuse me," Dennis says, starting to get away. "Champagne always makes me grumpy."

"Just like one of the seven little dwarfs," I say.

"Don't worry," he says. "Bashful and I will move my stuff out of our office."

"My office," I say. "Wow, I'll have an office." Wow, I'll have an office all my own. I think about this. Although I don't think very clearly on champagne.

"I guess this is a big day for you," Josie says. I nod. I take a deep breath.

"I'll go return some more phone calls," I say.

"Don't forget to write your cowboy boot copy," Dennis says. "Don't forget the little people who got you where you are."

"Don't worry, I'll work on it in my own office," I say, but I admit it sounds like I'm seven years old. Seven years old and a little drunk, that is. Not a wise combination.

*   *   *

I find Brendan by himself in my office, leaning against my desk.

"Do you really think I can win on *The Best Bachelor*?" he asks me.

"I don't really know what it entails," I say.

"Oh, it's not such a bad show. Everyone's pretty nice to each other. They're not vying for a million dollars or anything, so you actually see people express their true feelings once in a while."

"Not scripted true feelings?"

"Well, a script might come in handy, sometimes," Brendan says. I have to agree. I wouldn't have minded a script this morning. I wouldn't mind one now.

"I think you can do anything, Brendan," I tell him. I feel a little dizzy from the champagne, but not in a really bad way.

Brendan comes up and kisses me. This wasn't what I meant, but oh well. It's very quiet in the office, I notice. Brendan tastes of champagne and something sweet, bananas maybe. It's not a bad combination.

"We shouldn't do that here," I tell him, but I'm not sure if I mean we shouldn't kiss or that my office isn't a good place for it. He kisses me again. I guess he doesn't care which I meant. Just then I hear Perri head for the front door with a swoosh—she's wearing her red cape, which oddly, doesn't make her look at all like a superhero. She slams the front door, which makes me wonder if she walked by my office and noticed the kissing part. There's not exactly a place to hide in my office, not that I'm exactly trying to hide. And we don't have a policy against office kissing, or much else, really. Still, a slammed door is a slammed door.

I realize, as Brendan and I are still mid-kiss, mid-second kiss that is, that this really isn't my office yet, as Dennis is standing in the doorway. I turn to look at him smirking.

"I can come back later to move my work out," Dennis says.

"That would be fine," I say.

"You know, actual work," Dennis says.

"I should be going, anyway," Brendan says to me, as he gently rubs my right shoulder. Not a deep massage rub but an inquisitive pat. It wakes me up a little.

"Oh, right," I say. "I should get some solid food."

Brendan smiles and leaves. Dennis still stands and smirks.

"There's a little more champagne," Dennis says. "In case you haven't had enough."

I wobble past him, the two cups of champagne starting to settle somewhere between my ears.

"I'm just tipsy," I say.

"Tipsy, isn't that Snow White's eighth little dwarf?" he asks me. "The one with the red nose and really bad judgment?"

I try to walk around him through our doorway, but I can't help bumping into him as I go by. Despite that he's helped me to not fall over completely, Dennis has managed to not budge an inch.

Chapter 17

Someone's in the Kitchen with Brendan

"**O**h," Eleanor says, "I just love that show."

I'm getting my hair trimmed at Billie's. It's true, I could go to any of the five hair salons around our office for a trim, but that would cost over fifty dollars, per inch, it sometimes seems. Billie likes to charge me eight ninety-five, as that's the amount she charged for my first haircut, when I was seven. I wouldn't let anyone touch my hair before that even though the curls were getting a little out of control. My mother doesn't much love looking at my class pictures from that age, although we had a fine selection of hair clips, many of which are preserved in school photographs as dangling wildly from my hair.

Eleanor gets her hair lightened or what used to be called frosted. She is trimmed with foil, Christmas tree style. In fact, it adds a kind of modern look to her head. Foil becomes her.

"I haven't seen *The Best Bachelor*," I tell her.

"Oh, it's darling," Billie agrees with Eleanor. They nod enthusiastically. "That little Brendan would be a natural."

"I think he's a little nervous about it," I say. I know I am.

"Maybe I should come along?" Eleanor asks.

"Well—" I start to say.

"For support," Billie suggests.

"Such a nice boy," Eleanor says.

"But Mom," I say, although it's not the most mature phrase to come out of my mouth, I admit.

"I can be his personal bookkeeper," Eleanor says.

"And why would he need that to go on a show?" I ask.

"All right, not personal bookkeeper," Eleanor says. "Just part of the entourage."

"I don't think he needs an entourage," I say.

"Nonsense," Eleanor says, "everyone needs an entourage now and then." Billie nods. I still don't like the idea, despite that she may be right.

I look in the mirror before me and see a strange reflection of someone standing back at Billie's front desk. Not exactly strange, more like, well, perfect. I turn around.

"Heaven?" I say. Heaven waits at Billie's desk, looking around. She seems genuinely relieved to find me.

"Claire," she says and comes over. "I was walking by and saw all the flowers out front."

"It's not a flower shop," I say.

"It's beautiful here," Heaven says.

"This is Heaven," I tell my mother and Billie, who are edging toward Heaven and beginning to pat her snowy blonde hair. "One of our clients."

"Of course," Mom says. "I heard you sing at the county fair." Eleanor turns to Billie. "She has great range." Billie nods, impressed.

"I've always wanted to come in this shop," Heaven says. "Maybe you can help me."

"Sure," Billie says. "I'd have to think about how to improve on what you've got. Not that a trim ever hurt anyone," she says, back in my direction. She runs her hands through Heaven's hair. I've seen total strangers walk up to

Heaven and do the same, so it seems perfectly natural coming from Billie. She's a professional, after all.

"I want to make my hair seem, well," Heaven thinks a moment, "less noticeable. It sometimes seems like I'm just a head of blonde hair to people."

"Why don't you darken it?" I suggest. The idea has occurred to me before, although I can't imagine anyone actually agreeing to it. Maybe the idea has crossed the minds of tens of women who've seen Heaven's towhead hair and hated to admit how much they envied it. Or maybe I'm projecting again.

"That's it," Heaven says. "Let's make it darker."

My mother and Billie make a slight gasping sound in their throats, the kind you make when someone comes up behind you and startles you or when someone basically suggests something you'd never have thought of as a good idea.

"Are you sure?" they both ask. I'm starting to wonder the same thing.

"I want to be taken more seriously," Heaven says. "I want to be more than just the girl singer with blonde hair."

"Not that some of them don't do very well," I say, starting to backtrack. "You know, all the bus posters are done, with blonde hair," I say. I think of David and his artistic efforts. I think of Dennis, but just briefly. I refuse to think of what Dennis might say about Heaven changing her perfect hair.

"Can't I still be blonde, a darker blonde maybe? More like your color, Claire?" I'm a long way from towheaded with my light brown hair, although it's a little light right now as I've been out in the sun lately walking at lunch ("That's very bad," Eleanor has told me, and she always seems to leave a tube of sunscreen in my apartment after she visits). With a little sun, my hair is approaching a honey color, but it's pretty low on a sliding scale of blonde.

"More like my color," Eleanor suggests. It's true, Heaven would still look good in my mother's hair color, which I happen to know is called Honeybee Blonde.

"I can see it," Billie says, leading Heaven over to the chair next to me.

"No one ever thinks it's natural, anyway," Heaven says. "I want to look more natural."

"Even if it means applying unnatural colors to your hair?" I ask.

"Oh," Billie says, "not to worry. We have some plant-based colors that will work perfectly."

"Is there something you can do to add more curls?" asks Heaven. Her perfect blonde is the kind of straight all curly-haired girls want, the kind of straight even straight-haired girls want. She looks toward my slight curls, natural but somewhat feeble.

"Claire's always curls," she says, a little whiny. But never just right, I think but don't say, and I'm grateful that my mother doesn't say it, either. It's hard to believe a straight-haired blonde girl would envy my curls or much of anything about me.

Billie finishes cutting my hair. "I'll go yes on the darker shade," Billie says, "but you girls need to be happier with what you have in general. We're here to boost your spirits a little, not to make you into someone else. My philosophy."

"Your hair will never curl, dear," Eleanor says gently to Heaven. Heaven nods a little forlorn but with acceptance in the bounce of her head. A small crowd of Billie's customers and hairdressers begins to gather around Heaven. Billie instructs Gerty, one of the hairdressers.

"Just a smidge darker," she says. Women gasp. Heaven nods.

"It's every woman's right," Eleanor says to the crowd, patting Heaven's hand. I don't know the feminist philosophy of hair color—even plant-based hair color—but my mother seems pretty confident about this.

When they're done with Heaven, we all gather again. Heaven and my mother have nearly matching shades. Gone is the towheaded childishness, what Dennis and David refer to as the kitten in Heaven, although I hate when they say it. What we have here is a prouder cat with a pounce in her eye.

"I love this business," Billie says. Heaven smiles.

We're standing in a studio in Hollywood, not the kind of studio like Universal with a tour, more the old-fashioned kind where large men push big cameras around on shiny floors. No main attractions or roller coaster rides here. I'm standing with Brendan, who for some reason agreed enthusiastically to have my mother come along. Jackie is here for support as well, although not so much Brendan's.

"I'm wondering if it's a good show on which to place political candidates," she tells me. She's claimed it's her reasoning for wanting to come along.

"You just want to see the other bachelors," I tell her. "Check them out."

"Discuss their political affiliations," Jackie says.

"So to speak," I say. "Although I thought your affections were spoken for."

"They are," she says. "I'm strictly looking for votes at this point. Strictly professional," she says, fairly honestly and a little disappointedly.

"You're still allowed to look at the voters," I suggest. "From all sides." I don't want her too hung up on her married candidate, after all. This seems like such a good place for Jackie in her former man-searching condition. I hate to see her miss out.

"It would be too confusing," Jackie says. "I'm not good at dividing loyalties."

"You may be too loyal," I say.

"You just don't like politics," Jackie says.

"I guess I just hate an unfair race," I say. I think about Jackie's married-to-someone-else politician. "I like better odds."

"Me too," she admits.

We stand and watch them setting up. My mother is patting Brendan on the back in a calming way, I think, rather than in the way you might if you were trying to stop someone from choking, say. Although it's a fine line. We inspect the set.

"It's the *Dating Game*," I tell Jackie.

"It's not the *Dating Game*," Jackie tells me. "It's the *Dating Game Goes Postmodern*. No dress code."

"What will I have to do?" Brendan asks me.

A producer of the show, a woman in black named Therese, who accentuates the "ese" part of her name and is far younger than Jackie and me, tells us that Brendan will vie for the title of Best Bachelor tonight in the kitchen. We stand in front of a little kitchen set, although frankly, it's bigger than my kitchen.

"Wonderful pots and pans," Eleanor says, admiring them.

"They're copper," Jackie says. "Somebody's spent some bucks."

"All our equipment comes from A la Cuccina," Therese tells us. "In the Palisades," she says, as if it were paradise. Actually, it's a very pricey part of town that's hard to drive to. And harder to park in. All my pots come from Target, or from Eleanor, or from Eleanor after she's shopped at Target. They work just fine, too.

"What's your specialty?" Therese asks Brendan, who looks back to me as if I know what his specialty is, or even what she means by this.

"I sing kind of a cross between rock and rockabilly," Brendan says.

"Aren't they already a cross?" Jackie asks, but not meanly. I think she has a point.

"Maybe," Brendan thinks about this. "I'm somewhere in the middle."

"He has a lovely voice," Eleanor says.

"I mean in the kitchen," Therese says.

"I can sing in a kitchen," Brendan says. "I can try."

"What can you cook?" Therese spells it out for us.

"Oh," Brendan says, a little worried. "Well, cook—" he starts to think, but I can see it's a problem.

"What can you cook to entice that special someone?" Therese asks again.

Brendan thinks for a minute, then looks to me. Am I the special someone, or am I just here to put myself in the place of a special someone, or just here to help him think what to serve the special someone?

"An omelette?" I suggest.

"Every girl likes a nice omelette," my mother agrees.

"Sure," Brendan says.

"Scallions, spinach, peppers?" Therese asks.

"Shouldn't we have known about this ahead of time?" I ask Therese, since I'm supposed to be somewhat in charge.

"We don't want the bachelors preparing in advance," she tells me.

"I can make an omelette without preparing, much," Brendan says.

"Choose your pan," Therese says. Brendan looks up at the pan rack over the kitchen sink. There are quite a few up there.

"Hmm," he says.

Jackie grabs a small one and hands it to Brendan.

"Thanks," he says.

"A little butter in the pan, not too much," Eleanor whispers.

"There's really no coaching," Therese says.

"This isn't live, is it?" I ask.

"We'll tape," Therese says, "but we won't reshoot."

"Do you usually burn them?" I ask Brendan. I admit it's a problem I have.

Brendan shakes his head no, but he looks a little alarmed when Therese brings out an eighteen-pack of eggs.

"Not cage-free," Jackie says, shaking her head. Brendan rolls up his sleeves. The rest of us are sent to sit in some chairs, audience style, although Therese insists we make no noise.

"And no hand signals, please," she says to my mother, who smiles in her pretty Mom fashion that implies of course we wouldn't send signals and that Therese should really wear lower heels, all in one expression.

The producers usher in a young woman with a very flat stomach who's wearing low-rise jeans and a black top, I can't help but notice.

"She could use a nice little omelet," my mother says to me.

"Don't use the scallions, don't use the scallions," Jackie is whispering, mantralike, in Brendan's direction.

"Not on the first date," Mom agrees.

"This is like the *Dating Game* meets Julia Child," I say. "It's too weird. Why would anyone watch this?"

"Brendan leaves Julia Child in the dirt," my mother says. I'm a little shocked at her phrasing.

"Who wouldn't watch?" Jackie says, and I look at Brendan, who's getting his curls combed and looking better and better. The young woman, his date-to-be, I guess, seems to be eyeing him, too.

We sit and watch the whole segment, what turns out to be Brendan's portion of the show. It's a contest, and his role is to woo the girl (her name is Cristianna, and she's studying geology, an announcer I can't quite see tells us) by cooking a perfect, enticing meal. Then she'll see the next bachelor, who will woo with some other specialty, I guess. Or maybe make dessert. It's anyone's guess.

"I hope she's not a vegan," Jackie says.

Surprisingly, Brendan manages to sing a little while he cooks. Softly, almost just to himself, and with no prompting from me, although I can see now that I should have thought to mention it. We can all see Cristianna leaning in to Brendan, and not because she likes the smell of Monterey Jack cheese sizzling in eggs.

"She's smiling," Jackie says. "A good sign."

"She must not mind the smell of eggs cooking," I say. I'm a little sensitive to it.

"She's counting her blessings right now," Eleanor whispers.

"Maybe she's just counting the calories in the eggs," Jackie says. The girl is awfully thin.

"He only used a little butter," Mom says proudly, as if she'd taught Brendan everything he knows.

The "date" goes pretty smoothly. Brendan and Cristianna talk between his songs about her studies at the junior college. Brendan looks a lot more comfortable with an omelette pan than I would have guessed.

"And it's not even Teflon," Jackie says, as he scoots the omelette out of the pan.

It comes time to taste the omelette. We all lean forward. Cristianna takes a bite, then smiles, then turns to Brendan and kisses him on the cheek.

"She could have kissed him on the lips," my mother says. "I didn't see him put any scallions in."

"No one mentioned there would be kissing," I say, not jealous, exactly, just worried in general for Brendan. "I could have warned him," I say. "That's my job, isn't it?"

"To warn Brendan about kissing girls?" Eleanor asks.

"They don't have job descriptions at Claire's office," Jackie tells her.

"I see," Eleanor says, then looks at me with a question or two in her eyes.

"We're here to look after him, that's all," I tell her. "He's my client, I'm responsible."

My mother just sighs deeply. Cristianna feeds Brendan some omelette. I think she should have used a clean fork, but we're not allowed to make hand gestures. I just groan softly.

"A young man who can sing and make an omelette," Eleanor says a little dreamily. "Definitely the Best Bachelor, speaking as a mother, of course."

Brendan's segment comes to an end. We're invited to stay for the next one, and Cristianna goes off to meet her next candidate for Best Bachelor. Brendan shakes her hand good-bye, but she moves in and kisses him on the lips.

"And the camera's not even rolling," Jackie says. I thought of this, too.

Brendan comes out to us.

"That looked very fluffy, dear," Eleanor tells him.

"Not too much butter," Brendan says. "I could have done a nice spaghetti, too," he says.

"Not on the first date," Eleanor instructs. "All that slurping."

"You're not the type to wear a little spaghetti bib, are you?" Jackie asks.

Brendan shakes his head no. "Dark shirts," he says, pointing at his denim shirt, a rich deep blue. I do see a few spots, I think. Probably omelette spatterings.

We see Therese head over to another part of the set to get ready for segment two, and I feel a slight pull in my stomach, and not just because something smells bad from being left to burn in the kitchen.

"Perri?" I ask, although it's so clearly my boss, Perri, that asking isn't necessary.

Before us stands Perri with someone clearly ready to be Cristianna's bachelor number two for the night.

"I loved the idea," Perri says. "So I thought, since they have more than one contestant, why not fill up the show with all our gentlemen?"

Standing beside Perri is Ron, her workout guy, dressed well in tight black clothes but looking a little uncomfortable.

"I guess there's no conflict of interest in advertising?" Jackie asks me quietly.

"Not in Perri's interest, I guess," I say quietly. I turn to Ron. "Ron?" I ask him, implying any number of questions. He shrugs.

"I can use the money to open a yoga studio," Ron says.

"You get to win money?" Eleanor asks. "I thought this was just for exposure."

"Exposure is so important to developing an image," Perri says. "It's priceless."

"If you win the whole season, you get half a million," Ron says.

"And the girl?" my mother asks. We see Cristianna smiling at Ron.

"She looks like she could do yoga," Jackie says.

"I admit I noticed that," Ron says honestly.

"The girl is completely beside the point," Perri says, grabbing Ron by the elbow and leading him to his set.

"That's her trainer," I tell everyone.

"He seems very sweet for someone with so many muscles," Eleanor says.

Brendan groans a little this time.

"I didn't know you were representing him," Jackie says.

"Not me, exactly," I say. We've taken on clients with fewer abilities than Ron's, and he would be a good yoga instructor, not that Venice needs any more studios.

We watch Ron's segment. Perri stands apart, looking somewhat stage-motherly, not that I expect she'd like this description. Ron's part of the show is to give Cristianna a massage.

"Ooh," Jackie says. "I thought he was just yoga. I didn't know he gave massages."

"Isn't this sort of cheating? Ron's a professional," I say. I guess I still want Brendan to win, although I'm not certain about it.

"And there was no touching allowed in Brendan's segment," Eleanor says.

"There was a little touching," Brendan says.

"We couldn't see everything that went on behind the counter," Jackie says.

"I know," Brendan says. We watch Cristianna get her massage. Ron looks very expert.

"You have to admit," Jackie says, "she looks good in that towel."

"Who watches this show, anyhow?" I mumble again. Jackie pats me on the back lightly.

After commercials, Cristianna, dressed again in her low-risers with a black T that I recognize from the hemp store, chooses her bachelor. Brendan and Ron are forced to stand next to one another, Brendan, thin with his shy stance and curly hair, Ron, muscular with his romance-cover looks. They couldn't have more-different body types.

"Is it just me," Jackie asks quietly, "or does it just scream 'before and after?' "

"I'm a wreck," my mother says nervously.

Cristianna's job, along with looking like she's having a huge problem deciding—and maybe she is—is to hand the winner a white handkerchief with her initials on it.

"Kind of a Victorian quality to the show," my mother says.

"Kind of wimpy," Jackie says.

"She's having trouble deciding," Eleanor says.

"It might not have been wise to have that massage right after eating," Jackie says knowledgeably.

"It's not like she swam a marathon and is tired out," I say.

"You may not have had a massage in a while," Jackie says. She's right.

"I find towels too scratchy," I say. She nods.

"I saw some lovely Egyptian cotton ones at Macy's," my mother says. "You do have a birthday coming up." My mother's ability to multitask amazes me sometimes. Jackie bites her nails. Eleanor moves Jackie's hand away from her mouth, shaking her head no.

In the end, Cristianna hands her handkerchief to Brendan. Ron and Brendan shake hands.

"Nice-looking omelette," Ron tells Brendan.

I hear Perri huff in the corner, although you're not really allowed to make noise. Cristianna and Brendan hug as the show cameras fade out.

Perri marches Ron toward us. He waves good-naturedly.

"We should have used oils," Perri says to Ron.

"You're only allowed to use oils on cable," Jackie tells them. "Broadcast standards."

"Really?" I ask.

"I've done some investigating."

Cristianna goes off with several producers. Brendan comes over to us.

"You're the Best Bachelor," Jackie tells him.

"But we knew that," Eleanor says.

"Do I have to go on next week?" Brendan asks me.

"You don't have to do anything you don't want to do," Eleanor says, and he seems comforted.

"Two point five million young record buyers are watching," Jackie says. "I checked the demographics and Nielsen's, not to mention *Billboard*."

"We can teach you a nice quiche recipe," my mother tells

Brendan, and they walk off together. Brendan looks back at me.

"I just love your mom," he says to me, but I think I see his eyes saying something different. Or maybe I've just been blinded by so many bright studio lights.

Chapter 18

Something Tangy

I am front-page news. Okay, it's just *Advertising Today*, read only by people who work in advertising—all those future novelists, painters, and musicians trying to pay for over-priced L.A. and Westside apartments the only way they can. Ours is admittedly a very small agency, and *Advertising Today* has never much been interested in Jed's cowboy boots or Elvissa's crooning (not that it isn't first rate, because it is, it's just that trendy magazines find anything Elvis passé, if you ask me). Perri seems to love reading these magazines, but I don't pay much attention, usually. I have found that they're very useful to cover your head with when it rains and you've forgotten your umbrella, though.

But this week's issue features a front-page article on Brendan Baker and his Montana group. All five boys, or youngish men, if you like, smile behind their instruments in a photo across columns one, two, and three. Columns four and five, oddly enough, feature a larger-than-I'd-like photo of, well, me, along with the caption, "Claire Duncan, adver-tising executive, propels Brendan Baker and Montana to the top of the charts." At first I can't imagine where they got the picture, but after a little thought I know.

"Hey," I tell Josie, who stands over me reading the article, although she's already read it once. "This is the photo from the machine out front." It's true that in our lobby stands an aging photo machine where you can just barely fit with your best friend or someone you feel a bit stronger about, even, and make funny faces as the booth takes your photo. You can still get four shots for a quarter. It's an old machine.

"Yeah," Josie says. "These are the photos we all took last summer." It was a hot, hot day, and oddly enough, the photo booth is one of the coolest places in the building, so we all spent our quarters there.

"It's not exactly the kind of picture that's all that professional," I say. I admit I don't really like any photos of me that well. At least in this one I'm smiling happily. It was very cool in there.

"It's a terrific shot," David says, coming in to my cubicle. The one Dennis has vacated. It's now roomy enough for everyone in the office to gather here, which they're beginning to do. "A professional photographer would have charged you hundreds for that shot."

"It looks like a passport photo," I say.

"A passport photo taken in a 1950s photo booth," David says. "Very trendy."

"At least I'm not looking into the sun," I say.

"Advertising executives across the city are envying you right this minute," David says.

"Real advertising executives, you mean," I say.

"As if you'd really want to be one," he says.

"I'm messengering a copy over to Brendan," Josie says. "He'll want to see right away."

"When *People* magazine calls for your headshot," David says, "we'll go for something a little more natural, a little less photo booth."

"Good," I say. I wouldn't ever want my photo in *People*. I don't think I could live it down.

"At least you're not sticking your tongue out in this one," David says.

"That sounds more like something you save for *People*," I say.

"And only if your tongue is pierced," David says.

I head for the storeroom to look for something strong— tea, coffee, it doesn't really matter which. I take the long way around, which allows me to peek into the conference room where Dennis has set up his desk. He is typing away fiercely on his computer but looks up as I walk by.

"Hi," I say.

"Hi, leading advertising executive," Dennis says. "Nice photo," he says, not entirely sincerely, either.

"It's from the photo booth," I say. "Not my idea."

"It looks casual, like you're too busy to care about getting your photo taken," he says.

"I guess that's okay, then," I say.

"Too busy propelling boy singers to the top of the charts," Dennis says.

"I'm pretty sure the boy singers did that themselves," I say.

"Brendan came off pretty well on *The Best Bachelor*," Dennis says.

"Did you watch? We were there," I say. "I can't believe Perri put Ron on."

"It was a pretty enjoyable show."

"I'm surprised you watched. Why does anyone watch that?"

"Cristianna in a towel," Dennis says. "It's really very simple."

"Oh, good," I say. "We wouldn't want you wasting your time on any show that you found very challenging."

"I'm sure you have something executive to attend to," Dennis says. "In your spacious office."

"Yes," I say, not willing to admit I was only going to look for coffee. I do still have some less-than-glamorous cowboy boot copy to write today. Not that I'm not proud of my cowboy boot copy.

Josie pops her head in. "*Entertainment Tonight* is calling," she says to me.

"Give them Brendan's number," I say. "He won't mind."

"They want a story on you," she says. Dennis laughs, but not in the friendliest way.

"And *People* called, too. They wanted to know if there's a photo of you with your hair blowing in the wind slightly."

"I'm not the story," I say.

"We'd better put a fan out by the photo booth," Dennis says.

"Outside would work," Josie says. "There's an ocean breeze. The light in the photo booth is pretty harsh," she says.

Dennis holds up his copy of *Advertising Today*. I'm not sure how he got his own. Perri's usually the only one interested in it.

"That explains it," he says. I sneer in his direction, as he's hidden behind a too-large photo of me.

It is a long day of dodging calls—I really don't want an article about me in *People*, even if I am the only person in Los Angeles who feels this way. I've dodged calls from my mother, who sweetly suggested to Josie on the phone that I buy some blusher for the next photo shoot. Apparently she used the word photo shoot, Josie told me. I don't own blusher. I'm not willing to tell my mother this, though, as I know she'd be happy to buy me a whole range for day and evening.

David listened as Josie gave me the message.

"Next time we'll just pinch your cheeks for you," he said, not as malevolently as it sounds.

I've dodged three calls from Claire the Therapist. That is after canceling two sessions with her. Although I gave her lots of notice, it isn't the nicest thing to do, I know. I'm not sure if she's still dating Dennis, or really if she ever was. And it's not like I couldn't use a therapist now, what with my newfound fame, Brendan's newfound fame, and the office situation. It was wonderful to have a whole office to myself today, I tell myself over and over on the way home. Really, it was.

I arrive home to find somebody's been sitting on my couch, someone who has no doubt found it to be not quite right.

"What are you doing here?" I ask my landlord and former boyfriend, Andy. I haven't heard from him since our evening together. Or our part-of-the-evening together, as Jackie thinks of it. "You're not supposed to use your key except in emergencies," I tell him.

"Oh, it was an emergency," he says.

"Flood?" I ask, looking around. "Fire?" The place looks fine—not that neat, exactly, but untouched by acts of God, let's say.

"I had to use the bathroom," Andy says with a shrug.

"That would be *your* emergency," I say, "not mine. You could use the bathrooms at the beach," I suggest.

"No one is ever in that much of an emergency," Andy says. "Besides, I brought you French bread from San Francisco."

"They sell that at Ralph's here," I say. It's true. It's sometimes even warm, but I'm not sure how bread baked several hundred miles away can still be warm. I don't buy it for this very reason.

"That's not the same," Andy says, waving the loaf in my direction.

"Andy," I say, "I have plans for tonight. You need to go."

"I brought wine to go with the bread," he says. "We could talk. A real conversation. Can't you change your plans?"

"No," I say, "that would be inconsiderate of me."

Andy goes to the table and picks up his bottle of wine, already de-corked. He's big on letting wine breathe. He pours two glasses, all while I'm shaking my head and waving my hands. Drinking before a date with someone, someone else that is, isn't really a good idea I think. And tonight I have a date with Bobby Henry, our country-singing client. I'm not about to tell Andy that I have a date with a blind country singer. I don't even want to hint at it.

"I'm moving to Spain," Andy says.

"Um," I say, startled. "Good?"

"Good?" Andy asks. "Good? Can you say that after last week?"

"It was three weeks ago," I say.

"Really?" Andy asks. I nod.

"Come with me," he says.

"Move to Spain?" I say.

"It's gorgeous there, great food. Lots of people in the company you'd like. I'm sure they could find you a job, technical writing, or whatever, if you wanted to work."

"If I wanted to work?" I ask.

"You don't have to," Andy says. "I have quite a lot saved up."

"You must be one of those executives I've been reading about," I say.

Andy shrugs, a little proudly, then settles in. "I've missed you so much, Claire. I'm a better person when you're around. I want to be that person again. All the time." He seems sincere, not to mention proud of the person he thinks he can be. He hands me wine.

"In Spain?" I ask.

"I'm serious," Andy says. "I can be the man I'm supposed to be, but not without you. And it wouldn't be worth it."

"Do you really think you're a better person with me?" I ask.

"I know it," he says. "I love you, I love the way I feel when I'm with you," he says. "I don't say that to anyone else, you know, never have. Do you have someone else saying it to you? Someone else craving you like this?"

I want my therapist. Or someone else's. The answer of course is no.

"I have a date," I say, a little confused as I sip from the wine, which tastes expensive. Jackie and I usually go for the $4.99 special bottles that our local grocery store buys by the case. They're not too bad. This is a different liquid altogether.

Andy leans in and kisses me. There's not much I can do about it without spilling my wine, which I guess my mother has ingrained in me not to do. Although I'm not sure why it matters—it's Andy's rug. The kiss is more than familiar and more than good. Can a kiss be too good?

"Okay," Andy says. "You can go on your date, tell him good-bye. Let him down easy. I know you know what to do."

"I have a date with a blind musician," I say.

"It's so open-minded of you," Andy says. "It's what every-one loves about you."

I ignore this. "Why me?" I ask. "Why do you want me to go with you? You've never exactly had trouble meeting other girls." It's something I never much wanted to think about when we were together for nearly five years, but women flock to Andy, that combination of blonde curls and borderline Santa Monica real estate ownership. Something in his look oozes with success. Over the years, I came to find it a little scary. I try to think of that now. A little wine com-bined with someone insisting that they love you, well, it's a dangerous combination. One I'm not used to at all.

"No one is as easy to be with as you," Andy says. "Most women are so distrustful."

And smart, I think. Most women have caught on to Andy. "I don't think I love you, Andy," I say. "I did, and you didn't love me back."

"I did love you, I do love you," Andy says. He leans in again for another practiced, too-familiar kiss, but I step back and don't even spill anything.

"Not the right way," I say.

"That's not something you get to control, though," Andy says. "We love the best we can. Let's get rid of this place," he says, looking around, his eyes settling on my couch. "Start fresh in Spain."

"Do you think I could find a couch just like this in Spain?" I ask. *On sale?* I think but don't say.

"We'll get leather," Andy says. "You'll love it. I know what you like to do on couches."

"In Spain," I say.

Andy nods slowly, suggestively, and it's working. It's working on part of me, to see him look so handsome. There's a lot to say about being wanted. But it only works so far, because I know if I were dumb enough to fall for this, most of my friends would lose all respect for me. I'm old enough to know that despite all the statistics about how hard it is to meet men, it's probably easier to find someone better for me than Andy than it is to make all new close friends, not to mention family.

"I have to go on my date," I say.

"Dating shouldn't be an obligation," Andy says. "No matter the handicap."

"Yuck," I say. "That is just a yucky thing to say." I know I sound like a little kid, but it's my apartment—sort of—and after six o'clock you get to sound any way you want. Several self-help books say so. They're not really dating self-help books, but still.

I pack the loaf of bread under Andy's arm and place the bottle of wine in his other hand.

"I can't hug you like this," Andy says. "I so want to hug you."

I escort him to the door. It's funny, but somewhere in Los Angeles at this moment, maybe at a hair salon, maybe at a nail salon, maybe even on a yoga mat, I think I hear my mother applauding. It's a standing ovation.

In the end I meet Bobby Henry at a barbecue restaurant on Pico, near his place in West L.A. He can walk to the restaurant, and his white cane stands in a corner not too noticeably, not that it much matters. Bobby's known here, and the restaurant staff seems at ease with him.

I'm still a little nervous from my Andy encounter tonight, which I suppose has made me less nervous about tonight's actual date. Dinner, I mean. Just dinner, after all.

We sit at a little table off to the side. There's the smell of barbecuing in the air, and although I don't like to eat meat that often, I can understand why others do and why barbecuing has its allure. There's the smell of something sweet in the air.

"Claire!" Bobby greets me before I can say hello. I know it's the apricot shampoo I use (it's from Australia, although I don't see why they can't make a good one closer to home). He always tells me I smell like the farmer's market but in a really good way.

"Hi, Bobby," I say. I kiss him on the cheek and he hugs me. It's a hug I can use right now, nothing devious like Andy's hug would have been, had he not been encumbered by a loaf of bread and jug of wine.

We sit down at a small table. "Beer, wine, soda?" Bobby offers. A waitress has appeared who grabs Bobby by the hand in a greeting—they know each other by touch, but again, not in the way you'd think of if you were thinking about Andy, not that I want to be thinking about Andy. It's definitely time to focus on someone else, I remind myself.

"Oh, soda," I say. "I need soda, Coke."

"Extra caffeine?" Bobby suggests.

"Do they still make that?" The waitress shakes her head no. "It's been that kind of day," I say. More wine is out of the question.

Bobby orders a Coke as well then smiles at me.

"Go ahead and tell me about your day that leaves you longing for extra caffeine," he says encouragingly.

"I think my whole life could use a little extra boost," I say. "What about you?'

"I think my life is going great," Bobby says. The waitress returns with our drinks. Bobby tells me he's thinking of ordering a Number 5 off the menu that appears under the glass on the tables.

"Interesting glass menus," I say.

"Keeps the barbecue sauce off them," Bobby says. The waitress nods. "Do you mind if I eat meat?" he asks me.

"I don't mind," I say. "I don't eat red meat, but I do eat chicken, which most vegetarians find incredibly confused on my part. I have to say I'm confused about it myself." I point to a Number 3 to the waitress. A no doubt huge plate of chicken smothered in something.

"I'm ordering ribs," Bobby says. "Okay?"

"Ribs are the food of my childhood," I say. "I don't eat them anymore, although I'm not above taking a bite off someone else's entrée. I'm heartless when little animals are covered in barbecue sauce."

"It's the California girl in you," Bobby says. "Take heart. It's free-range pork anyhow."

"So it was a happy pig?" I ask.

"At some point. And I'll be eating most of the plateful anyhow. You're really absolved of any wrongdoing," Bobby says.

"If only life were that easy," I say.

"Maybe it is," Bobby says.

"Maybe I should just cover my whole life with barbecue sauce, you mean?"

"In a manner of speaking," Bobby says, "maybe you should."

I think about this. A life less plain. A life covered with something a little sweet, a little sour, and in the right combination.

Bobby and I listen to the sounds of the barbecue place. Jukebox in the corner. Waiters dropping things in the background, utensils mixing against bowls in the kitchen. I find it relaxing to listen, to absorb. I'm not uncomfortable with the silence at all, because it isn't really silent. Bobby seems to enjoy letting me hear the restaurant in full.

"It's all in the way you look at things," Bobby says, as the waitress approaches with our quickly cooked meal. They must have a very hot grill. "Get it?" he says to both of us, "look at things? Blind guy joke," Bobby says, pointing to his face.

"Blind guy joke!" the waitress yells to the kitchen.

"Blind guy joke," echo two cooks back there. Someone rings a bell.

"No wonder you like this place," I say softly to Bobby. He laughs.

"I'm trusting you to take only one bite of my ribs," Bobby says.

"You don't know me well enough to trust me with your dinner," I say.

"It's not that I wouldn't let you have a whole rib," he says, "just that I don't want you fighting with your conscience," he says.

"Thanks," I say.

"Not about a rib, at least," Bobby says, raising an eyebrow. If he only knew how much my conscience and I have to discuss.

"The sauce is delicious," I tell him.

"You can take a bottle home," Bobby suggests.

"Maybe I should carry one around with me," I say. "As a symbolic gesture."

"Believe me," Bobby says, "a girl can never have too much barbecue sauce."

"A girl with a very big purse, you mean."

"I only date girls with very big purses," Bobby says.

"You haven't seen mine," I say. "How can you tell?" It's big, I admit it. The kind with the strap you can wear across your chest. The kind you can put seven textbooks in, if you're in school, and the kind you can never seem to stop carrying if you were the kind of girl in school who carried seven textbooks around. I'm sure my back has suffered dearly, but I love my purse.

"Some things a guy can just tell," Bobby says. "Big purse, huh?"

"I guess I carry a lot of baggage," I say.

"Better get two bottles of sauce, then," Bobby suggests.

After our dinner, I drive Bobby back to his house around the block. I stop at his door.

"You're not going to try anything funny, are you?" Bobby asks.

"I might," I say. He looks at me. He has a wonderful face, even if he's never had the chance to see it himself. "You have a good face," I tell him.

"That's what all the girls tell me," he says. "But I won't ask you in."

"Really?" I ask, although I wouldn't come in. It's been too long a day.

"Oh, no," Bobby says. "I think you need to go home, think."

"Wash my hair?" I suggest. "Isn't that what girls say, 'I have to wash my hair.' "

Bobby leans over and smells my hair. I somehow feel like all my life, I've been wishing someone would lean in to smell my hair. Andy had a weak sense of smell—he never noticed the apricot shampoo, although he did use it when he ran out of guy shampoo.

"I won't make you go to all that trouble," Bobby says. "I think I'm going to let you off easy."

"Why's that?" I ask.

"Because I've been to your office. I've listened. You should listen sometime. You guys are all pretty close around there."

"It's a small office," I say.

"Well, that has its advantages."

"So no kiss goodnight because I work in a small office?" I ask.

"Pretty much," Bobby says. "Besides, all you agreed to was dinner."

"How noble," I say.

"Not really, just paying attention," Bobby says. I kiss him on the cheek anyway.

"That'll do me," he says, getting out of the car and waving. He walks up his driveway. I watch him go in before driving off. I head for home with my heavy bag and bottle of sweet and sour barbeque sauce, an extra gift from Bobby. I feel the need to be alone with something tangy.

Chapter 19

The Good Claire

Because I like to think of myself as a responsible person, I know there is someone in my life that I have to deal with. Face to face, that is. I'm old enough to know when it's time to resolve conflicts. Not that this is a particular strength of mine, more of something that's on my personal wish list of qualities to attain, a list something like the one with resolutions that we all make around New Year's, but a little more permanent. It's the list of qualities for the person I most want to be, someday. "The Good Claire," my therapist sometimes calls it, which makes me wonder, as we're both named Claire, if one of us is "the Bad Claire." Not that I haven't been wondering this lately anyhow.

With such thoughts in mind, I head to my therapist's office. There's really no good way around it. I'm wearing my comfort jeans—some people go in for soft foods for comfort—I tend toward soft denim. Claire the Therapist wears what must be a very soft skirt, faded and flowery. I can imagine myself wearing that skirt, although this may be more transference than simple psychotherapy really requires.

"Sit anywhere," Claire the Therapist greets me. So I do. I choose her usual chair. I notice she chooses not to sit on the couch in my old place but instead to pull up her desk chair to face me. Not that she couldn't sit on the floor, also. Just that I can't imagine it being very comfortable, let alone professional. I guess I'm hoping a new seat will give me a different outlook. And we are definitely face to face.

"Tell me what's been happening," my therapist says. "In the last few weeks."

I could ask her the same. I sit there a moment.

"I noticed you cancelled some appointments," she says, leading.

"I did," I admit.

"Do you want to talk about why?" she asks.

"Are you still dating Dennis?" I ask.

"Oh," Claire the Therapist says. "Dennis your office-mate?"

"Actually the only Dennis I know," I say. "Why, are you dating more than one Dennis?" I ask.

"We should probably take it one question at a time," my therapist says, which makes me wonder if she actually is dating more than one guy named Dennis. I meant it as a joke.

"I don't really feel comfortable with you seeing someone I've been discussing," I say.

"Do you feel you've been talking a lot about Dennis?" she asks.

"He's in my office, we're friends. He's part of my life," I say. "Isn't it natural that I should talk about him?"

"I think it's perfectly natural," my therapist says. "Tell me your problems with my dating Dennis," she says.

"This particular Dennis, you mean?" I ask. My therapist nods.

"I've talked about Dennis," I say.

"That would seem more like a problem Dennis would have with dating me, not a problem you would have," Claire the Therapist says. I catch her looking at her nail. A woman looking at her nail while talking with me has something of the same effect as a man looking at another woman while talking to me. Or maybe I only feel that way in this case, the case of a woman I'm paying to talk to me. I may be getting off the subject.

"I've talked about Dennis being my friend, someone I confide in, someone who comes over to my house and eats my leftovers while standing in front of the refrigerator and never, never, questions how old they are or whether green is their natural color."

"I don't remember your talking about Dennis in connection with your refrigerator," Claire the Therapist says.

"Would it make you feel differently about him?" I ask.

"I'm not sure you should be asking me that question," my therapist says.

"Which question?" I ask. "Whether you'd mind Dennis eating out of my refrigerator or whether you're bothered by Dennis's not caring whether his food is spoiled?"

"Maybe it's the same thing," she says, but I don't think so at all.

"Are you going to date my friend?" I ask. "The friend of one of your clients?"

"I think this is good for you," she says. "I think it's good for you to consider your relationship with Dennis," she says.

"Actually," I say, "I was considering your relationship with Dennis."

"Maybe it's the same thing," Claire the Therapist says again. And again, I don't think it is.

"Has he asked you out again?" I ask.

"I think you need to put some thought into this," Claire the Therapist says. As if I haven't been thinking about it. "Ask yourself why this is such a concern. Not worry so much about my part of the relationship."

"Is there a relationship?" I ask.

Claire the Therapist waves away my question. "Relationships come in many forms," she says.

"That sounds textbooky," I say, but my therapist takes no offense, as she isn't thin-skinned. I wish I weren't.

"Tell me what else has gone on in the last few weeks," she says. I take a deep breath. She's going to charge me for the session anyway, so I might as well go on.

"My client is succeeding in his music career and was watched by millions of people on television," I say. Although Brendan chose not to continue as the Best Bachelor, this only got him even more attention from several more magazines. Seemed no one ever said "No, thank you" before. Cristianna, I hear, was devastated.

"And how does this person's success relate to your life?" she asks. It's not a question I really like, although it is one I'd expect from a therapist, even one dating my officemate.

"He's my client," I say. "It's his talent, I take no credit for that. But it's nice to see him succeed."

"And what does he mean to you personally?" she asks.

"Brendan is young," I say.

"Young," she leads me.

"He may have ideas about us," I admit.

"Has he done anything about these ideas?" she asks. I don't like to kiss and tell, not that I dislike the kissing part, but still.

"Brendan may be a little confused about our relationship," I say.

"But you've taken steps to straighten him out?"

"I've been kind of busy," I say.

"You're going to take steps to straighten him out?" she asks. I look away. "Or," she says, "maybe you're enjoying the confusion a little?"

I take a deep breath.

"Aren't you entitled," my therapist asks, "to enjoy your own life?"

"I'm entitled," I say, "not to hurt others."

"Maybe you just worry too much," my therapist says, but

it makes her sound like my mother. Actually, even worse than my mother.

"I also slept with my old boyfriend," I say.

"And did this seem like a good idea?" Claire the Therapist asks. "Afterward, I mean."

"Afterward," I say, "well, three weeks afterward, I told him to go away."

"He stayed for three weeks?"

"No, about three hours," I say. "Maybe less. I mean I told him when I saw him again. It's over, really."

"This is the man whose apartment you're living in."

"I pay a hefty rent," I say. "It's not like he gives me a break."

"He must be very cute," Claire the Therapist says, staring off over my head a little.

"Like Dennis?" I ask.

"Interesting," my therapist says, grabbing her notebook to jot something down. "Does your ex-boyfriend, with whom you lived for five or so years, look like Dennis?" She's pretty excited about this.

"Exact opposites," I say. "Andy is blonde, Dennis with that dark brown hair."

"And the soft beard," my therapist says.

"And the beard," I say, although I'm back to not liking that my therapist may have touched my officemate's beard.

"I don't think it's right that you know someone I'm talking about well enough to ascribe adjectives to his beard," I say.

"You need to think about *you* more," she says.

"Sorry?" I say, confused.

"Think what Claire needs."

"Me Claire, not you Claire, right?"

"I can take care of myself," my therapist says. "Now it's your turn."

"I can take care of myself, too," I say, but it comes out kind of whiny.

"That's our goal," Claire the Therapist says.

"Then I think I'm there," I say.

"Oh, well, no, not yet," my therapist backtracks.

"Yes," I say. "I think I'm ready to move on, take control."

"You mean end therapy?" she asks.

I nod. "Yep. Not that I'm not grateful, just that I'm taking it from here."

"Oh, but there's still so much in your life to straighten out. Your missing your father, for instance. Your work life. Your indecision about men."

"Well," I say. "There are self-help books, right?"

She shakes her head like a musty smell has just entered the room.

"And I'm not so indecisive about men," I say.

"Your officemate," she says. "You slept with your ex and are interested in a very young man. A boy singer."

She's left off the blind musician, but I don't say anything. I'm in enough trouble, it sounds like.

"You realize," she says, "that as your therapist, my job is to talk you out of quitting therapy."

"Really?" I ask. "I didn't know that."

"Oh, yes. I took a whole course about it. Clients leaving before they're ready."

"Don't I decide if I'm ready?"

"Not entirely," she says. "It's a collaboration."

"I think you've been collaborating a little too much in my life," I say.

"Back to Dennis, again," she says.

"Yes," I say.

"But if I'm not your therapist anymore, doesn't that give me free rein on Dennis?" Claire asks. I hadn't thought of this.

"Wouldn't it be weird for you if I dated someone you work with?" I ask her.

"I work alone," she says.

"Someone you were close to, someone who knew almost everything about you?"

"I'm not sure you have the best perception of how Dennis sees you," my therapist says, "and how he sees me."

"But you want me to stay on and work on it a while?"

"I think it would be an interesting turn, yes," she says.

"I think you should stay away from members of my personal life," I tell her.

"That's very aggressive of you, Claire, very much taking control. We've really made progress."

"But that's not a yes, is it?" I ask.

My therapist closes her notebook and points to the clock. Time flies when you're challenging your therapist about her dating behavior.

"I guess we have something to talk about next time," she says.

I shake my head and get ready to leave, for good I think, even though it will mean I won't get to ask Claire the Therapist where she got her flowery skirt. I know it would look good on me, as we have much the same body type, although it might be a problem having us share not just a name but also an exact duplicate wardrobe. I can't help but wonder what Dennis would think about it, but I do know that even if Claire the Therapist and I share a name, and a penchant for all things flowery, I don't want to share certain things.

Which isn't to say that when I get home, I'm not still thinking about all my therapist has said. About my needing to recover from Dad's death. About Andy—although I sent him to Spain, didn't I? Isn't that far enough away? About Brendan and his kisses, although really, doesn't half the country want to kiss him after *The Best Bachelor* success? For all I know, my therapist saw the show and has been fantasizing about Brendan in her spare time. In the time she isn't fantasizing about Dennis, that is.

I have a sick feeling in my stomach, so I go in the kitchen and make myself a cup of chocolate milk. I admit I use soy milk, because it's healthy and I can't drink real milk after a certain hour and not have a stomachache. I put in enough Quick so that I can't much tell what kind of milk I've used. I am above drinking Quick with plain water, but just barely.

There is something so comforting, still, about a container of Quick. It makes that little pop sound when you lift the lid with a spoon. My mother always insisted that I open it this way, saying that to use your hands invites nail breaking. It's a rule with her, but it makes sense, as the lid is pretty tough to lift. Then there's that powdery chocolate whiff that goes straight up my nostrils and sends soothing memories to someplace just beside my right ear. It's really my drug of choice. I know that Quick is no answer for dinner in these health-conscious times. My dad used to like to dip a banana in his chocolate milk, and this might be the solution, but the only fruit I have is a bunch of grapes, which isn't nearly the same thing.

I take my Quicked-up soy milk to my couch and pull out the box of photos of my dad that my mother left some time back, the box that has remained untouched on my coffee table. Graduation photos, birthday photos. A photo of us washing my old dog, Baxter, a really smelly basset hound who liked to sleep on my legs, which I only let him do when it got very cold. Basset hounds are not lightweight creatures. I admit it wasn't his only character flaw, but we loved him anyway. He'd follow my father anywhere, but then, we had that in common.

The photos make me cry into my Quick. I don't stop

myself at all, and not just because I know it won't really affect the taste. I make piles of photos, not chronological, more by theme. Dad and I engaged in hobbies—building a raft for the beach, building my dollhouse, watering the yard. Dad and I at events—parties, school plays. And just a pile of Dad himself—a photo I took of him with my new camera when I was ten, Dad at his desk, drawing circuitry, intensely focused. It is one of my favorite shots.

I spend what seems like hours sorting, then put rubber bands around the piles and place them back in the box. There are so many photos that they become a blur. I know I wanted to keep some out, maybe frame one or two where my father and I shared a certain look, but I can't remember what pile I've put them in. Still, the boxful—not to mention the Quick—has brought me back to my father. It is the best I'm going to get, and I have to learn to make it be enough.

I go to my stereo and play a tape of music I made for my father when he was sick. He was fond of certain girl singers from the early sixties—not hippy girl singers, more the kind with a little weight to them, a little gravel in their voices. What my dad called bossa nova in their boots. My father used to dance me around on his feet. I'm sure all fathers did, or I like to hope so, because if you've never been danced around on your father's feet, you have missed something. Something that you'll want to look back on, after drinking all the Quick in the glass, packing up all the photos, and listening to the sounds of women singing. Women singing to your father.

Chapter 20

Things That Go Wrong When You Dress Up

"This isn't the prom," I tell Jackie. "You didn't have to come over and do my hair," I say, even though she's halfway through working me over with her curling iron. Mine broke years ago. "And besides, isn't my hair curly enough?"

"Something about the iron gets it to curl even better," Jackie says. "And I need you to do me next."

"We're grown women," I say. "Shouldn't we be capable of curling our hair ourselves?"

"I always burn myself when I do my own hair," she says. I nod, understanding completely. "Then I have to go to parties with big red marks on my face."

"Not the look you're going for?" I ask.

"People at these fund-raisers tend to take me aside and ask if I've been abused," Jackie says.

"They mean well," I say.

It's true. This evening, Jackie and I are headed for a large fund-raiser being held at the Santa Monica Airport. Not in the middle of a terminal, of course, but in an empty huge hangar that will be heavily decorated (Jackie swears) and not remind us of aircraft in any way. None of that thick fuel smell, Jackie assures me. The airport charges heartily for renting these facilities, I know, as I have also been in on the planning. It is a fund-raiser for a local charitable organization—HELPUS, which stands for Helping Each Live Peacefully Under the Sun, although I think they've left a *T* out of the acronym, even if it's just a small *t*. Jackie's candidate and sort-of-a-secret boyfriend, Theo, will be speaking, as will his opponent (HELPUS is open-minded and in need of support from whichever candidate wins). To top off the evening, Brendan will be singing with his boy band. Jackie and I have worked together on this. You could say both our careers ride on it, if you wanted to use a cliché, not to mention exaggerate slightly. Our personal lives are a little involved, too. Jackie wouldn't bother curling her hair for anything less.

"You're not nervous, right?" I ask her.

"I don't really get nervous," Jackie says, and I believe her. She's calm but agitated, but not nail-biting nervous. Still, there's something about her that seems a little pale.

"I'm more fatalistic," she says, thinking. "Not really anxious, just pragmatically wondering how many things can go wrong when you're wearing your dress-up clothes."

"You always turn things into mathematical exercises," I say. "Do we have to add up the plusses and minuses of tonight before it even happens?"

"My mind is basically kind of a pie chart that way, or at the least a table of plusses and minuses," Jackie says. "The right-brain left-brain idea never really worked for me. My brain is more of an abacus."

"You know, we're headed to what's basically a big warehouse," I say. "Can't we just put things that go wrong over to one side and ignore them?"

"Isn't that one of life's big questions?" Jackie says. "Why can't we just compartmentalize the little things that go wrong and be happy with our lives?"

"I wasn't thinking in such general terms," I say. "But okay."

"Maybe nothing will go wrong at all," Jackie says, as I

take the curling iron to her hair. She thinks to herself while
I try to curl her impossibly straight red hair. I manage to
give it a little body, which is all Jackie really could hope for,
I know.

We're keeping our expectations low yet somehow hoping for the best.

Jackie and I walk into the hangar, which has been converted
into the very meaning of the word festivity. Hanging all
around us are those twinkly little white lights, what I imagine a Parisian street looks like, although I know this is a huge
hangar and would undoubtedly take up many a Parisian
cobblestoned street. Someone under Jackie's command has
draped soft fabrics across the ceiling, swoops of fabric here
and there. So we've got soft purple fabrics with blue moons
and stars, plus the twinkle of lights. It's the soothing kind of
festivity that makes you want to donate large sums, or at
least that's what the fund-raisers are hoping.

"Maybe we should have gotten our hair professionally
done," I tell Jackie.

"It does feel like we should have paid a lot to get in, doesn't
it?" Jackie asks. "It has that feeling of charitable yet tax-
deductible contribution in the air."

"That and something I can't quite describe," I say.

"It's probably just a draft," Jackie says. It is vast in here.

But no, what I'm sensing is something that can't be cured
by putting on a little sweater, although maybe my mother
wouldn't agree, as not only does she carry an extra sweater
for herself in the car, she has an extra in the trunk for me,
even though I've recently passed thirty years old and have
had my own car for years.

But a sweater isn't a cure-all, especially in an awkward
social situation, and lately it's begun to feel as if there just
isn't any other kind. Jackie and I walk forward to meet

Dennis, who I can't help but notice has a fresh—yet not too short—haircut. And maybe a beard trimming. And Claire the Therapist hinged at his side. Her curling iron seems to have worked just fine.

"Hi," Dennis says, not looking particularly happy.

"Hi," Jackie says, looking curiously from Dennis to me to Claire the Therapist.

"This is Claire," Dennis says to Jackie, nodding to his side.

"This is Claire," I say to Jackie, who has seen my therapist but never been introduced.

"As in Claire the Therapist?"

"I am a therapist," Claire the Therapist says, not catching on to our nickname for her.

"You're dating Claire the Therapist?" Jackie asks Dennis. It's a large room, and I'd like to be on the other side right now, although I can't say whether it would be the plus or minus side we'd been imagining earlier. Maybe I can choose to be in a different hangar altogether. Not that Jackie's question doesn't need to be asked, not to mention answered.

"Oh, well," Dennis says, "we just met up, over by the whale."

We all look over. There's a life-sized statue of a whale owned by the organization. I don't know how they got it in here, but considering its girth, it really doesn't take up as much room in the hangar as you'd think.

"Whales are so symbolic of our need to conserve," Claire the Therapist says. "I'm a long-standing member of HELP-US."

"And you're dating Dennis?" Jackie asks, not about to be thrown off guard by environmentalism or the sound of a rain forest in the distance. I'm hoping it's just a tape and that there won't be a real mist somewhere over there. My hair curling will be for nothing in a mist.

"Dennis and I have gotten to know one another," Claire the Therapist says.

Jackie looks to me. "Didn't I mention?" I say, although I'm pretty sure I did. "But then Dennis and I see so little of each other nowadays." Jackie looks to Dennis.

"I've changed my office to the conference room," he says. "Things were getting crowded."

"It's important to have your own space," Claire the Therapist says.

"So now I have my own office," I say to Jackie.

"I've had my own office for years," Jackie says, not at all bragging. "It's not all that great."

"It's essential to explore your own possibilities," Claire the Therapist says, although she's sounding a little more new-agey than usual.

"I always liked that your office was crowded," Jackie says to me, then Dennis. "It had a sense of togetherness." She smiles at him. He smiles back.

"We're a little busy for that these days," Dennis says. "Much more solo work."

"The price of success," I say.

"Solo work is overrated," Jackie says. "No one to throw your balled-up trash at."

"And no need to," Dennis says.

"Champagne?" Claire the Therapist asks, but clearly she means only Dennis, and he seems not ready to break away.

"Wow, my therapists have never actually met the men in my life," Jackie says to me boldly. "Your life is getting complicated," she adds.

"That's why I want her to continue therapy," Claire the Therapist says. "Among other reasons, of course."

"This doesn't seem quite professional, does it?" I ask. I'm not sure whether I mean the discussion or the whole meeting in general. Maybe both.

"The meaning of professionalism can be subjective," my therapist says.

"It's true," Jackie agrees, although I'm not pleased to hear it. "A therapist's utilizing her clients to meet men?" Jackie asks. "It may be way out of line. Or, it may be the next big wave in psychotherapy." Claire the Therapist nods. Jackie considers this, but then I notice her expression change, for the worse. Kind of like mine did when I saw my therapist. My therapist stroking the arm of my officemate, or maybe just his suit. Not that the difference matters.

Jackie and I spot her politician, her married-yet-still-sexual-partner politician, coming through the door. Theo looks elegant with his gray hair and expensive suit. He looks like he's up on the issues. He looks electable. His wife beside him looks nice, too.

"Wow," I say. "I didn't know she was coming."

"I didn't know she was coming," Jackie says. Jackie seems focused on their hands, which are clasped in a not-very-impending-divorcelike way.

"They don't look very unmarried, I'm sorry to say," I tell her gently.

"They look like they just had sex," she says.

"No," I say. "No, not at all," I try to comfort her. "They're not even wrinkled."

"Without-clothes sex," Jackie says.

"Oh," I say. She's right. "Maybe she just has good skin tone," I say, but Jackie looks convinced with her assessment.

"They do have a postcoital glow," my therapist says. "I see it a lot in my work. Do we know them?"

"You don't," I suggest, "since they're not people I may have discussed at length in sessions."

"So you'd say you've discussed me at length?" Dennis asks me.

"I've had to explain a lot of coffee stains on my clothes," I say.

"Oh," he says. Dennis knows he spills too much.

Claire the Therapist studies Theo and his wife. "Are one or more of you involved with him?" she asks. "Or her, no offense intended."

Jackie makes an ambiguous yet slightly possessive noise recognized world round by all women who've been involved with someone who may not be acting the way you like, or may still be holding hands with his wife.

"That's Theo," Dennis says. "He's running for Congress."

"Democrat?" Claire the Therapist asks.

"Yes," Jackie says.

"It's his one good quality," Dennis says. "Although he also has a wife and children."

"Democrats can be family men," Claire the Therapist says. "And still have other interests."

"It's getting to be a little clichéd, don't you think?" Dennis asks, but not that meanly. "Married Democrat with other interests?"

"Maybe. Nice hair, though," my therapist says, looking dreamy.

"Do you think he could get elected without it, maybe with a plain old brown crew cut?" Dennis asks us.

"He's more than just hair," Jackie says, then hesitates. "I think."

"Who needs more?" Claire the Therapist says. Jackie looks at her distrustfully.

"This is a thing with you," I say to my therapist, who looks at me inquisitively, but just barely. It occurs to me that my therapist, young and attractive, has some kind of antennae tuned in for whenever an attractive man enters the room. Even an airplane hangar-size room.

"Hello, dears." Our spell is broken by my mother, who looks beautiful in a black fitted jacket-and-skirt combo. It's not that unlike my own black suit jacket-and-skirt combo, although my skirt is long. I consider Mom's shorter skirt, which suits my fifty-three-year-old mom just fine. It's even shorter than Jackie's black skirt worn under a close-fitting black sweater, as Jackie ignores the fashion for very mini skirts and always tries to cover a large patch of freckles two inches above her left knee, even when she's wearing stockings.

"Eleanor," Dennis says, coming out of his funk a little. "You look terrific."

Claire the Therapist looks displeased to be out of his thoughts, not that she's necessarily been in them. The woman in front of her is clearly old enough to be Dennis's mother, but this doesn't much put her at ease.

"Claire, you look wonderful," my mom says.

"Thank you," both of us Claires echo.

"This is getting icky," Jackie mumbles to me.

"Mom, this is Claire. She's a therapist," I say.

"Oh," Claire the Therapist says, "this is your mother?" She reaches out to shake hands. Eleanor does, but cautiously.

"This is your therapist, dear?" Eleanor looks back and forth.

"Yes," I admit. This isn't going well at all.

"Your therapist's name is also Claire?" Mom asks.

"Yes," I admit.

"Well, that would send me into therapy right there," my mom says. She shrugs at Dennis. He shrugs back, as if he still can't believe it, and I'm not sure it's really sunk into him, actually. Claire the Therapist still hangs on Dennis's arm, but he's started leaning in Eleanor's direction. We're all close enough to hold hands and sing, not that I think anyone's about to.

"You girls could be sisters," Mom says to me and my therapist.

"No we couldn't," we both say in a way that sounds sisterlike, and not for the first time, either.

"It's a strange, strange coincidence," Dennis says.

"Coincidences aren't statistically significant," Jackie says, coming back around. She turns to Dennis. "You might want to keep that in mind."

"Meaning?" he asks her.

"Not everything happens by chance." She looks at my therapist, who is gazing around the room. I'd think she would have a few questions for my mother, but then I remember she's off duty. And I'm not at the top of her priorities right now.

"Where's our politician?" Mom asks Jackie. Eleanor has been advising Jackie on her relationship with Theo. Gently and ineffectively, just like me. Jackie is still enthralled. She points Theo out.

"And that's his wife," my therapist says indiscreetly.

"Well," Eleanor says. "There's always one of those, isn't there? At least she's in Donna Karan."

"I never know what that means," Dennis says. We don't enlighten him. It's actually something I like about him, at the moment.

"It's not a topic men usually discuss at parties," I hint to him.

"Oh," he says, a little alarmed. My therapist laughs and pats him on the arm, which makes him look a little more alarmed.

Our art director, David, approaches the group, an odd smile on his face. "You all look cozy," he says. He gives my mother a little kiss on the cheek. "Beautiful Eleanor and her daughter," David says.

"Kiss-up," I say.

"Works every time," Eleanor says, smiling at David.

"Moms love me," David says.

"Why do you suppose that is?" Claire the Therapist asks.

David looks at her, then at me. "You remember Claire the Therapist," I say.

"And you are?" she says to David, clearly forgetting she ever met him, as she did, the day we happened to be spying on them at the health food store.

"David the Art Director, remember?" he reminds her. She smiles and tilts her head to one side. It's an attractive move. Jackie groans. David catches on.

"David the gay Art Director," he tells her.

"Oh," Claire the Therapist says, and puts her head back on straight.

"It's our little nickname for him," Dennis teases, and my therapist looks alarmed at last.

"You shouldn't, you know," she tells Dennis. "Hostilities have to be addressed directly."

"Especially in our office," David says, looking from Dennis to me. I ignore him, which I'm very experienced at.

"Is there a problem at your office?" Eleanor asks us. "You can always ask the mother, you know, for help."

"Well that's not always—" Claire the Therapist starts to say.

"We know, dear," Mom cuts her off.

"Two points to the mom," I hear David whisper to Jackie, who has taken to following Theo around the room with her eyes.

"Claire and Dennis have divided up their office space," David says. "Although I can't see how they're going to get any work done now at all."

"There's much more room," Dennis says.

"Personal space is important for professional growth," my therapist says.

"Are you married, dear?" my mother asks her.

"Of course not," my therapist says.

"She doesn't even work with anybody," I tell my mother.

"It's not that I can't work with anybody," my therapist says. "It's a personal choice." She almost stamps her foot.

My mother pats her on the arm and takes a card from her

small purse. "Here's my card, dear. You might want to stop by Billie's for some advice. You girls just can't do it all on your own, you know." Claire the Therapist studies my mother's card. I admire my mom for carrying business cards in her purse at a fund-raiser and for managing to get them out of such a small bag without having to tug at all.

"Eleanor has much to teach," David says.

But we all turn our attention away from my therapist to the approaching Theo, although Jackie seems to be trying to look away.

"Hello, everyone," Theo says.

"We haven't met," Claire the Therapist says, extending her hand.

"Well, we definitely should," Theo says, although he places a hand briefly on Jackie's shoulder. She doesn't move much, except a slight sinking into her low-yet-respectable heels. Only a best friend would notice such a slight movement. I sense she wishes the hand would stay on her shoulder longer. I can almost feel the pressure, slight but reassuring, affectionate even. I just wish she didn't feel that way about it.

"Theo MacArthur," Theo says.

"For Congress," Dennis says. "That's what the signs say."

"Nice bus art," David says.

"Thanks," Theo says all around. "Jackie's handled all our campaigning."

"I thought you just stuck to numbers," I tell her.

"Strategizing takes many forms," Jackie says with a shrug.

"To say the least," my mom adds.

"Theo," I say, "this is my mother, Eleanor Duncan."

"It's a pleasure," Theo says to her, lifting her hand.

"So I've heard," Eleanor says. Theo blushes, but only slightly.

"I'm glad to hear you're a supporter of HELPUS," my

therapist says, undeterred. I have to admire her persistence, sort of.

"They are a terrific organization, but of course, our part of California focuses heavily on the environment. It's really the issue for the millennium," Theo says.

"I've always wondered—" Dennis begins, not meanly, but with real curiosity.

"Yes," Theo turns to him.

"Where, exactly, do you guys learn to talk that way. Is it in college? Do they have Political Speaking 101 or something?"

"It's crucial to be able to express your thoughts concisely to your public, to see their thoughts and get right to the answers they need," Theo says, completely unoffended.

"And a good suit goes a long way," Eleanor says.

"It's true," Jackie says. "It's twelve points on the rating scale either way, a little more for an Italian suit. And the statistical error's only three point five."

"Thought so," Eleanor says.

"Jackie's not just a great number cruncher, she's my fashion expert. She's molded my whole presentation, even the way I've begun to think about my career, my goals for myself and all of us, really."

"Wow," I say. "You have goals for all of us?"

"As a politician, it's a requirement," Theo says.

"Your wife's coming over," Dennis says. "Want to discuss your plans for her?"

Theo just looks at Dennis, but his attention is quickly taken away by the woman we call Mrs. Theo and, sometimes, Mrs. Married to the Politician. Her real name is Elise. She's what Mom calls well coiffed, although I've always found that hard to say.

"Speaking of a woman in a good suit," Theo says, moving toward his wife with what would look to most people like real affection and may even be real affection. Makes you sick, though.

"My wife, Elise," Theo says to us.

"Hello," David says, "we're six possible constituents."

"It's nice to meet you all," Elise says. "I do hope you'll vote for Theo. He's really an ideal candidate." I don't know what this means, but on some level it still seems true.

"He certainly looks like an ideal candidate," Claire the Therapist says.

Elise turns to Jackie. "And little Jackie," she says. "Such an important member of our staff." I know for a fact Jackie isn't a staff member. She's a respected demographer in a large, well-paid firm. And she's five foot eight and hasn't been little in a long, long time. She's actually just about head to head with Elise, in height, at least.

"Well," my mother says, "little Jackie here is practically one of my daughters, so naturally I've been paying very close attention to your candidate."

"You must be so proud," David says to Elise, who has turned away from us and is watching a group of actors standing nearby. As I look at them, I realize each one of them was in a TV show that was cancelled this last year, which only reminds me that I watch far too much TV. Still, it's an odd coincidence.

"Our support base," Elise says, then waves good-bye to us. "Come, Theo. He really must mingle. Even your demographer would have to insist, I'm sure." Really, the way she says demographer. It almost sounds like pornographer.

"I'm sure there're a few things your demographer would like to insist on," Eleanor says, but the politician and wife head off toward the out-of-work celebrity crowd.

"I thought somebody said there was champagne," Jackie says.

"There is," Dennis says. "It's squirting out of the top of the whale fountain over there."

"Let's go rescue some," I tell Jackie. "A spurting whale fountain filled with inebriants may be just what you need."

"Funny," Eleanor says, "I was thinking more of a large punching glove, but I suppose it would clash with your outfit."

"And then I might lose all of my statistical significance," Jackie says. None of us is much of a statistician, but I still think we all know just what she means.

Chapter 21

It's My Party

The whale-spurting champagne fountain should not be confused with the life-sized whale sculpture, which is the first whale we have to pass in search of sparkling liquids, the kind that promise the soothing numbness you really want when the person you love has just walked off with his wife. Even if you're experiencing this vicariously.

We locate the right whale, which makes whale-crying sounds—those deep moans that reverberate through your whole body, or mine, anyway. The moaning whale spurts champagne, but it's the expensive kind, so I'm not about to criticize.

"I'm drinking this on an empty stomach," Jackie says as my mother hands her a nearly overflowing glass of champagne.

"Good," Mom says, although I shoot her a look of surprise. "It'll go right to where it's needed. None of that dallying around the baked crab cakes." Jackie shrugs and drinks.

"I didn't know there were crab cakes," I say.

"You'd think they wouldn't be eating creatures from the

sea," Jackie says, "what with all the creatures they're trying to save."

"Maybe these crabs were all particularly mean ones," I say. I love a crab cake.

"Still," Jackie says, "I may have to speak to the caterers. I think this was supposed to be vegan night."

"Which only means it really could have been worse," I say. My mother hands us more champagne.

"Mom," I say, "are you trying to get us drunk?"

"I'll see that you get rides home, if the potion hasn't worn off," she says. "I think a little mind-numbing is in order."

"As if the evening hasn't been mind-numbing enough," Jackie mumbles. I happen to know champagne doesn't have much effect on her, although I'm not sure why. Something about metabolism, I guess, although I suspect it may be sheer stubbornness on her part. I sip my champagne slowly and decline the second glass, as I'm not nearly as stubborn or metabolic.

"Nice eligible rides home," Mom says. Jackie looks almost open to the idea.

"Please, Mom," I say. "We've been designating our own drivers for at least ten years."

"And not doing a very good job of it, if you ask me," Mom says. Scarily, she may be right.

It is time for the entertainment portion of the evening, not that Theo and his odd wife aren't thoroughly entertaining, just not so much to me. Or Jackie.

Unfortunately, the entertainment begins with Theo, who greets the crowd with a perfect smile.

"His dentist should get a cut of whatever money he makes," my mother says to us. "A lot of teeth-whitening there."

"A lot of caps," Jackie admits.

"And do you think this is something you really need to know about your future representative?" I ask her.

"It's only the start of what I know," Jackie says.

Theo welcomes us to the event. "I can't tell you how important groups such as HELPUS are to our future," he goes on, "but since you're all here, I guess we agree. Even my opponent and I agree—the environment is not something to be taken lightly." Theo gestures to his opponent, who will speak next. It's the first I've seen of him. I jab Jackie with my elbow. I think my mother is jabbing her from the other side, too. Sometimes we think alike.

"Dish on the opponent?" I ask. It should be clear by this point that I wouldn't bother asking if he weren't just extremely cute. My mother, I can see, agrees.

"His name is Frankie Phelps," Jackie says.

"Alliterate," I say.

"Adorable," Eleanor says.

"Actually, I've only seen him in black-and-white photos before," Jackie says. "He looks better larger than four-by-six." It's safe to say we are all three enchanted. Frankie is mid-thirties, not that tall, and muscular, but not like he lives for it or anything.

"Single?" Mom asks. "Not that that's such a criterion these days, I realize, but still."

"Single," Jackie says. "Berkeley-educated, likes to play pick-up basketball on Sundays. At least, that's what his brochures say."

"Look at the freckles," Mom says. Actually, Frankie looks a little like Jackie. Dark red hair and freckles.

"We know what your children would look like," I say.

"He's the opposition," Jackie says.

"It's getting so hard to tell," my mother says.

"Republican, huh?" I ask.

"He leans toward center," Jackie says, a little wishy-washy for a political demographer.

"With the love of a good woman," my mother says, "he could move a little to the left. Anyone could."

"And he really goes by Frankie? Not Frank or Francis or anything?" I ask.

Jackie nods. "Family nickname."

"I like a man not embarrassed by his mother's baby name for him," Eleanor says.

Frankie Phelps gets up to speak. "I'd like to welcome you also tonight, putting politics aside, which I have to say is awfully refreshing in the middle of a campaign."

"Me, too," Eleanor whispers.

"So let's enjoy ourselves this evening," Frankie continues. "Mingle and check out the exhibits set up by the local marine society and our friends at HELPUS."

"Tell me again why we can't vote for him?" Mom asks.

"He's not our kind," Jackie says.

"Well, not yet," Eleanor says softly, a little promise in her voice. I raise my eyebrows at her. She raises hers back at me.

It's not lost on me that, basically, everyone I know is here. Dennis stands with my therapist not far across the room, a sentence I never thought would ever occur to me, and yet there they are. Dennis looks unhappy. My therapist Claire watches Frankie, no doubt noticing his slightly cleft chin and ignoring his to-the-right tendencies, but who isn't. Our art director, David, stands nearby, watching Claire the Therapist watch Frankie the just-barely Republican, and shoots me funny faces I refuse to return. I notice my mother returns one to him. They have that kind of relationship. This room of course is hangar-size, and I can't possibly know enough people to fill it, but it's large enough to hold everyone I've ever met. This doesn't mean they all had to show up, though. In another spot stands my boss, Perri, draped in black velvet, although I'm not sure it's exactly in style. To her right is Ron, her personal trainer and not-quite-Best Bachelor. Perri's son, Malcolm, glowers over near a table filled with crab cakes, but I can't imagine why anyone would glower, because they look tasty even from here. I try to figure out if it would be rude to cross the room for crab cakes while the presenters are speaking, then I wonder if I've had too much champagne to cross the room discretely anyway.

I notice that Josie stands near the stage with her clipboard. I don't think she's in charge of the entertainment, exactly, but I do feel comforted by the clipboard. I wish I had one myself, but all I have is this useless little black beaded purse on a shoulder strap, and although it's perfectly nice (a gift from my mom), it's just not the same. It gives me absolutely no sense of control. Not even a false sense.

With my attention on crab cakes, I've missed the introduction for the musical part of our evening. I'm sure I can walk around during music and eat, as I don't think there are rules in manner books about chewing while boy bands take the stage, even when you're the girl representing the boys. Josie puts her clipboard down as Montana takes the stage with Brendan out front. Members of the audience, the front portion of which somehow has become composed entirely of young women in black tights and tight black dresses, are screaming, or maybe cooing is the right word for it. Actually, they sound a little like the whales. Brendan begins to sing his new hit.

"Maybe he should run for office," Eleanor tells Jackie.

"He'd get extra points for the cowboy hat," she says. "Among a certain demographic."

"A certain demographic not old enough to vote," I say.

"They look eighteen to me," Mom says.

"They look eighteen when they're eleven now," I say, although I sound just like my mom. I guess I'm at that age.

Brendan, however, doesn't much notice the girls in black. He's looking right at us. At me, that is.

"I think that boy likes you," Mom says.

"We don't talk about it," I say.

"Not even in therapy?" Mom asks me. "Even though I realize it's confidential." We look over to Claire the Therapist. She's thoroughly enjoying the boy band. Dennis is staring at his drink, but not in a hopeful way.

"It might be time for a new kind of therapy," I say.

"Aromatherapy is nice," Mom says. "And reasonable. Target has its own line, now—four ninety-nine buys enough to last you the month."

"You don't even have to bill your insurance company," Jackie says to me.

"Cut-rate therapy," I say.

"And the little bottles hardly ever try to date your friends," Mom says.

"I like that in a lotion," Jackie says.

"Aren't we being rude by talking?" I ask.

"We're whispering, dear. Plus, we aren't bothering those girls who are still meowing in front of Brendan."

We listen as Brendan finishes his first song. "I'd just like to say how happy we are to be here," he starts, then is greeted by a cheer among the well-dressed girls assembled by the stage. One of them jostles Josie, who maintains her position near Brendan's feet. She bats the girl off with her clipboard a little.

"Go, Josie, go," I whisper in her direction. I look around the room to see everyone enjoying the music, and I notice a large, smiling man approaching, the kind of man who makes you sigh deeply in relief, even if you hadn't realized you felt nervous and worried, although I'm perfectly aware

I've been feeling this way. I look over to see my mother looking as well. And I feel suddenly very dumb, a little ashamed of myself, mad about what I could have done. After all the fix-ups my mother has taken me along on of late, each of which has ended badly, and after whatever ones she may have tried without me, I suddenly realize that I may have an answer for her. I've had it all along. I can fix up my mother.

"Mom," I say. "Have you met my friend Jed?"

"Well, no," Eleanor says, but it's the only thing about her saying no at the moment.

"That's Jed, of Jeds Round Em Up," he says, extending his hand to my mother, gracefully for such a large, large man.

"I'm Eleanor Duncan," says Eleanor Duncan.

"She's my mom," I say, proudly. I look to Jackie, who is intrigued, suddenly alert by the idea of possible dating material for anyone, especially someone else at the moment.

"That's the cowboy store!" Eleanor says.

"It's one of several," Jed admits.

"Plus the café next door," I say.

"That's one of several, too," Jed says. "But it's really more of a pub."

"Darts?" Eleanor asks.

"Why, yes," Jed says.

"I love darts," Mom says.

"I didn't know that about you, Mom," I say, not that it isn't probably true. This is a woman who is learning to play handball, I've recently learned, a sport I equate with little pink rubber balls and five-year-old girls, not that I had any proficiency at it when I was five. Darts aren't at all out of the question when it comes to my mom.

I notice Jed and Eleanor looking at one another, smiling.

"Eleanor," Jed says, hanging a large arm around my neck and lassoing me in, "you have a terrific girl here. Why not bring her by for a nice family game of darts?"

It sounds like a plan. And not the worst one I've heard.

Just then Brendan taps on his mike, "Here's our next release. I hope you all like it. And we'd like to dedicate it to someone special, someone who's, well, changed my life around. Instructed me how to feel about things."

"Oh, yikes," I say quietly.

"It's your moment," Jackie says.

"I should have gone for crab cakes," I say.

"A woman," Brendan goes on loudly, it seems to me, "who's helped us deal with our new success." Brendan looks our way. "Thank you, Eleanor."

People applaud. Mom takes a little shy bow, and the band strikes up their next tune, a song from the sixties or so, I think, called "Eleanor." I'm too surprised to say anything and almost a little disappointed, maybe. I'm really not sure how many more surprises I'm up for.

"Wasn't this a Turtles song?" Jackie asks.

"Yes, I think so," Mom says, fixing her hair a little.

"Mom," I say. "What have you done?"

"You girls," my mother says. "I've just been helping out. Just motherly advice Brendan could get from any mom in the room."

"He's a fine boy. We dressed him," Jed says.

"It's an excellent hat," my mother says of the cowboy hat Brendan and Montana wear, one of Jed's specialties. Jed bows to her.

The girl crowd seems to like the song, an oldie none of them has heard before, no doubt.

"Maybe *People* magazine will be calling you," I tell my mother.

"The woman behind the boy," Jackie says.

"So to speak," Eleanor says, before shushing us completely.

*　*　*

Brendan finishes his tribute to my mother. I admit feeling a little proud, not to mention overwhelmingly surprised. And besides, if Brendan feels this way about my mother, what does this mean for his feelings toward me? And should this bother me at all? These are things I'd love to go home and soak for a while thinking about. But it seems the entertainment must go on. As an advertising not-quite executive, no matter what the papers say, you'd think I'd understand this, or even encourage it.

Dennis and Claire the Therapist, trailed by Malcolm and David, seem to have made their way over to our part of the room, although I think they're going the wrong way, as there's no food over here that I've found. I've noticed Dennis drifting this way and wondered if he was trying to sneak away from Claire the Therapist, who has drifted with him. I just can't tell. David and Malcolm seem to have come along this way as if part of an ocean wave. Just drifting along. David hands me a crab cake, for which I'm eternally grateful, even though it's a little cold. Brendan on stage prepares to speak. He adjusts his mike.

"And now, one of my compatriots, a woman who's on her way to becoming an important musician of her own," he says. I can't think who he means.

"Folks," Brendan says casually, "please welcome our friend, Heaven."

"Oh," our entire group says softly.

"I thought you planned this," my mother says. I just shrug.

"Oh, no," Dennis says as Heaven approaches the stage, and I know why.

Heaven is very properly dressed, white blouse buttoned to the top in a style not that unlike what I might wear, actually. She's wearing a nice and not skin-tight jacket and flowy pants. I've never seen Heaven not in tight jeans, especially pink. But most notably, at least for those of us who know her, is the hair. Still pretty, still fair, but not towheaded any-more. Just a basic dark blondish color. Not something to fantasize about, at long last.

"She looks lovely," Eleanor says.

"It can't be her," David says.

"Oh, no," Dennis says again.

"I think it's becoming," I say.

"The suit could use a little fringe," Jed says, "but other-wise she's a peach."

"Who is she?" Claire the Therapist asks.

"That's Heaven," Dennis says.

"What do you mean by that?" my therapist asks him.

"Oh, no," Dennis can only say. "Did you know about this?" He means me.

"I helped with the color," I say. "A little."

"She's starting to look like someone we might talk to," Jackie says. "Willingly."

"It's important to be able to relate to a musician," I say.

"Baloney," Dennis says.

"Yes, I think you're underrating the appeal of bleached blonde," David says.

"It wasn't bleached, though," I say.

"All that bus art is wrong now," Dennis says. David groans.

"Will it wash out?" David asks.

"We're not going to let her," my mother says firmly.

"Perri doesn't look at all happy," David says. We all look over to Perri's side of the room. Perri is looking around frantically, then finally finds who she's looking for and glares. She's glaring at us.

"Uh oh," Jackie says.

"Heaven sings very well, actually." It's the sudden voice of reason, my therapist Claire, of all people. And she's right. The audience is attentively listening to Heaven sing.

Not looking at her hair or her breasts. She's still beautiful, but no one is ogling.

"She sounds wonderful," Eleanor says. Heaven finishes one song, then begins to sing a duet with Brendan. I don't know the song, but I don't really have time to think about this, as Perri is in front of us. The term "in your face" comes to mind, although I admit I'm too old to really use the term out loud.

"Your boss is here," Jackie says drolly. Perri doesn't do much for Jackie, especially when Perri has her hair dyed as red as Jackie's is naturally, a color that Perri is clearly shooting for at the moment, but missing slightly. Jackie's a natural redhead. Perri doesn't much intimidate her.

"Who's responsible for this?" Perri asks. Ron follows her but seems not at all upset.

"Define *this*," David says.

"Heaven's look. Where's Heaven's hair?" Perri asks us, although she clearly doesn't mean this exactly.

"Well," my mother starts, "my hairdresser did the shade, and terrifically, I must say, too. Oh, and it's nice to see you, too, Perri."

"This is hardly the time to be gracious," Perri says. She turns to me. "Were you there when this happened?"

"Heaven felt bad about her own hair color," I say.

"Imagine that," I hear Malcolm whisper. His own mother has changed hair color what must be thousands of times.

"Heaven is a natural towhead," Perri says. "This is unconscionable."

"Now Perri," says Jed, one of her oldest clients and despite all the cowboy hats, a very wealthy customer. "I think you need to take a deep breath."

"I've been telling her that," Ron says. "Repeatedly."

"Heaven wanted a change." I tell Perri. "She wanted to feel more natural."

"Isn't there a song about that?" Dennis asks. "A natural woman."

"Maybe Heaven could sing it," David says. "Maybe on a hair color commercial!" The boys are pretty excited about this.

"I think it's been done," Jackie says. I agree. You'd think Dennis would remember this with all the TV he's watched. Much of it on my couch.

"I want it changed back, pronto," Perri says. She uses the word pronto often. She even snaps her fingers.

"That seems like Heaven's decision," I say. "And she's already make it."

"She's twenty," Perri says. "We make her decisions for her."

"That doesn't sound very respectful of her self-image," says Claire the Therapist.

"But it does sound like my mother," Malcolm says.

"And you are?" Perri asks my therapist, ignoring Malcolm.

"I'm Claire's therapist," she says.

"Her name is Claire, too," everyone but me says. Seems like everyone, anyway.

"You brought your therapist?" Perri asks me. "Oh, and your mommy?"

"Not that there's anything wrong with that—" my mommy says aggressively.

"And her personal demographer," Jackie says. "But then, you brought your masseuse," Jackie says.

"I'm a personal trainer, mostly," Ron says.

"Oh, no offense," Jackie says.

"None taken. I teach yoga, also," Ron says.

"I love yoga," Eleanor says.

"I love yoga, too," Jed says. He and my mother share a look that says something I don't think I'm supposed to see.

"Claire, you're fired," Perri says. "I'll fix this myself."

"I'm fired?" I ask.

My therapist turns to me. "Now is the time for con-frontation. Don't hold back."

"You're firing me for helping Heaven?" I ask. I push my therapist out of the way slightly. But then she asked for it. She goes to stand with my mother. They both look ready for a good girl fight, actually.

"You can't fire Claire," pipes up Malcolm, who until now has been hidden by someone. Maybe Perri. Usually Perri.

"I can fire any of you, even you," Perri says to her son.

"Not really," Malcolm says.

"You're fired, too, Malcolm," says Perri.

"Nope, can't be done," Malcolm says, then he turns to me. "I think Heaven's look is just right for her. Look how happy she is. Look how tuned-in the audience is. It's as if she sounds even better, that the new look has boosted her confidence and really turned up her volume, her power over people."

"You're very perceptive," Claire the Therapist tells Malcolm. "Very evolved for a young man."

"Well I can't think since when," Perri says. And I have to agree a bit. That may be more than I've heard Malcolm say the entire time I've known him.

"What was that about Perri not being able to fire Claire?" Dennis says.

"Um, yeah?" I say, although it's not very elaborate after Malcolm's little speech.

"That's nonsense," Perri says. "Would you like to be fired, too?" she asks Dennis.

"Only if everybody else is," Dennis says. "I mean, I hate to be left out."

"It's because you come from a large family," Claire the Therapist tells him.

"You can't fire us," Malcolm says. "It's in the contracts."

"That's impossible," Perri says. "You don't have contracts."

"Yep, we have contracts, you signed them, and you can't fire us," Malcolm says.

"I don't remember signing anything of the sort," she says.

"You don't pay much attention," Malcolm says.

Josie has joined us, clipboard to her side. "What's going on?" she asks. "Why aren't you listening to them singing? They're very good."

"We're all fired," I say.

"I'm not fired!" Josie says, then turns to Perri, an unspoken *Am I?* in the air.

"Do you know anything about employment contracts?" Perri asks her. Josie looks quickly to Malcolm, then back to Perri.

"Could you be more specific?" Josie asks.

"Do you all have contracts that I signed without my knowledge?"

"I don't think you can sign something without your knowledge," Jackie says.

"Are you a lawyer?" Perri asks her.

"I'm a demographer," Jackie says. "I rely on numbers and facts. Lawyers cringe at my approach."

"And there are hardly any jokes about demographers," David says. Jackie nods.

"But it's changing," she says.

"I don't want to be fired," I say. "Am I the only one getting upset?"

"You go right ahead, dear," my mother says.

"You just didn't have enough crab cakes," David says.

"I'm going to have my lawyer look into this," Perri says. "Have those contracts on my desk in the morning," she says to Josie.

"Then I'm not fired?" Josie asks.

"After that, you're fired," she says. "Consider it your two-hour notice."

"You can't do that either," Malcolm says with a shrug.

Perri turns back to me. "Don't even bother showing up," she says. "You're definitely out." She storms off.

"I'll go have a little chat with Perri," Jed says. He turns to Mom. "I'll see you, Eleanor." My mom gives a little wave as Jed leaves us.

"We have contracts?" Dennis asks Malcolm.

"Yep," he says. "I wrote them all."

"And job descriptions?" Dennis asks.

"Yes," Malcolm says.

"Hey, you guys?" I ask. "I just got fired," I say. "I'd like a little attention."

"Good for you for asking for what you need," my therapist says.

"I'd like you to combust," I say. "No hard feelings."

"I'm not sure hostility is what we're going for here," says my therapist.

"But it's not a bad place to start," says my mother to my therapist.

"You could maybe just mingle," David suggests to Claire the Therapist. "Way over there."

"Could I see my job description?" Dennis asks Malcolm.

"Sure," he says.

"I wonder if you had benefits you didn't even know about," Jackie says.

"I can't believe you wrote contracts for us," Dennis says to Malcolm.

"I've been going to law school at night," he says.

"That's wonderful, Malcolm," my mother says.

"I'm not having a good time," I say.

"It's your party, you can cry if you want to," Jackie says. "I already have."

"I wonder if Brendan knows that song," my mother says. She turns to Josie. "May I?" She takes Josie's clipboard and makes a note. Josie looks at me.

"None of this was on my schedule for tonight," Josie says.

"None of this ever is, dear," my mother tells her, or all of us, it seems.

Chapter 22

The Designated Driver

Late at night, our office building, which is really just a big warehouse of a place converted into smaller offices, isn't nearly as spooky as I might have thought. I find something comforting about the place empty, with the buzz of the overhead lights and a kind of stillness all around me. Plus the echo when I walk. It's a comforting sound, reminding me that I have weight, that maybe I'm important enough to still make a little *plunk plunk* sound. Even if I'm the only one who hears it.

I arrive here tonight after a fairly disastrous evening because I can't quite face going home. I didn't need any one to drive me, as the evening's proceedings sobered me up entirely, not that I'd really had that much champagne. And only one lonely cold crab cake. A small one. Really, things didn't go well at all.

I stop just inside the warehouse's front doors at the four old coin-operated rides, the kind that stood outside the grocery stores of our childhood: a horsey ride, an elephant, a yellow car for two with side-by-side seating, and a petite merry-go-round for three. And all for a nickel a piece. As I was raised properly, I always have change in my purse—

even when it's a little black beaded bag, especially when it's a little black beaded bag only big enough for change—and I always have nickels, as you just never know when you'll need a horsey ride. That's been my experience, at least.

I sit on my horse and remove the Out of Order sign put there for tourists and others who don't belong here, as we who practically live here know that the rides work fine. The horse is yellow with a white mane and big smile on its face. It's hard to be depressed on a smiling horsey ride. I'm hoping this, at least. I insert my nickel and go for a gentle ride, a rocking that's reminiscent of something I'm too old to remember but that I value just the same.

I hear someone else coming in to the warehouse, and maybe I'd be worried at the sound of footsteps outside on this dark night, but seeing how I hear the person drop his keys, then pick them up, then drop them again before entering, I don't have to worry. Some people are so identifiable just by their sounds. Their exasperating sounds.

Dennis drops his keys again after entering the warehouse. "Oops!" he says, slightly angry.

My horse stops rocking. I remain seated on it, though, and I'm not even sidesaddle, which in my long black skirt may not be the best look for me, but it's a wide skirt, and I'm not about to fix myself up any. I knew there was a reason I avoided miniskirts.

Dennis looks at me. "Howdy, partner," he actually says.

"Original," I say.

"Hey, I'm a well-paid copywriter," he says.

"That makes one of us," I say, since I lost my job tonight, whereas Dennis's probably still exists in the maze we think of as Perri's mind.

Dennis sits down on the elephant, which I happen to know is his favorite. I'm more of a pony girl, myself, but the elephant has a certain charm, as it looks like it's laughing hysterically.

"What's the worst that could happen?" Dennis says. "Let's analyze."

"I prefer to just sit and mope," I say.

"Yeah," Dennis says, "but you could have done that at home on a comfy couch."

"I do love my couch," I say.

"I know," Dennis says. "Yet here you are, sitting on a mechanical object."

"This is a horsey," I say. "It's different. It knows how to gallop gently."

"Without ever really getting anywhere?" Dennis asks.

"We have a lot in common, my horsey and me," I say.

"Is it my horsey and me or my horsey and I?" Dennis asks.

"I'm an out-of-work former English major," I say. "So I don't have to care."

"But I know you do," Dennis says. He's right. I consider the grammar for a while and insert another nickel. I go for a ride.

Dennis searches his pockets and comes up with a nickel. "Aha!" he says, then goes on an elephant ride. We're sitting in an abandoned office warehouse riding nickel rides in our dress-up clothes. Maybe it doesn't get any better than this.

After the ride, Dennis says, "Wait here," and goes into our office. *As if I were going anywhere*, I tell myself. Although I should go in and pack up my things. All the personal items I've collected over the years working in advertising. My cat mug and samples of my work, not that I'll ever work again, but still. Shouldn't I have been saving examples, putting together a portfolio? Have I been utterly foolish?

I'm out of nickels. There's another roll of them in my office drawer, I realize. My soon-to-be-former drawer in my soon to be former desk.

I go into the office. I don't know what Dennis is doing, but then I hear the sounds from our kitchen/stockroom, the *pop pop pop* of microwaved popcorn. Leave it to Dennis to think of food at a time like this. And thank goodness.

In my office I look around for personal items, things that I need to take home, things I would someday regret having left behind. My cat mug (chipped). My collection of bandanas in the top drawer, courtesy of Jed, who often brought one for me. I've never known what to do with them. I sit down at my desk and am surprised, suddenly, by a personal object from my past, but one I haven't put here. It's the picture of me with my father, me curtsying to him, taken long ago in the happy days of my childhood, before anyone ever asked me to write copy or help a boy singer change his image. Before I was ever fired. It's the picture I was looking for and couldn't find—the picture I couldn't even remember to keep track of. It has been placed in a silvery frame with something sparkly to it, not diamonds of course, but little flecks of metallic shine. They make the picture look magical, not that it wasn't already, to me at least. I pick it up and hold on to it, rubbing it slightly. Making a wish I can't quite express, even to myself.

Dennis stands behind me. I turn around.

"You did this?" I ask, waving the photo.

"You did that," Dennis says. "I just framed it."

I put my head down on my desk, which smells of cinnamon. I can't imagine why, and it's not something I've ever noticed before. Probably something Dennis spilled. I know I'll miss the smell immensely.

"Oh, no, come on," Dennis says. He grabs me with the arm not embracing his bag of popcorn and takes me out to the hallway again. We get into the yellow car, Dennis taking the driver's seat. I've never sat in this ride, mostly, I suspect, because it has a car seat that's a bench for two people. This ride is built for two, and it has always seemed just too sad to sit here alone. Especially tonight. Although I'm not alone tonight.

Dennis and I sit quietly in the yellow car. He offers me some popcorn.

"I don't remember having popcorn in the office," I say. "It must be very old."

"Not that that's going to stop you from eating it," Dennis says.

"Well, no," I say. "I'm running on one crab cake. A cold one."

"Eech," Dennis says. He doesn't like seafood. He inserts a couple of nickels.

"Will it run longer if you put more money in?" I ask.

Dennis smiles.

"How do you know this?"

"I don't have much of a social life," Dennis says.

"I'll say," I say. "Unless you count my therapist."

"I don't, actually," Dennis says. "Count your therapist."

"I'm sure she'd love to hear that," I say. Dennis crams some popcorn in my mouth, which from anyone else I suspect would be a sign of hostility. It's actually just his way of sharing. I know he could eat the whole bag.

"You're not feeling better, yet," he says, sticking more food in my face. "I just met your therapist, and I didn't know she was your therapist, and I didn't know she was coming tonight."

"And you didn't buy that new suit for her, either," I say, not really a question.

"How'd you know it was a new suit?" Dennis asks.

"I don't have a social life either," I say. I know Dennis's wardrobe by heart. This is a new suit. The old one has holes, but it's very possible Dennis doesn't even know that.

"I didn't invite her, and I didn't dress for her," Dennis says. "I did, however, tell her I thought it wasn't right for us to date, since I know you and she knows you."

"I stopped seeing her," I say.

"Well," Dennis says. "That makes two of us."

He puts another nickel in.

"This isn't making you carsick, is it?" Dennis asks me. "I mean, it's a new suit, I'd like to keep it clean." He rubs at a speck of something on his suit. Too late, I guess.

"I can eat in any car going any velocity," I say. "It's one of my good points."

"I know," Dennis says. "I've ridden in your car."

I give him a look.

"At least if you're in an emergency and need to eat, you can always find scraps in your car," he says.

"Sometimes I spill sunflower seeds," I say. "That's all. And I may need to eat them soon, as I'm going to be poor and out of work."

"Poorer," Dennis says. It's true, we really don't make a lot of money here, but enough to buy sunflower seeds.

We rock awhile. "Why are these machines here?" I ask.

"It's an ageless question," Dennis says. He doesn't know, either.

"So you're not dating Claire the Therapist?" I ask.

"No," Dennis says. "I'm not nearly mature enough to date someone who would question my every thought. I haven't even been mature enough to date anyone for a while."

"She dresses well," I say.

"She copies you," Dennis says.

"No, I don't think so," I say.

"She told me," he says. I'm taken by surprise. All this time I thought I was emulating her. Well, the skirts anyhow.

"She holds you in great awe," Dennis says.

"Wow," I say.

"We all hold you in great awe," Dennis says.

"I'm an unemployed copywriter with too many bandanas," I say.

"You say it like it's a bad thing," Dennis says, placing several pieces of popcorn in my mouth.

"Societal pressure tends to frown on such a person," I say, after swallowing.

"Not when sitting in a race car ride," Dennis says. He puts the popcorn bag down, inserts another nickel, and kisses me. All in one fairly graceful move for someone known around here as Mr. Fumbly Fingers. David even made him a plaque for the door, but we don't really have an office door, so I don't know what happened to it. Not that this is especially important now.

I know there must have been times, over the years, when I've somehow (inadvertently?) brushed up against Dennis's beard, because I know how soft it will be. And it is. We sit this way for a long time, kissing and riding the race car of our childhood, the slow rocking adding nicely to our movements in a way no doubt far more subversive than the creators of the kiddie ride intended. Dennis kisses me, covering my face with equal and undivided attention, my top lip, bottom lip, both lips together, then round about and back again, not ignoring my neck, of course. Eventually, we begin to toss parts of our dress clothes by the side of the road, so to speak.

"Oops," Dennis says, jokingly, as he drops my jacket over the side of the race car.

"You're always dropping things," I say, tossing his tie overboard as he kisses my neck while unsnapping my bra (it's in the back)—with one graceful movement. No big snap or anything startling, just a gentle gesture barely even noticeable, no doubt, to a girl more used to having her bra undone by someone else. A bearded someone else. While sitting in a race car ride that's rocking at the moment. It's new, but I like it.

Dennis takes out more nickels. I knew there was something I was saving this car ride for.

* * *

In the morning, Malcolm finds Dennis and me sleeping on the small black sofa in the conference room. We have somehow reassembled ourselves into some of our clothes (my bra is in my desk drawer, though, as who really wants to put a bra back on at a time like that). So it's not like we're naked. And it's not like Malcolm would really care.

"Hi," he says casually, waking us.

We're all wrapped up in each other. It's a small couch. We're covered in bandanas, too. Malcolm doesn't ask.

"Hi, Malcolm," Dennis says casually back.

"There's a meeting," Malcolm says. He looks well rested and, well, almost happy, for Malcolm. He looks employed. I think I'd resent this if I felt any less happy and comfortable myself at the moment. This couch isn't bad at all. I would have thought too small, but I would have been wrong.

"I hope it's not here in the conference room," Dennis says, tossing aside bandanas.

"Nope," Malcolm says. "It's at Jeds Lunch Place."

"When?" Dennis and I ask at the same time, then look at each other with one of those looks that nauseates other people, those looks that say, *Ooh, we spoke at the same time. We share the same thoughts.* Clearly, romantic morning-after looks, although I've had much worse morning-afters and really don't mind a bit.

Malcolm is unphased. "Pronto," he says facetiously. It's Perri's word, but it sounds good on him.

"Hey," I say. "Doesn't this surprise you at all?" I point to me and Dennis, and to bandanas. Dennis's shirt is all crumpled. I couldn't say where his jacket is. I'm not sure he could either.

"Please," Malcolm only says.

We meet everyone at Jeds Lunch Place, next to the Round Em Up.

"It's a little early for darts," I say, my hands wrapped around a large cup of latte. Jed features extra-large mugs with cowboy motifs. Mine has a cowgirl with a devilish smile, and the latte goes a long way on a morning like this, a morning that finds me still wearing my clothes from last night. I haven't done that in a long time, and for some reason, I hear my mother's voice saying, *Too long*. I'm shocked at her, even though she's only inside my head at the moment speaking thoughts I'm too afraid to attribute to myself.

Dennis sits groggily beside me, very close by, actually. We're touching in several places under the table. I feel like telling people this. I feel like I need to giggle amongst a group of girls, whispering about all kinds of kisses from the night before. I feel about twelve years old. It could be because I left my bra at the office. But I don't think that's it.

Dennis wears his suit pants and good shirt from last night, both very wrinkled, not that this is an unusual look for him. Everyone else here seems to have found time to change clothes. I find myself feeling a little sorry for them.

Josie sits down looking energized. She places her clipboard in front of her. Malcolm joins us with a large basket of French fries.

"That's not good for you," Josie says. Malcolm shrugs.

"They say breakfast is the most important meal," Malcolm says.

"You should read the fine print," Josie says.

David joins us with two cups of coffee and a basket of muffins, enough for all of us. He keeps both cups of coffee, though, to himself.

"These are real muffins," David says to us. "Not low-fat, not good-for-you muffins. No healthy grains or berries."

"Thank goodness," Dennis says, taking one.

David looks from Dennis to me, then back again. We smile at him nonchalantly.

"I certainly hope we're not going to have to hear details," he says dryly. Dennis shrugs at him.

Jed joins us. For a moment, I'm terrified my mother will be with him, not that she's that kind of girl to spend the night with someone and appear in rumpled clothes in front of nearly everyone she knows. I'm sure she'd at least change clothes first. But thankfully, Jed is alone.

"Is Perri coming?" I ask. "I may need something stronger than latte."

"We could get you a chocolate chip muffin," David says. He looks through the basket and pulls one out for me. I treasure my friends at times like these.

"It's a start," I say. Dennis looks at me longingly, which I really like at the moment, even though most of this particular desire is for my chocolate chips. I break off some for him. His muffin smells like banana, which I know just isn't the same.

"I guess this means I'll be helping you move your desk back into your shared office," David says to Dennis.

"I don't have an office anymore, remember?" I tell him. "I'm fired."

"I wouldn't say that," Jed says. He gets all our attention, and not just because he's the tallest, even without the ten-gallon hat he's wearing. No one can pull off a cowboy hat like Jed, especially not at 8:30 in the morning.

"Claire," he starts, "you still have a job, if you'd consider staying."

"I do?"

"Seems Perri has decided to move on. She and Ron are moving to New York to open a yoga studio for celebrities. Quite a market for it, it seems," Jed tells us.

"Really?" David, Dennis, and I all say together.

"Wow," Malcolm says. "I'll miss Ron."

"How do you know this?" Dennis asks Jed.

Jed stirs his coffee slowly, gathering our attention as he does. "I bought the place from Perri last night."

"Our place?" Malcolm says.

"Our office?" Josie asks.

"The name Persephonia! has got to go," Jed says. "No offense," he says to Malcolm, Persephone's own son.

"None taken at all," Malcolm says.

Josie flips a page on her clipboard, ready to take notes.

"I'll need you kids to come up with a new name," he says to Dennis and me, and all of us really.

"And new art," David says. David drew Perri's logo, sort of a long-haired nymph looking like a much younger Perri. With wings. And multicolor hair. None of us much liked it.

"There's more changes in store," Jed says, so we all lean in. "I'm on the board of HELPUS," he says, "you know, the organization that held the soiree last night."

"Ugh," I say softly. Last night. The bad part, at least.

"No, they were pleased with how it went. Raised a bundle. But we're going to take them on at our new agency. You're going to take them on. Help them get their message where it needs to go."

"What about our musicians?" Josie says. I know she's thinking about Brendan. It's the first I've thought of him in a while. He suddenly seems very, very young.

"We can keep our musical folks and work for the community," Jed says.

"An agency for the new millennium," Malcolm says.

"I like it," Jed says. "And first thing, would somebody please come up with a new name for HELPUS?"

"Oh, yes," Dennis says. I nod as well. I would hate to have to call someone up and say, "Hello, this is Claire Duncan, representing HELPUS." Although the idea of calling someone up and saying, "Hello, this is Claire Duncan, unemployed," sounds a lot worse. It's nice to have options, suddenly. I take another bite of my high-calorie muffin. It's excellent.

"Claire and Dennis, I'm putting you in charge of HELP-

US, or whatever," Jed says. "Malcolm, you take over Heaven."

"So to speak," David says.

"No problem," Malcolm says.

"Josie, you need a project," Jed begins, and Josie snaps to attention.

"Josie could take over for Brendan and Montana," I say. "Nobody knows more about them." Josie smiles.

"Sounds good," Jed says. "Eat up, kids, then back to work."

"Does this mean we get to wear cowboy boots to work?" Dennis asks.

"You mean you haven't been?" Jed looks a little affronted.

"We could use some fringed shirts, too," I suggest.

Jed nudges Josie. She writes it all down. I look at Dennis. I have to admit, I'd like to see him in a little fringe.

"I already have boots," I say to Dennis tauntingly. "Pink leather. Pointy toes."

"Ooh, boots," Josie whispers.

"Employee discount, too," Jed says. Josie's eyes light up. Jed orders more latte all around.

"I'll draw up the contracts," Malcolm says. We all clink cowboy mugs in agreement.

Chapter 23

Love and the Margin of Error

It's our grand opening, so to speak, a housewarming of sorts for our new office, which looks a lot like our old office but with a few much-needed changes. Best of all, Perri is gone, and with her goes a nervousness and tension to the office that no one really needed. I'm not sure I could have pointed it out before, named it, but now I think of it as something called Essence of Perri—like a perfume you may have accidentally gotten sprayed with at Macy's, passing by one of those imposing women with a glistening bottle, but something you'd never buy. Something you scrub off as soon as you get home. We are so much more productive without Perri, so much more relaxed yet more focused. It has surprised us all. We find ourselves smiling, even when the copier jams up. These are good times.

Dennis and I share our office once again, and we still tease one another over spilt latte and other things, as the need arises.

"I'm bringing in a new file cabinet," I told Dennis while he moved his papers, stacks and stacks of them, back into our shared space.

"Too much change at once is bad for you," Dennis said.

"It's a half-size file cabinet," I said. "It's just a half a change."

"So this is where it starts," Dennis said. "Women trying to change their men."

"I've actually been trying to change this about you for years," I said.

"Oh," Dennis said. "I guess I'll have to throw out that self-help book I read that from."

"I have a few myself," I said. "Bonfire material. I'll throw out mine if you throw out yours," I said.

"Deal," Dennis said. It's a date.

"The new file cabinet is mahogany," I said, temptingly. I whisked away a sheet from the half-size file cabinet I'd been hiding, a *Let's Make a Deal* kind of gesture. Dennis has watched the show with me on one of those oldies TV channels, for senior citizens, no doubt. We like those shows.

"Hmm," Dennis said, surveying the small cabinet and running his hands over it. "Mahogany." Good wood is the way to a man's heart, I know. Kind of like a home-roasted chicken (this also worked wonders on Dennis last night). And I didn't even have to read any of this in a self-help book. Maybe I should write my own.

As my former therapist might have said, such behavior is appropriate between officemates who've probably loved one another for years but have been too stupid to admit it. Not that she ever used the word stupid, and not that she'd be all that pleased, I think, with the way things turned out. With the Claire that ended up with Dennis after all.

Jed likes to come by and work out of what he calls "the new office," which for us is the same old place. We've re-arranged, somewhat, removing some of the fake walls (and there really was hay in there, and it really did make me sneeze when we removed it, even though we wore those little dust masks you're supposed to wear when you dust, not that I dust very often). So now Dennis and I have a little larger space. And just when we didn't really need one. Still, it's nice. Malcolm has his own office, instead of having to work out of the storeroom, which by the way has been re-modeled to include a cappuccino machine that sounds like a dragon spewing something hot yet frothy. A small dragon. Someone bought new checkers for the checkerboard table, too, so it's a full set.

"Where's the challenge in that?" Dennis said. I had to agree. Still, the table looks nice, and we can all follow the same rules now, at least. I have noticed Dennis and David trying to hide some of the checkers. I happen to know there are extras, but I hate to spoil their fun.

Josie also has a new office space, next to David our art director's, and I notice they've developed a special relation-ship of throwing wadded paper at one another through their shared archway. It's a big step for Josie, I know, feeling comfortable enough here to throw something. She's taken her responsibilities with Brendan seriously, too, and has propelled him to new fame through several late-night TV appearances. They've been spotted together in a few late-night appearances around town, too.

"They make a cute couple," Jackie said at tea with my mother and me one day. "Although I think she needs to lose the clipboard."

"Never underestimate the value of a good accessory," my mother said. She bought Josie a nice leather-backed clip-board, which Josie carries proudly. I'd never seen a leather-backed clipboard before.

"I thought he was interested in you," Jackie said to me. My mother leaned in to hear about this as well.

"I don't have good accessories," I said. "I think I was more of a passing fad."

"Maybe you were just practice," Jackie kidded me, but

Brendan and I have seen each other in the office, and we both seem to know it was just a few kisses. Just after the move, Brendan came in and shook my hand.

"Congratulations on the new office," Brendan said. "And everything."

"You, too," I said. "The success, and everything."

"And thanks," Brendan said.

We stood there and shook hands, just holding on for a minute, our way of moving on. Sometimes a kiss is just a kiss after all. Maybe we were both practicing.

"Not that you didn't come out of things just fine," my mother said at tea, referring to Dennis, who she likes more and more every time I see her. "But not that you couldn't use a nice new leather purse," she said. Mom never passes up a chance to dress me, or at least accessorize me.

My mom has become a bit of a fixture here, too, and surprisingly, it hasn't bothered me having her in the office. She's only here once a week or so, of course. Dennis and David like to tease her.

"What's your official function?" David has asked her.

"It almost sounds dirty the way you say it," Eleanor said, "but I'm the bookkeeper. Just dotting the i's and crossing the t's."

"It sounds dirty the way you say it," David said, admiringly.

"That's because I'm good at it, dear," my mother said. I just leave the room when they talk like this, but I can't say I really mind. Because even better than seeing my mother fulfilled with new employment is seeing her with Jed. She stands beside him this evening at our office party.

It has occurred to me that after the last party, the HELP-US Disaster, as I sometimes think of it, I should be a little wary of another "event." But Jed can really throw a party, especially, it turns out, with Josie in charge.

"Who'd have thought she'd be a party girl?" David says

of Josie, the once prim office assistant, who has let her hair grow and wears a short flippy skirt and tall cowgirl boots. She and Brendan dance in a corner, and it really looks great the way she waves that leather clipboard around. I wouldn't have thought so, but there it is.

But if Josie is the princess tonight, the Cinderella released from her dingy obligation of cleaning up after Perri, freed to dance at the ball with her prince in her princessy slippers-turned-boots, still, my mother is the queen.

"Eleanor," Dennis says, "love becomes you." My mother kisses him on one of his bearded cheeks.

"You're right—it is softer than I'd thought," my mother says to me, and I feel my face redden.

"Mom," I say, sounding ten years old.

My mother and Jed have been "dating," as my mother calls it. I admit I've heard a little more than I want to know about my mother's ideas on dating. She's sat me down and told me where she thinks are good places to go on a first date (a boisterous barbecue restaurant, where they went), what the proper dinner is to serve on your first "cooking for him" date, as she calls it (anything hot from the oven, but no green veggies that might make him think you think he needs to eat more healthfully, not yet, at least), and appropriate weekend spots for the first "weekend get-together," as she's called it (anyplace up the coast with three stars). Thankfully, the details stop there. I'm sure I'd lose all respect for her if she told me any more, although sometimes she looks tempted. As for Dennis and me, we still eat popcorn and go to movies and snuggle on the couch. Some things don't change, except that everything has, really.

Jackie joins us at the party for our new office, which we've named simply, Public Beach Access. It's still a strange name, I admit. David thinks it sounds dirty, somehow, but it emphasizes that we're going to work on community issues along with our beloved musicians, the little people who support us so we can work cheap for the greater public good, as the politicians like to say. Plus, the name beats some others that were in the running, which included Millennium Agency (Malcolm's idea), Saltwater PR (Josie's suggestion, and not too bad, either), Jed's Advertising Agency (Jed's idea, although of course he vetoed the apostrophe), Boy Howdy (a joke, we think, from David, and no one really knows why), and We're Your Advertising Agency (no one admitted to this—it just appeared on the list one night). So Public Beach Access it is. It suits us, situated as we are a few short blocks from Venice Beach. And if a little sand gets in the office, we don't have to clean. It looks like part of the motif.

But we still struggle with renaming HELPUS. We're still trying to come up with a good suggestion, plus get the organization to go along.

"How about Create Responsible Alternative Businesses?" Dennis suggested.

"That's CRAB," I said.

"You know how they love sea creatures," he said with a shrug. It's the best we've come up with so far, which I know doesn't say a lot for our English major skills.

"Acronyms aren't really an English major thing," I've said to Jackie in defense.

"They're more like military science," she's agreed, letting me off the hook. After all, if acronyms were easy to come up with, they wouldn't have been called HELPUS in the first place. The weird thing, of course, is that they really like the name CRAB. So far.

I'll admit that I was set to comfort Jackie this evening. Jackie's candidate, the still-married Theo, lost by a surprisingly wide margin. Dennis and I made cocoa that night for Jackie as she sat at my kitchen table, with Dennis putting marshmallow after marshmallow in her cup. It didn't much seem to help. And of course the cocoa finally spilled over. I didn't say anything, but Dennis got a sponge anyhow.

"You did everything you could for him," Dennis said to Jackie. Jackie just gave him a look.

"That didn't really sound the way I wanted it to," Dennis said.

"Which doesn't mean it isn't true," Jackie said. "Unfortunately."

"I thought you had the election called," I said.

"Must have been the margin of error," Jackie said. "Gets me every time."

"Love and the Margin of Error," I said.

"That's right," Jackie said, "reduce my life to a *Cosmo* article."

"Again," I said.

"Again," she said.

But things are different at our party tonight, with the twinkling little white lights we've draped all around the hallway and over the kiddie rides. (Dennis has placed an "Out of Order" sign on our race car, as he says he can't stand to see anyone else in it.) From the look of things tonight, Jackie may have moved on. In an unexpected if not entirely bad direction.

Jackie stands in front of us with Frankie Phelps, the winner of the recent election and one of the cutest men I've ever seen, my copywriting partner excepted, of course. The red-haired, freckle-faced young Congressman-to-be might just be what my mother would call the perfect accessory. He and Jackie look exactly right standing together.

"Aren't you a Republican?" Dennis says to him, shaking his hand anyway.

"Well, Jackie's working on me," Frankie says. "I'm not sure the old ideologies mean so much anymore. I want to be able to look at each issue on its own."

"Frankie's thinking of becoming an Independent," Jackie says.

"And you've only been dating a week," my mother tells Jackie. Jackie nods. Mom seems impressed.

We look to the little stage we've set up, where Malcolm is about to introduce Heaven, whose hand he's been holding all night. They are an unexpected and yet instantly casual couple, as though they've known each other all their lives, which actually, they have. I stand with Dennis. Mom stands very close to big Jed. The twinlike Jackie and Frankie stand side by side, red hair merging. Someone should take a picture.

"What a pair," Dennis says, and I wonder if he means Malcolm and Heaven, or maybe Jackie and Frankie. Or maybe us.

I'm back at home the next night, still recovering from dancing with Dennis for hours but also for the first time, dancing to Heaven singing, then to Brendan singing, then even to Bobby Henry, one of my personal favorites, and not just because, after he winked at Dennis and me about twenty times to let me know how much he approved when I told him, he dedicated a song to us. This is of course corny and embarrassing, but it's never happened to me before. I liked it.

Although back at home isn't exactly the right phrase, because I'm in my new apartment. Maybe it was something my former therapist said, or something my mother said, or Jackie said, or a look from Dennis. Maybe, just maybe, I'd had enough. I like to think I did it all on my own, but one day I just packed up and left Andy's old apartment and all memories of Andy, I like to think. Of course, I scouted around plenty and rented a very nice apartment for myself first. I'm not really all that impulsive, and I wasn't about to move home with my mother. I don't think she'd have much liked it, either.

My new apartment is a cottage in Santa Monica, in what my mother considers a very respectable neighborhood, and

I have to admit it is very nice. There are little lights on the trees outside everyone's buildings, much like the ones from our party, and flower boxes filled with geraniums. My old building had one giant cactus and a burned-out bulb hanging outside the door. But I don't need to think of that anymore. The burned out bulb is someone else's problem. And I'll never again rip my tights on that vicious cactus.

I have a wood-burning fireplace, although it burns other things too, such as paper. Paper ripped from old self-help books. Which is what Dennis and I are doing tonight. Jackie joins us to burn up files and files of old lists she's had, lists I've looked through. Lists we're done with.

"Potential men are going up in smoke," I tell her.

"It's cathartic," she says. "Not that we're disgruntled women."

"We're just being fuel efficient," I say.

"Recycling men," Jackie says.

"And really bad advice," I say, tossing in pages from a book about how to choose the right therapist for you. The amazing thing, of course, is that I read it.

"I just wish," says Dennis, who may someday soon move into my new apartment, but not quite yet, "that you'd have gotten your love life together a little sooner," he says to Jackie.

"Don't we all," I say.

"Then we'd have a few marshmallows left to roast, instead of losing them to all the cocoa you drank."

"Is it roast, or toast?" Jackie asks.

"We're out of chocolate and graham crackers, too," I say, "so it's neither."

"This is a roast of a kind," Jackie says, tossing more pages into the fire.

"It gives a new meaning to the term Campfire Girls," I say.

"It's a whole new trend in fireplace starters," Dennis says.

He adds a few chapters of a book entitled *You and Your Inner You*. I give him a look.

"Christmas gift," Dennis says.

"Sure it was," I say. Still, it doesn't look like he's ever opened it, as he seems to be having trouble getting the pages to separate. I take this as a good sign. I admit I've checked the book out of the library. I can't remember what it might have said.

"Good-bye poor choices and desperate Saturday-night reading," I say.

"You will not be missed," Dennis says.

"I think this is the most use we've gotten out of this stuff," I say.

"It's a good thing it's getting to be wintertime, or it'd be awfully hot in here," Dennis says. Really, there's a lot to burn for just three formerly unattached thirty-year-olds. Actually, Dennis turns thirty next week. I have big plans for this.

Jackie picks up another book. "They're all useless, it's true," she says, paging through an old self-help tome, then watching it burn, a satisfied look on her face. "Still, they give off a nice glow."

"Maybe it should say that on the book jacket," says my copywriter of a boyfriend.

We watch the pages burn and listen to the crackle, lights twinkling outside my windows, so content and philosophical that we forget to turn on the TV entirely. We have come so far.